In the Interest of Faye

In the Interest of Faye

A Novel

by

Lisa Brognano

Golden Antelope Press
715 E. McPherson
Kirksville, Missouri 63501
2017

Copyright ©2017 by Lisa Brognano
Cover Design by Russell Nelson
Cover Image by Elena Barenbaum (Shutterstock 526349296)

ISBN   978-1-936135-48-6 (1-936135-48-5)

Library of Congress Control Number: 2017963500

Published by:
Golden Antelope Press
715 E. McPherson
Kirksville, Missouri 63501

Available at:
Golden Antelope Press
715 E. McPherson
Kirksville, Missouri, 63501
Phone: (660) 665-0273
http://www.goldenantelope.com
Email: ndelmoni@gmail.com

To my parents, Ralph and Marie;
it is my pleasure to be your daughter
and to love you with all my heart.

Acknowledgements

Special thanks to my wonderful, handsome husband, James, for his love and support. I'm indebted to my mother, an expert proofreader and a terrific sounding board for plot points. I thank my father for reading all of my published work. Thanks to my sister, Maria, for being my dearest friend, and to our beautiful sister, Josie, who watches over us from Heaven. Thanks to my nephews, Tyler and Noah, who are discovering the joy of reading as a ten- and eight-year old, respectively. Many thanks to Neal and Betsy Delmonico for their literary expertise and everyone at the press. I especially thank S. Max Kolbe. Above all, I thank God and Mary.

In the Interest of Faye

Chapter One

Mrs. DuPont started off slowly. "I've been approached by a businessman," she said and interlaced her hands on the table. "In the beginning his proposal didn't interest me. Eventually, though, he started to talk numbers. The figures were staggering. I had no idea this place was worth that much." She paused, perhaps considering how to tell the rest.

"The man's name," she continued, "is Bobby Sterling, a veritable shark when it comes to investments. His millions can vouch for that. And his unique brand of cafés has taken the Eastern Seaboard by storm. The demands of his business require him to move quickly when he sees something promising. He strikes while the iron is hot, make no mistake about that. Sterling will stop at nothing to attain his goal." She smiled weakly, the red of her lipstick too bright for the circumstances.

"I have something he wants," she said firmly and shifted in her seat. "This building will house his one-hundredth café. A milestone for his company. He's signing the papers tomorrow, and aims to get operations up and running by late February." She unwrapped the white fur shawl from around her shoulders and laid it in her lap.

"Extending my regrets to you in person is why I've come all this way. I thought it might soften the blow. You must know I pondered this decision for quite some time. I've always seen this place"—she twisted around to take in more of the colorful paintings—"as a haven of beauty and good taste. Certainly, my initial intentions were for the gallery to remain rooted in this spot for decades. Five years may only seem like a split second, but I'm grateful for all your hard work. Hirsch Gallery has acquired a measure of success, and I attribute that to you."

Faye glanced across the folding table at the gallery's founder and owner, Margaret Hirsch DuPont. The silver-haired woman's thin, pointy nose and high cheekbones accentuated a perpetual look of controlled disdain. She wore a red, tailored dress that flattered her figure, and Faye supposed it had taken many nips and tucks to raise the woman's rear end up to where it was now.

"Faye, I say this with a heavy heart, but I've made up my mind to sell to Sterling."

Mrs. DP's personal assistant, Ronald, bald and dressed all in black, returned with hot drinks from the coffee hut down the block. Faye got the feeling he'd waited in the lobby until his boss delivered the final blow. How could this be happening? The Vincent Van Gogh exhibit was scheduled for March. Her most noteworthy acquisition to date would have no outlet if the gallery closed its doors. She sat up straighter and accepted the coffee Ronald handed to her.

"As much as I understand your decision, and realize that you have every right to sell this building, I feel strongly that this gallery, which is an integral part of the community, should remain the cultural hub everyone has known it to be for the past five years." She stared at her coffee cup. "I guess I'm asking if there's any way to stop this from happening."

Mrs. DuPont covered Faye's hand with her own. "I've always liked your spunk," she said. "But somehow I don't think you could win a bidding war with Bobby Sterling. The man put the multi in multi-millionaire." As though the older woman saw the devastation in the pretty young woman's hazel eyes, she suggested a meeting between Sterling and Faye, on the off chance it could accomplish something.

"I'm not saying he'll agree to it," she said, "but I will put in a call and see where it takes us. Regardless of how impractical it is and how futile the final outcome may be, I'll set up a meeting for some time this week, providing Bobby can free up his busy schedule."

Honestly, Faye didn't know whether to thank Mrs. DuPont or to fume. Would anything come of meeting with a high-powered businessman who owned ninety-nine cafés? More importantly, would she have to make an awkward call to Anouk De Ven in Holland to cancel the Van Gogh drawings and letters being loaned from Amsterdam?

Never one to set foot in the Northeast during the winter months, Mrs. DuPont looked out of place in early December's chill; she could have sat by the pool in Boca Raton and revealed her plans over the phone, but instead she had trekked to the gallery's doorstep to lay out the circumstances directly in front of Faye. If nothing else, Faye admired that.

"I've taken up enough of your time," Mrs. DuPont said finally and rose from her chair. "Consider taking the day off to think everything through. It doesn't have to be the end of the road if you look at other opportunities. Think of New York City. The art scene there is five times what it is here. Broadening your career might be the best thing for you."

"My career," Faye murmured. Her career had just slipped through her fingers, hadn't it?

"Trust me," DuPont added. "You'll want to speak with Bobby. He's the one with the big ideas. Who knows, maybe he'll allow you to hang art in his café on commission. It might not be what you're used to, but change isn't always bad, now is it?"

Ronald assisted his boss in wrapping the fur shawl around her shoulders. "You'll land on your feet, Faye," she said, with a thinness to her voice. "I can guarantee you that."

Faye heard the message behind her boss's pep talk loud and clear. Soon she would be out of a job. And she knew that the potential to get another job of higher stature hinged on showing the Van Gogh works. A resumé with that type of acquisition on it could land her a directorship almost anywhere. Without it, though, she would merely float to another gallery and start from the bottom.

Faye scanned the paintings all around her. "Do me a favor," she asked Mrs. DuPont, and pointed to a large canvas. "Tell me what you see."

The woman gazed at the work as if it was a flying saucer pinned to the wall. "My goodness," she stammered, "you're putting me on the spot, aren't you? If you must know...my interpretation would be...well I think it's...I'm guessing that...It's lovely. Is that enough?"

Ronald and Faye exchanged smirks that went unseen by Mrs. DuPont who stared intently at the painting.

Once he cleared his throat, Ronald suggested that the meaning of any abstract painting varied with the viewer's set of personal experiences, and said that for him, this one was about the inner turmoil inside of every individual.

"Oh no it can't mean that," Mrs. DuPont said quickly. "If anything, it's about beauty and running free. Don't you see all those swirls there? They mean freedom."

Faye sighed. Five minutes ago she would have staked her reputation on anyone's ability to be enriched by a painting, but at the moment she was at a loss for words. Clearly, Mrs. DuPont had owned this gallery just for the prestige of owning it. Her passion didn't extend beyond the sign above the door. Art for her was not worth the fight, which was why she was selling out to some weasel who wanted people to order their lattes from an illuminated bar. It seemed so senseless that Faye's head ached.

"Let me see you both out," Faye said, a glimmer of a smile in the corners of her mouth. The sooner she got rid of them, the faster she could concoct a plan that would at least extend the life of the gallery through the springtime. The Van Gogh exhibit had to be shown.

"Remember what I said," Mrs. DuPont reiterated as she left. "You'll land on your feet. I can feel it."

Ronald handed Mrs. DuPont into a big black Yukon at the curb where Faye stood and peered up at the sky. The enormous rental car lumbered down the one-way street as the puffy clouds drifted overhead. It was obvious to Faye that things were slowly moving in a new direction. Whether or not she could save the gallery remained to be seen, but she knew without a doubt that she would fight for Hirsch Gallery.

***

A few hours later, her best friend, Norman, stopped walking and turned to face her. "I'm having a little trouble understanding this," he said. The darkness of the street made his eyes the brightest part of his face, and his large nose deepened the shadow on his undersized mouth.

"Join the club," Faye replied. She moved a few feet forward to capture the glow from the streetlamp. "Take a look at this—" She pulled a folded piece of paper from her purse. "That's him."

Norman set down his briefcase on the sidewalk, his striped tie swinging forward. Then he smoothed out the paper. It showed a small photo of a man in a business suit holding a shovel, ready to break ground. The top of the page read: 'Bobby Sterling's Trendy Café Revitalizes South Beach.' "If you want me to read the article," he said as he pushed the paper closer to his eyes, "it may be best to wait until we get to the brownstone."

Faye snatched the paper back and shoved it deep into her bag. "Not necessary. I can tell you what it says. Things like Bobby knows his clientele and Everything he touches makes a profit and It's best not to stand in his way. People think he's the savior of the frothy latte simply because he provides them with a swanky place to drink their coffees. Something tells me the man will give new meaning to the word arrogant, but I can't say for sure until I meet him." They neared the next streetlamp and Faye picked up the pace.

"Slow down, will you?"

She had a habit of walking quickly when she was deep in thought. Today her world had been upended, and in order to lend meaning to everything that had happened, she needed to sort it out in her head. If there was a way to fix this mess, it might hinge on Mrs. DuPont keeping her promise to set up a meeting with Sterling.

Norman switched his briefcase into his other hand and doubled his speed. "My God, Faye, it's not a race. I'm supposed to be walking you home, not chasing after you."

Huffing from the exertion, he glanced down at his dress shoes—made with the finest Italian leather—as if realizing they wouldn't spring into action like a pair of sneakers. Furthermore, his business suit lacked the flexibility of a pair of sweat pants. When he caught up to her, he reached out for her wrist. "Were you out to prove I'm not in shape after all?"

Faye shrugged her shoulders. "Sorry, Norman. I didn't mean to rush off."

In this region along the Hudson River, most streets ran parallel to the water; those that veered off and twisted toward downtown Albany where Faye and Norman lived were considered chic and desirable for the under-thirty-five crowd. The cozy walk-up Faye called home was a brownstone connected to other brownstones that stretched down the length of the street. These beautifully maintained row houses extended for several blocks.

She climbed up the wide brownstone steps. "I won't lose the gallery, Norman."

He took a deep breath. "It never crossed my mind that you would."

Chapter Two

Faye gave a twisted smile, "Please, sit down."

Had Norman been present he would have recognized that phony grin of hers. She only used it to express severe annoyance—like when someone arrived notably late to a meeting and then held up his hand several times to ask for her patience while he took a few "urgent" calls.

They sat at the same card table where she and Mrs. DuPont had sat a week before. Originally, she'd thought it was ingenious to have Sterling meet her at the gallery on a Saturday afternoon, but it only left her disappointed when the man failed to admire the artwork. He'd shaken hands with her at the door, and then sat down at the table, eyes forward.

Now, he paced around the table, the phone at his ear.

When he veered toward the entrance, apparently looking to get more privacy for his call, which was the third one he'd answered in fifteen minutes, it was assumed that Faye would patiently wait for him to be finished.

By the time he strolled back to the table, Faye was having second thoughts about the efficacy of the meeting, much less her tolerance for a man who seemed only to value his own time and no one else's. It was obvious that the handsome Bobby Sterling made people wait on purpose because he was that important.

She had to admit she'd imagined him differently, a man with thinning hair and a pudgy belly perhaps. But his figure was surprisingly trim and his straight, dark hair showed no signs of re-treating toward the back of his skull. His broad shoulders and short neck produced a bulldoggish appearance, but only because his height was below average. On the face of things, the man was as handsome as they come, only lacking a tall physique to be considered dashing.

"Shall we get down to business?" he finally asked her, and waved his hand in the air, perhaps to focus her attention.

She'd been staring at the painting several feet beyond Sterling's backside, and wondered if the walls of his home were adorned with commissioned canvases of him riding horses or at the helm of a yacht. Expensive hobbies for a man who made millions seemed appropriate.

"Ms. Brooks," Sterling said, the muscle in his jaw working. "I'd like to hear what you have to say. Shall we get on with it?"

Faye raised her eyebrows. Clearly, he expected her to snap to attention when he was ready. "Uh yes, I suppose so." As she began explaining why she'd asked Mrs. DuPont to call this meeting in the first place, she didn't break eye contact with him.

Norman had coached her last night about the best way to make an impact on a man like Sterling. "You need to show him you mean business," Norman had said as he'd handed her the bowl of popcorn and paused the movie they were watching.

Faye wasn't about to blow this chance. She'd stared at her face in the mirror all morning, practicing a variety of looks: curling her lips and then uncurling them, fixing her gaze and then unfixing it. She supposed there was a method to looking confident, poised and determined, and she hoped to present herself that way to Sterling.

She angled her chin a notch higher and leveled her voice. "The benefits this gallery brings to the community can't be measured in the number of lattes sold in a café. It's been a cultural icon for the past five years, which means removing people's access to its fine art would leave a gaping hole. A trendy café can't heal that type of wound."

Sterling leaned forward, his chest touching the table. "How has a latte ever wounded anybody?"

"Surely you can see the detriment this will cause." Her eyes narrowed and then softened. "People in this area are inspired by this place. The works of art give them hope and light and fulfillment." In one delicate motion, she pushed her honey-colored hair back from her face. "Anyone who wants to minimize the power of art is doing so for their own wallet."

"A businessman tends to make money on purpose, you're right about that. But I think you're failing to see the bigger picture."

Faye uncrossed her legs under the table and took a deep breath. "Far be it from me to fail to see something." She knew he wouldn't get her intended meaning simply because he hadn't even glanced at the art which surrounded him.

Sterling's phone buzzed. Faye expected him to answer it and rush off, but instead he grimaced when he checked the caller ID. For several seconds he peered down at the screen and then tapped the end call button. "This isn't my first rodeo," he said, and grabbed hold of the knot in his tie and tugged down on it.

Faye wondered who had called and what power the person had over Sterling. The way he yanked on his tie suggested he needed more room around his throat to breathe. She was reminded of something Norman had told her last night. Find his weakness and use it against him. Well, this seemed to qualify as a weakness, but since she couldn't identify the caller, how exactly could she use it against him?

When he stopped fiddling with his tie and leaned his elbows on the table, his heavy-looking Rolex slid up his arm. "This building's in a perfect location. And it's the perfect size—a single-story space with hardwood floors and a brick exterior. Because of those things, I'm paying top dollar for it. I didn't expect to encounter any obstacles. But here you are."

For the first time he looked at Faye with a smile. "You are impassioned about saving this gallery. It means something to you and I am the one trying to take it away. I suppose that makes me the bad guy in all of this. So let me apologize," he said, and extended his arm across the table to pat the top of her hand.

As brief as the touch was, Faye started to weaken. Perhaps the man wasn't so bad after all. Maybe he wasn't the heinous developer of trendy cafés she'd anticipated.

"I did get a verbal warning from Mrs. DuPont not to upset you," he continued, slowly removing his hand from on top of hers. "The woman seems to think you're a gallery guru."

"She doesn't even know the half of it." Faye closed her eyes for a moment and sighed. "Recently I received permission to exhibit some artwork from overseas. Letters and drawings will be meticulously packaged and flown here from Amsterdam. It took all of my persuasive skills to bend the ear of the curator's assistant. Once or twice I thought she was going to hang up on me. And the paperwork has been endless. I feel as though I'm signing my life away. No little gallery in this area has ever received Van Gogh works on loan." She waited for him to show signs of being impressed but his face remained blank.

"I see," he said finally. "You can show them beforehand. I mean the renovations won't begin for another month or two. All your hard work doesn't have to go to waste."

"The loan is for March." Her voice sounded hollow. "There just isn't time," she added. "Unless—" Instantly, her face brightened and she sat up straighter. "I could dip into my savings. I could rent out the space month by month until after the show."

Bobby chuckled. "How far in advance did you request those Van Gogh pictures from—where was it—Amsterdam?"

Faye tilted her head in thought. "Oh gee, I started contacting them in the summertime. Last week I sent back the final bits of paperwork."

"Well, the teams of men I've got coming to overhaul this place were contracted two months ago. If I canceled now, I'd look like a damn fool." He rubbed his jaw. "It would put the entire project at risk."

Faye responded in an even tone. "Delaying the start of a project may not be ideal but it's not out of the ordinary, is it? My father's an architect in San Diego, and projects get delayed there all the time."

"Your father, huh." He twisted his watch around to see the time. "Wait a minute. Isn't your last name Brooks? Don't tell me your father is Wellington Brooks."

Faye gave a half smile. "Okay, I won't tell you."

"I've had dealings with his firm over a structure I plan to have built in San Diego. It's still in the planning phase, of course, but as soon as I finish the café here, I'm looking to expand on the west coast."

Faye tapped her fingertips on the table. "How about you cancel the café here and focus your energies on the west coast."

However briefly, Sterling's eyes twinkled. "Mrs. DuPont and I have signed papers. It's quite official: I own the building."

Faye put one hand under her chin to think.

"A change in plans now would only confuse things," he added.

"Well I disagree. The way I look at it, you've got more cafés in more cities than you know what to do with and I, on the other hand, only have Hirsch. The disparity is alarming; don't you agree?"

"I'm a businessman, Ms. Brooks. Surely you can see that. My perspective on this place is monetary while yours is emotional. I didn't expect us to see eye to eye. Nevertheless, my full possession of this"—he waved his hand to indicate the space all around— "takes hold on February first. Seeing as I've got the paperwork to back that up, there's really little else to discuss."

He straightened one arm over the table and pulled down on his sleeve, one gold cuff link winking in the light. "Your commitment to this gallery is honorable."

Obviously, she hadn't gotten through to him. He'd bombarded her with ineffectual jibber jabber for forty minutes, but the only words she longed to hear would provide assurance that the gallery would remain open indefinitely. If he couldn't promise her even a two-month delay, then it seemed useless to banter on and on. She stood up and placed one hand on her hip. She wasn't about to give up.

Then another one of Norman's suggestions from last night popped back into her head. *If all else fails, flirt a little…men love that.* Quite frankly, Faye chastised herself for not unbuttoning her blouse within an inch of her bosom before this meeting started. To do it now would be inappropriate. Beforehand she'd seen little point in using her looks to sway Sterling's opinion, but now she loosened her ethical stance to save the gallery.

"Before you go," she said with a lazy smile, "let me show you around."

Sterling cleared his throat. "Good to see you're accepting the circumstances. I'd love a look around."

"We should start over here." She led him to a large canvas in the corner of the gallery. "This one isn't my favorite. I'm saving that for last. However, look at the brushwork."

Sterling leaned his head closer to the surface and said, "Ah yes, really thick paint."

Faye positioned herself close to him and let the scent of her perfume do some of the work. She'd worn a tight-fitting skirt in deep purple that stopped above her knee. The fuzzy belt around her small waist was mohair. The large lavender flowers on her blouse were pale and the thin fabric allowed the straps of her camisole to show thru underneath. The outfit had won Norman's approval last night when he'd convinced her that a male point of view had value. "It's the subliminal advertising you'll need to get a guy like Sterling in your corner," he'd said and pointed to Faye's bosom.

"I didn't plan on wearing jeans and a tee shirt," she'd shot back at him. "Besides, my attire has nothing to do with getting the man to see the validity of my argument."

Boy, how the tables had turned. Either Faye had reached a new low in what she was willing to do for her career, or she was finally grasping a solution to save Hirsch. She wasn't proud of it, of course, but a woman had to level the playing field when art and beauty were up against delicious lattes.

With her hip movements exaggerated, Faye sashayed to the next canvas, her strappy heels clicking across the floor. And Bobby—he'd insisted she call him by his first name—trotted right next to her. "So Bobby," she said, slowly putting her hair behind one ear and letting her lips part slightly, "what do you think of this one?"

It seemed to take him a moment to release his gaze, as if he was fascinated by her earlobe. "Oh gosh, well gee, it's very bright. Lots of different colors, for sure."

Faye grazed her fingertips along the base of her throat where a pendant in the shape of a circle hung. The slow movement of her hand must have intrigued Bobby; she could tell by the way his eyes softened and then narrowed. "It's electric...if I had to choose a term," she said softly. "The colors create a form of brilliance for the viewer. Something akin to sparks, wouldn't you say?"

When he didn't answer, Faye led him into her office, in one corner of the storage room. She reached for a folder on her desk. "See this," she said and shared the contents with him.

He tilted his head and held the papers in his hand. "I notice some paragraphs written in a foreign language, possibly Dutch, and three signatures at the bottom of the page next to an official-looking stamp in bluish ink." He paused. "Are these the documents allowing the Van Gogh works to travel to America?"

They were standing shoulder to shoulder, so she turned her head to smile at him. "They are. You're holding Mrs. DuPont's copy. Anyway, more than once I thought about framing every single page. Finally, I realized how silly I was being."

Bobby laughed, the type of laugh that suggested he knew exactly what she meant. "The first café I ever built had me over the moon. I spend half the profits plastering the walls in my office with every article written about its success. When I counted thirty-three frames, I knew it'd gotten out of hand."

Her smile widened. "That's pretty bad."

"I'll tell you what I'm going to do," Sterling said as he closed the folder and handed it back to her. "I'll have my foreman look into a delay. If it seems feasible—and I'm not making any judgments until I get a report from him—I'll rent you this space during February, March, and April–until after your precious Van Gogh pictures go back to Holland. Sound fair?"

Faye jumped into his arms. Against all odds, Hirsch Gallery would remain open for a while longer. The community would get to see the Van Gogh drawings and letters after all. She'd won.

The only thing that gave her pause was how her slinky movements may have tipped the scales. A part of her disliked the notion that she'd used her feminine wiles to bring his thinking in line with hers. She'd achieved her goal, underhandedly or not, and for the sake of the gallery she would find a way to live with that.

Her chin rested on his shoulder. Then Bobby put his arms around her waist and said, "Seems like I said the right thing for once."

She smiled into his collarbone, the softness of his lapel making her realize the garment was made of expensive material. "Wait until I tell Isaac and Zoe," she said, and explained that they were the gallery's guard and attendant.

"We should celebrate," he said and pulled away from her to look into her eyes. Then he glanced around the space. "Any champagne around here?"

She laughed. "We serve punch, brie, and crackers at openings. No alcohol allowed."

"I thought you artist types were supposed to be wild and crazy."

"Art history major. We tend to keep tight reins on our wild sides."

Bobby rested his buttocks on her desk and pulled Faye into his arms so her back was against his chest. "So tell me...What's the wildest thing you've ever done?"

The question struck her as pillow talk after mindboggling sex, only they hadn't had any, so she took her time in answering. "I'd have to say my experience in Italy. My father took me there as a child and we climbed the smaller volcanoes at the base of Mount Etna."

Bobby shrugged his shoulders, as if in disbelief. "Are you kidding me? There must be something else—something that could've gotten you arrested or thrown out of a place? Think harder." Gently resting his palms on the top of her head, he wiggled his fingers to massage her scalp. "This should help you call forth some tantalizing memories." Then he put his lips next to her ear and added, "The spicier the better."

The way his hands poked around her noggin felt luxurious, only she grew so relaxed that recalling her own name seemed difficult, much less bringing to mind some wild event to impress Bobby. "How about you?" she said finally.

"Me?" He took one hand off her head to scratch his own jaw. "Well, I'm a sensible businessman, of course. There's no room in my life for shenanigans. I was hoping to get some spectacular stories out of you."

"Oh no, that's not the way it works, not by a long shot. If I have to think of something to share, then so do you, Mr. Sterling."

"Back to calling me Mr. Sterling, are you?"

She pivoted to face him. "Mr. Sterling isn't so bad, is it?" And with her disheveled hair looking like a lion's mane around her face, she planted a kiss on the end of his nose.

Bobby had been seduced by enough women—usually female CEO's of companies who wanted to buy him out, and in some instances the wives of the men in charge—to know that Faye had laid it on rather thick. She'd gone from giving him pointed stares throughout the first half of their meeting, as though she wanted to divest him of his heart and lungs, to teasing him with that lock of hair she had wrapped around her finger.

A part of him had hoped she would continue the little charade all the way until breakfast the next morning at his place. But honestly, her temptress skills needed a bit of work. Case in point, when she'd thought he wasn't looking, he'd caught her relaxing her pouty lips and reversing the roundness of the hip that she had stuck out. Too bad for her that he had excellent peripheral vision.

The more effort she put into playing the part of a siren the easier it would be for him to suggest a lousy offer, one that she'd have no choice but to accept because the gallery was her life. And for that reason alone, he wanted the games to continue...for now. Not until he thought the moment was right would he reveal what he planned to do.

In fact, when she had led him into the storage room, he'd been all smiles. Perhaps she wants to do it on her desk, he'd thought. But apparently the sight of her desk had the opposite effect on her. She had become all business. Instead of shoving the stacks of papers off the surface to make room for their lovemaking, the woman had reached for a folder and opened it. That was when she'd shown him the acquisition papers for the Van Gogh show.

And there was one moment when the tip of his nose touched a wave of her hair. The fruitiness of the scent had made him wonder if the soap she used to cleanse her body had a similar fragrance. Being levelheaded enough to know he wouldn't find out right then did nothing to abate his interest in unraveling that mystery someday. After all, he'd noticed her slender, cute figure and that amazing light brown hair: it looked almost blonde under the track lighting. He even found her little earlobes quite adorable.

Chapter Three

In the two weeks it took for things to go south with Bobby Sterling, Faye had consumed two dinners with the man, and broken the heel of her brand new stilettos during an evening of dancing. Things had started unraveling that night as they stepped onto the nightclub's terrace for some fresh air, and Bobby's phone rang. The Head Foreman was returning his call about the cost estimates for delaying the project. Faye stood close to Bobby because she needed to hold onto his arm to steady herself. The broken heel was a nuisance, but at least she could hear bits and pieces of the conversation.

None of it sounded good. At one point the foreman raised his voice and Faye heard his words clearly: "Stop thinking with your pecker, Bob. Don't be a damn fool. No woman's worth it."

During the cab ride home, Faye peered out the window at the dark sky and willed herself not to cry. Her angry refusal to let Bobby drive her home only confirmed that she needed to cool down. It crossed her mind that a man like Sterling would expect to rekindle what they'd started in a few days' time, but she wanted nothing to do with him.

"How could he?" she asked the cab driver, her voice a little shaky.

"You've got to get him between the eyes," the man responded and took the right-hand turn sharply. "And, trust me, there are plenty of ways to do it."

Faye sniffled. "I'm not following. How do you mean?"

The cabby glanced at Faye in the rear view mirror as she unzipped her handbag, pulled out a tissue, and dabbed her eyes. "I'm not in the habit of sticking my nose in other people's business, but the last young lady I saw so distraught in the back of my cab was running from a malicious boyfriend. And now you're sitting in that same spot pretending not to cry."

For a man in his late fifties, Ray had several inches of muscle on him. "I'd like to grab this Bobby fellow by the scruff of the neck and pound him into the shape of a belt buckle. I can't help but think if I had a daughter your age, and if nobody helped her...."

Ray's gravelly voice somehow matched the black leather vest he wore, motorcycle patches all down the back. Faye noticed the one on his shoulder when he hunched over the steering wheel to see if the light had turned green.

"What do you have that he wants?" Ray asked her.

"That's the problem. He has something I want. The gallery."

Ray coughed and then spit out the window. "Sweetheart, with the way you look, there's gotta be somethin' you can hold over him. Is he married? You could mention it to his wife."

The breeze from the open window jostled Faye's hair. "No wife."

"Okay. What about some crooked business dealings? Expose him for a crook and he'll back down."

Ray closed the window and Faye's hair stopped blowing. "I don't think so."

"Plenty more options," he said, and cut off the oncoming car to make a left-hand turn. "Same to you, moron," he shouted to the other driver, who had blared his horn.

Once they were safely through the intersection, Faye asked him, "Do you know what the worst part is?"

"Never been good at guessing games."

"I thought he was leaning in to kiss me." Faye looked down at her lap and realized she still held her broken heel in one hand. "The next thing I knew he was going on and on about it costing thirty grand to delay the project, which meant I would have to pay ten grand a month to rent the space until after the show is over. Can you believe that?"

"And you've got no way to raise that kind of money, am I right?"

"My savings won't spread that far."

"Not many folks' would." He coughed but didn't spit. "You're in quite a pickle; I'll grant you that. But I wouldn't give up just yet."

Ray's sentiments stayed with Faye all week. She began to think he was her Christmas angel, especially since he swung by with the cab every night to drive her down the block to her brownstone. Norman couldn't walk her home this week because he was in charge of babysitting his niece and nephew while his sister went last-minute Christmas shopping for their toys.

"Get in," he said.

"This is so unnecessary," Faye said but settled herself in the back seat. "I wish you'd let me pay the fare at least." She watched Ray's side profile as he grabbed something off the passenger's seat.

"Not on your life." He extended his arm over the top of the seat to hand Faye a small white envelope.

"What's this?" She could feel the thickness of it between her fingertips.

He pulled away from the curb. "See for yourself."

She peeled back the flap and saw a stack of bills, twenties and fifties mostly. "I don't understand. Why are you showing me this?"

"Count it," he said and picked up speed.

In the dim light she had to hold the bills up to the window and catch the reflection of the streetlights to count it properly. "Okay, there seems to be—three, three-twenty, four, four-fifty— about five hundred here. Not too shabby if these are your tips for tonight."

"Let's call them your tips." He pulled over in front of her brownstone and put his flashers on. "Some motorcycle brothers of mine were happy to empty their pockets for an art collection. Turns out they all wanted to do their part to save your gallery. It ain't much—" He twisted around to look at her. "But it'll cover some of the rent."

Her mouth dropped open. "Oh Ray." She lunged forward to kiss his cheek and squeeze him around the shoulders. "That's the sweetest thing anyone's ever done for me, but I can't possibly let you do it. It's too kind."

"You've got no choice. I won't take the money back."

With the envelope against her chest, she scooted back into her seat. "You're a spectacular man; do you know that?"

"Keep talking...."

"The kindest, most generous, strongest man I know."

He waved his hand at her. "Go on, get out of here."

"I'm not finished. You're a superhero, only you don't know it."

Ray laughed. "I don't own a single red cape. So I know you're mistaken."

Faye didn't have time to convince him otherwise because a call from dispatch came through and Ray needed to drive to the airport to pick someone up. So she opened the door and got out, briefly pausing at his front window until he pushed the button to roll it down. "Until tomorrow night, big guy."

He let the car idle until Faye disappeared into the brownstone. The chilly night air coming through the window must have reminded him that he needed to get back to work—a fare waited to be picked up—and he drove off.

The brownstone's interior staircase ran up the left side of the foyer. There were two apartments on the second floor, one Norman's and the other Faye's, which meant it was just as easy for Faye to pop in to say hello to her neighbor as it would be for her to unlock her own door and scrounge for something to eat.

There was a momentary silence after Faye knocked on 2B, and

then the pounding of feet, and the shouts of children's voices grew louder as they scurried toward the door.

"Don't open it yet. I've got to see who it is first," Norman was saying. "...Oh look, it's Auntie Faye." He'd barely cracked the door an inch when his niece and nephew wiggled through to hug Faye.

"Auntie Faye, did you bring us anything?" Their round faces peered up at her.

Faye submerged her hand in the deep pocket of her coat and extracted two candy canes. "Here, Lily. And there's one for you, Benjamin."

Both candy canes had sustained hairline cracks from being in her coat pocket since yesterday. So when the children held them up, the curved parts flopped over.

"Mine's broken," Benjamin said.

Lily frowned. "Mine too."

"Sorry, guys."

Norman knelt down on one knee and told the children that Auntie Faye only understands 'fragile' when it applies to paintings and sculptures. They gave him a puzzled looked and then dashed off to watch television on the sofa.

Norman led Faye into the kitchen and immediately grabbed whitish bowls from the cabinet, below which was an eighteen-jar spice rack. He pointed to the spices. "My sister gave me this several months ago for my birthday. I just took it out of the box before you came. According to her, it's the touch my kitchen needs to entice a woman into thinking I'm a suitable mate. Jacklyn says spices indicate to a lady that a man is willing to prepare a meal once in a while to save her the trouble." He set the bowls on the table. "In other words, now that I'm thirty-eight, it's supposed to be bait to attract a quality female. How else will I produce cousins for Lily and Benjamin if I don't settle down soon?"

Faye unstacked the bowls and put one in front of herself and one on Norman's side of the table. "She means well."

He ducked into the refrigerator and grabbed several cartons of Chinese food, and stacked them against his chest for carrying to the table. He positioned the cartons like chess pieces and moved some forward and some back, advancing the dishes he knew Faye preferred. "Dig in," he said and scooped pork fried rice into his bowl.

Faye shoved a forkful of noodles into her mouth. "This is soooo good."

"We aim to please here at Maynard's twenty-four-hour dining chalet."

Faye looped her hair behind one ear. "Very funny. I thought you might need some help watching the kids. What time is Jacklyn getting back?"

"She phoned an hour ago. With all the background noise at the mall, I could only catch every other word." Norman chuckled. "And true to form, I distinctly heard my sister shouting at someone before she hung up. From what I could gather, she demanded so-and-so put down the last Glam-O-Doll on the planet because she planned to buy it for Lily."

"At this time of year," Faye said, and dabbed the corner of her mouth with a napkin, "the mall shoppers show their ugly sides."

Norman held his fork out with a strip of chicken on it for Faye to try. "Never stand between a mother and a toy for her precious child," he said. "Staying out of the fray is the most basic survival skill I can think of."

"Yummy," Faye said of the spicy chicken.

"Uncle Norman, I'm thirsty." Lily entered the kitchen dragging a stuffed bear behind her, and climbed onto Faye's lap.

"Milk? Juice?" her uncle asked as he waited to pull open the refrigerator door.

The child rubbed her eyes. "Juuuicy."

Faye attempted to untangle the knots in the six-year-old's hair. "You look tired, Lily. What time does Mommy usually put you to bed?"

"Dunno." As soon as her uncle put the juice box in front of her, she sipped from the tiny straw until the flimsy sides caved in. "All gone," she muttered.

"Wow, you were thirsty," Faye said, and wove a loose braid into the child's hair. Then she looked around for something to secure it with.

Norman pulled a rubber band out of the drawer. "Will this work?"

"It's not a pink ribbon, but yes."

Lily slid down from Faye's lap and twirled around. "Look at me, Uncle Norman. I'm a big girl with a braid."

"I can see that. You look very pretty." Norman picked Lily's bear up off the floor where she'd abandoned it and asked her to go play with Benjamin.

"Do I have to?"

"Yes you have to."

"I had a very interesting drive home," Faye said once Lily had stopped peeking into the room from the doorway. Norman had clearly lost his patience when she did it three times in a row. Faye had watched him leap up from the table and carry the child like a sack of potatoes against his hip into the living room. Giggling and squealing, Lily told the horsey to go faster. Shortly after they were out of sight, Faye faintly heard Norman telling her to stay put or else she wasn't getting any more juice boxes tonight, pretty little miss. Obviously, the tactic worked because Lily hadn't snuck up on them again.

"You won't believe what Ray did," she continued.

"Talked you into buying one of those smaller motorcycles for women?"

She shot him a look. "No, of course not."

"It might be better if you just tell me because I can throw out guesses all night."

Her purse was on the counter so she brought it over to the table and searched inside for the envelope. "Ah, here it is." She pushed it halfway across the table and used a nod of her head to indicate Norman should slide it toward himself and take a look.

There wasn't exactly a clear path with all the food containers in the way, so Norman used his forearm to roughly clear everything to one side. "Of course you could've handed it to me across the table, but it's just like you to build up suspense over a silly little envelope."

Once he turned back the flap and peeked inside, his eyes got wide and he gave a low whistle. "You rob a bank?"

"Ray took up a collection for the gallery. A group of his friends chipped in."

With the trained eye of an accountant, Norman fanned his fingertip across the edges of the bills. "Around five hundred, I'd say."

Faye rested her elbows on the table and let her head drop into her hands. In a muffled voice, she said, "It's wrong for me to accept it, I know."

"Difficult times call for drastic measures. You're not the type of person who'd ever grow accustomed to handouts. However, this time a lot of people are counting on you to swallow your pride."

She lifted her head. "Maybe you're right. But it's still a long way toward the thirty grand I need."

"Speaking of that exorbitant amount, have you heard from Sterling?"

Faye's lips twisted and she repeated what Norman had just said. "Have I heard from Sterling? It's safe to say he's not getting the hint that I don't want to speak with him. Fifteen messages are a bit excessive, don't you think?"

"What does he say?"

"Oh Faye, please take my calls. Oh Faye, I need to speak to you. Oh Faye, I understand how deeply angry you must be...." So that Norman didn't notice the sadness mixed with fury in her eyes, she let her gaze float above his right shoulder, not making direct eye contact with him. "The man is pathetic."

He seemed to give her a moment to collect her thoughts before he asked another question, and this time he reached his arm across the table to briefly pat her shoulder. "He's still in California?"

"Of all places, yes."

"And he's hired your father's firm to expand his business on the west coast?"

"It's maddening, but I'm afraid so. The only good news is that he'll probably be in San Diego through Christmas. My dad, on the other hand, is scheduled to fly up in a couple of days. I'm hoping the two of them won't have the opportunity to engage in much conversation. Besides, I think he's working with Jack or Ron, the other partners in the firm."

Norman leaned in. "You know, Faye, this might be a good thing. Maybe your father can convince Sterling to ease up on the rent."

She shook her head and stuck her hand out. "Absolutely not. The last thing I want is somebody fighting my battles for me. Besides, this is something I have to do on my own."

Norman leaned back in his chair and locked his hands behind his head. "You do realize your father isn't poor, right? An architectural firm like his brings in clients from all over the world. He's at the forefront of his field, which means money is flowing in all directions. It would be no skin off his nose to write you a check for thirty thousand dollars. Knowing Wellington, he'd want to come to your rescue."

"That's just it. I don't need rescuing. I'm perfectly capable of raising the money myself."

"Will you take a loan from me, then?" He tilted his head, softened his shoulders and raised his eyebrows. "Pleeeease?"

"Your puppy dog eyes don't work on me, remember? Anyway, you sound like Benjamin."

Norman balled up his fists in mock frustration. "You're a stubborn woman, Faye. Has anyone ever told you that?"

"You, my dad, Isaac, Zoe, Mrs. DuPont."

"And do you ever listen to any of us?"

She looked directly at him. "Shouldn't you go check on the kids?"

Norman stomped off. Faye closed the partially-full cartons of food and tossed out the empty ones. She took a sponge from the sink to wipe down the table. "I could always get a second job," she said out loud.

Chapter Four

Three Weeks Earlier

Broad-shouldered and in a hurry, a man brushed passed Faye on the dark city street and in no time at all she realized her purse was gone, snatched off her shoulder with a fairly delicate yank. She stifled the impulse to scream because this had happened before. Nothing of importance was in her handbag anyway. Three folded twenties, two credit cards, and her driver's license were safely lodged in her bra, tucked against her bosom.

It gave her a fair amount of pleasure to imagine the crook ducking into an alley to unzip her bag, only to find a hairbrush with Van Gogh's Starry Night painted on the handle, a notepad with an attached pen, a tin of breath mints, the tangerine she hadn't had time to eat at lunch, and some postcard announcements for the show at the gallery.

Too many notches down from high fashion, the oversized handbag was not worth stealing in its own right. Faye had deliberately stopped buying designer brands after the second theft. It had been on the same street, only a different thug, and many months before. So on the nights she planned to walk home from the gallery after dark, she carried a faux crocodile purse, one of the ugliest ones she could find.

Unseasonably mild weather for early December had not allowed the river to freeze over yet, but Faye couldn't see the water from here. With no snow on the ground, the approaching winter was off to a slow start. Dutifully, the nights churned out their darkness at four-thirty, which didn't leave Faye sufficient time to complete her work at the gallery and stroll home in the daylight.

Faye slowed down as she neared her brownstone and looked over her shoulder. Slightly mesmerized by the way the street-light's glow danced in front of a pair of lovers who walked arm in arm, Faye wondered if it might be time to get one of those—a man to drape her arm around. Realistically, though, a man required more momentum than her stalled love life had to offer at this point.

Long hours at the gallery made it a challenge to carry out simple errands like lugging dirty clothes to the laundromat. The fact that laundering her outfits didn't coincide with putting on the last clean blouse and skirt in the closet spoke volumes about her ability to juggle a man at the present time. To squeeze a lover into her schedule was out of the question.

As the director of Hirsch Gallery on State Street, she was knee deep in arranging exhibits of art from all over the globe, and she often promoted the paintings and sculptures that hung on the walls or stood on the pedestals to the position of cherished family members. Most recently, she'd obtained three Chagall paintings from Lincoln Center, on loan for three months.

Faye walked up the front steps of the brownstone, followed the interior set of stairs that led to her apartment door on the second floor, and set about sticking her head in the freezer to locate something to defrost. Breaded shrimp would only take twelve minutes in the oven, so she decided on those, along with a salad.

Meanwhile, she sauntered into the bathroom to tie back her honey-colored hair and slip into her robe. It felt good to relax after a long day of negotiations. She'd been on the phone for part of the afternoon with Anouk De Ven from the Van Gogh Museum in Amsterdam. When it came to their beloved Post-Impressionist artist, the Dutch could be sticklers, and Faye had known it would be easier to deal with the smaller of the two prize museums in the Netherlands; the Rijksmuseum had simply been too grand to tackle.

As she made herself a cup of oolong tea a few minutes later, her cell phone rang. She jerked her shoulder up to hold the device steady against her ear. It was her father, reiterating his plans to visit her for Christmas. He would be on a plane flying east in a few weeks to see his only child. With a bit of sadness in his voice, he reminded her how long it had been since the two of them had shared a holiday.

"I'm not a little girl anymore," Faye said as she set her teacup down and leaned into the oven to grab the tray of shrimp. Her statement was in response to Wellington inquiring about her safety in that neighborhood of hers. Faye had mistakenly told her father about the purse-snatching from a few months ago and he seemed to be worrying about it still. Little did he know it had happened again tonight.

"I don't like the idea of you walking home late at night unattended," he said with an edge to his voice.

Faye crinkled her mouth. "My apartment is a block away. I can practically see it from the gallery door. Nothing's going to happen to me."

"If I lived closer, I'd walk you home myself," he said, as if it made perfect sense. "But since that isn't an option, I will have to settle for your word. Promise me you'll keep your eyes open, Faye. Who knows what's in the mind of a criminal. Today they grab purses; tomorrow they may want more."

Faye sunk her teeth into the end of the oven mitt to pull it off, and then said, "Dad, you worry too much. I'll see you soon."

They ended their conversation with Wellington giving an audible humph sound. Faye scooped several shrimp onto her plate and smiled. Certainly her father's intention to protect her from afar was commendable and she didn't mind reveling in the knowledge that he would do anything to ensure her wellbeing and happiness.

She settled on the sofa and plopped one shrimp after another into her mouth. Eventually, the late broadcast of the news came on. A short segment showed the taverns and shops along Lark Street. Several purse snatchings had occurred in the last week. Others were being robbed of their ugly purses too, Faye thought. A part of her realized she shouldn't be making light of it, but even the anchorwoman mentioned that the snatcher was nonviolent and appeared only to be looking for cash.

By the time Faye eased under the covers and drifted off to sleep, she'd forgotten about her eventful day. Walking home in the dark after work and being unburdened of her purse was not the subject of her dreams, and neither were her dealings with the Dutch woman from the museum in the Netherlands. Oddly enough, her sleepy thoughts wandered back to that young couple she'd seen under the streetlight.

***

As usual, Faye entered the gallery the next morning with a little bag in her hand. She paused at the guard's desk to say good morning to Isaac Thomas, an older man of African descent. "Don't tell me you don't want this," she said to him, and set the brown bag on his desk. "It's blueberry. I thought I'd mix it up a little."

Tall and thin, Issac leaned forward in his chair. "The way you spoil me is shameful, Miss Faye." He reached for the bag. "Don't get me wrong. I like it a lot. Now of course I doubt my cardiologist sees it our way. If he knew about this muffin, well my Lord, he'd probably sit us both down and have a little chat about cholesterol, sugar, and all the rest of it. But I won't tell him if you won't."

Faye swept one finger across her lips to show they were sealed, and then strolled into the main space. It had white walls and tall, white partitions that created areas of interest in the otherwise rectangular room. Colorful eight-foot-high canvases—big and imposing—lined the walls. Technically, they were abstract oils, but Faye was fond of staring at them for extended periods of time until she found people and objects hidden in the swirls of paint.

At the back of the gallery was the storage space which doubled as her office, a desk in one corner. A row of windows along the back wall looked out on an alley with a gravel path that sprouted every sort of weed and a handful of trees. Drafty warehouse type windows, with mullions that created four panes down and eleven across, had hinged metal bars to prop the middle panes open for air. The narrow space had the feel of an artist's studio in Manhattan. Gray metal shelves ran along the front—leaving a gap for the door—and held an assortment of items: stretcher bars, rolled canvas, power drills, dry wall tape, cans of white paint, brushes in all sizes, extra track lights, art hanging cables, freestanding barrier poles (to keep patrons at a safe distance from expensive artwork), stacks of 4"x 6" Plexiglas (to cover information cards), and more....

Faye heard a knock on the door, and a moment later Zoe Bowen, the gallery attendant who was an art student from a local college, poked her head in to say hello. "Hey, Faye. We're out of postcards on the desk." With dyed blood-red hair, the twenty-year-old had piercings on her eyebrow, in her nose, and at the tip of her ear. A tattoo of a paint palette adorned the underside of her forearm and Faye saw it as the student held up her arm to wave before disappearing into the gallery.

Certain that she hadn't placed all of the postcards in her purse on the evening it was snatched, Faye dug around in her desk to locate another stack.

"This should hold you for a while," Faye said as she went into the gallery and placed the postcards on the uppermost ledge. The desk had a high counter and a low writing surface beneath that, which made it difficult to see the top of Zoe's head if she leaned forward in the chair.

The attendant's desk being located at the back of the gallery, directly outside of the storage room, gave patrons the opportunity to experience the artwork before coming in contact with a human entity. When the gallery first opened its doors five years ago, every sort of discussion had taken place about where to position the desk, but no amount of Isaac dragging it to different locations had made it feel right; that was when Mrs. DuPont had waved her handkerchief in the air, signaling time for the nonsense to stop. With her mouth in a straight line and her hands folded in her lap, the owner sided with Faye. The desk would remain in the back. For Faye, it meant her new employer had faith in her abilities.

"How are your studies going?" Faye asked Zoe, who pulled a thick art history book out of her knapsack.

"We've got a test coming up on Baroque architecture."

"I remember those days. All the late nights studying." Faye leaned her elbows over the desk's high ledge to get a better look at the book's cover. "Not that I'm proud to admit it, but I spent entire days and nights with my art history book by my side while I pursued my degree. I'd hoped to commit every noteworthy item in the book to memory. My fellow students called it my hardcover boyfriend. But to me, art history was worth it."

"Whoa, that's pretty intense. I'm lead singer in a garage band. That doesn't leave a lot of time to acquaint myself with every page in this book." She flipped through to a chapter entitled Italian Baroque Architecture. On the left-hand side was a picture of St. Peter's Basilica in Rome.

Faye looked down at the book and smiled. "A thing of beauty," she commented, even though the picture was upside down to her. "And you should bear in mind that St. Peter's is a mix of Renaissance and Baroque."

"Feel free to take the test for me. It's a big lecture hall. The professor will never know."

With a wave of her hand, Faye dismissed the silly offer and went back to her office.

Chapter Five

When the weekend finally arrived, Faye tossed her dirty clothes into a wheeled laundry cart and pushed it down the sidewalk. Each brownstone that she passed looked identical to hers. The wind gusted in spurts, enough to make Faye zip up her jacket and put on the hood.

"You're off early this morning," Norman said as he came in the opposite direction and stopped in front of her cart.

"Norman, hi. Yes, I'm headed to the laundromat." She pointed to her cart.

"I can see that," he said, and flashed a smile. "I was out for a walk. No harm in going back the way I came, if you'd like some company, that is."

Faye nodded and accepted his kind offer to wheel the cart. They headed toward Lark Street, chatted about the weather, their respective Christmas plans, their jobs, and the recent purse snatchings. "I saw it on the news, too," Faye said, "three weeks ago, on the same night it happened to me."

Norman stopped the cart. "Are you telling me you were robbed? Dear God, Faye, this is serious. What did the police say? Did you give them a description of the man? Tell me you're not hurt."

Faye looked away from his searching eyes for a moment. "Um, well, I didn't exactly inform the authorities. There was no need.

I'm perfectly fine. If you take into account how ugly the purse was, the guy actually did me a favor."

Because people were going by, Norman lowered his voice. "How can you say that?"

She walked forward a few steps and waited for Norman to follow. "There's no need to worry. My valuables weren't inside the purse at the time."

Norman turned to look at Faye. "They weren't? Do you mind telling me how you managed that?"

Faye chuckled. "A woman has her ways."

Norman took that to mean she'd left the important things out of her purse that day. Perhaps home in her apartment. But as they walked further up the street to the next block, it dawned on him that perhaps Faye referred to her womanly parts. Didn't women hide money in their bras? Had Faye done that? The thought of it made Norman more alert, as if he'd been slapped in the face. This lovely woman walking next to him with hair the color of honey and hazel eyes that he found ever so captivating had evaded a robber by placing her valuables next to her bosom. Clever and sexy, he thought.

"The most important thing is that you're okay," he said in an uneven tone, still amused by the thought of her deception, her beating a robber at his own game. "I would still urge you to contact the police, but I would probably have better luck lassoing the moon than getting you to heed my request." He unclenched one hand from the cart handle and buttoned the top part of his coat. "If you don't mind my asking, does Wellington know?"

Faye shrugged. "Not about this most recent one."

Norman's eyes widened and his words came out gruffly: "There have been other times? I should walk you directly to the police station right now."

The Albany Police Station was on the corner of Western and Madison Avenues, quite a distance from where they were now. "As much as I appreciate the architecture of that old brick building, which truly does resemble a stationhouse from an earlier century, I have laundry to do. On this very fine Saturday morning that's chilly but clear, my laundry must come first. I know you mean well, but I won't be swayed from washing my favorite sweater and a cozy pair of flannel pajama bottoms that have candy canes scattered in all directions."

After a small silence, she added, "He'll be here for Christmas."

Norman was confused until Faye explained she meant her father. "That's wonderful news," he said and aimed the cart down another street, the laundromat's sign visible in the distance. "Last year he was dating some woman, wasn't he? I believe you mentioned he couldn't get away to come see you."

Faye appeared to focus on closing the distance between themselves and the door to the laundromat. "He caught Lucinda in bed with her tennis instructor."

"As a means of improving her game, no doubt."

Faye laughed. "As much as I don't like to see my father get his heart broken, I don't think she was right for him. I can't tell you how many times she forgot about the time difference and called me in the middle of the night."

Norman held the door to the laundromat open for Faye and then walked in behind her with the cart. "What do you have planned for the two of you?"

She located a washing machine and then grabbed armloads of her clothing from the cart, tossing the garments into the basin. "A nice dinner. Maybe something catered or I'll make reservations at a fancy restaurant."

The two washers on either side of Faye's were in various stages of a spin cycle. There was an Asian woman with a small child sitting on the bench in front of the big window. And aside from the attendant who read a magazine with his feet up on the counter, no one else was around.

"You know, you could always buy a spiral ham and the rest of the fixings to cook a traditional Christmas dinner. I wouldn't mind the savory aromas wafting over to my apartment."

With one hand on her hip and the other holding a pink oxford shirt, Faye looked at him pointedly. "You said you were going to your sister's house. Your nose will be too far away to appreciate anything I might cook."

Norman leaned against a dryer and watched Faye shove the pink shirt in with the rest of the garments. "That may be true," he said and held out his arms to take her coat, which she had draped over the top of the washer, only it kept sliding off. "But I have a distinct feeling that I could be the recipient of leftovers in the days following Christmas. And I, for one, am not going to give that up without a fight."

She slammed the door to the washing machine closed and giggled. "How much trouble do you expect me to go through to satisfy your distorted notion that I should be thinking about your stomach before my own?"

With Faye's coat tucked under his arm and his hands crammed into his pockets, he gave a wobbly smile. "Well...that depends. We've been living in the same brownstone for what...five years now? I think you moved in the year after I did—and a lucky thing, too. The woman who used to rent your place had half a dozen cats." He cleared his throat. "So I expect it isn't asking too much to have a plateful of leftovers after the holidays, considering how long we've been living across the hall from one another."

Faye motioned for Norman to follow her to a bench at the back of the laundromat. "Is that why I found so many balls of yarn in the oddest places when I moved in?"

"Wouldn't doubt it." He sat down and crossed one ankle over his knee before laying Faye's coat in his lap. As though it were yesterday, he remembered the evening when Faye had come after work to look at the place for rent. He'd been climbing the stairs to the second floor when he looked up and saw the landlord and a pretty lady coming toward him. Naturally, he said hello to the landlord who grunted a response before reluctantly introducing him to Faye. After they shook hands, Faye gave a wide smile and told him she worked down the block at Hirsch Gallery. He couldn't help but think that she looked like a painting herself.

For some reason, the subtle waves in her hair and the belted raincoat she wore that day reminded him of Lois Lane, not from the comic books but from a movie version. He half expected her to receive a mysterious call and then provide an odd excuse to run off to help Superman. But she stayed where she was—halfway down the stairs—even after the landlord walked away. "Does he mean it?" she asked Norman, referring to the landlord's parting warning that he'd cash her security deposit check in two days and if it bounced he wouldn't rent to her.

"Afraid he does," Norman replied and rested a bag of groceries on the banister. "Spence Adler runs this brownstone like a general in the army. If you want to live here, you may have to act the part of a soldier."

Faye's mouth tilted. "Not a forgiving man, then?"

"Considering he has a strict policy about bounced checks, you could say that."

"Oh goodness, I'm holding you up," she said, and pointed at his grocery bag. "I've taken up enough of your time, but it eases my heart to know I've got a nice neighbor at least, even if the landlord is a bit harsh."

He invited her up to his place for a bite to eat since he had enough ingredients in his bag for two pasta alfredo dinners, but she declined. Norman figured it was because they'd just met and she was being cautious. He guessed her age to be about twenty-seven and he wondered if she thought he was old at thirty-three.

"Maybe I should get a cat," Faye said before she stood up and walked over to the machine to remove her wet clothes. It jostled Norman from remembering anything else about that night.

She shook out each item to free the wrinkles and then formed one of her shirts into a loose ball. Norman watched her hurl shirts, pants, sweaters, and skirts into the dryer with the accuracy of a MLB pitcher. It appeared that she made a game of transferring her laundry into the other machine and called out her score as each of the items went in. The distance between the washers and driers, which were directly across from one another, was about three feet.

"Norman, I want you to try this." She motioned for him to come over, and once he stood beside her, she offered him a balled up sweater. "Show me what you've got," she said, a glint in her eyes.

Norman chuckled as he prepared his aim. "Now may not be the best time to mention my successful athletic career in high school…. Surely, you couldn't have known." The sweater whooshed into the dryer with speed and grace.

She cocked her head. "You played ball?"

He released his tight grip on a pair of leggings and they shot through the hole. "Ah, wrestling actually. But apparently my athletic aptitude translates into throwing women's clothing as well. You just saw that, didn't you? I'm a natural."

"Oh really? In my opinion, your technique could use some work." The little Asian girl scampered toward them. "Well hello there," Faye said to her and looked down. "Something tells me you'd like to give this a try." She handed the girl a shirt, picked her up, helped her to aim, and with a little added force…the shirt sailed in. "Awesome job. Can you tell me your name?"

"I'm four," she said in a serious tone and held up three fingers to show Faye. "I'm not going to be five until after Santa comes." She pushed her long, dark hair out of her eyes and smiled broadly. "My name is Tomiko."

"Well, I'm Faye and this is Norman…and we couldn't have done it without you." Faye high-fived the child who took off giggling and skipping toward her mother.

Faye waved to the girl's mother who still sat in front of the big window on the bench. The outdoor brightness darkened the woman's silhouette.

"Why would you want to get a cat?" Norman asked. He was still thinking about what she'd said five minutes ago.

"Cats are excellent companions."

Norman pushed the dryer door closed. "You're confusing them with dogs, Faye. Cats are suspicious little creatures who hide from you when you get home. A warm greeting comes from a dog; I can tell you that much."

"First you're an expert on pitching balls of clothing into the dryer and now you know which pets are the most companionable?"

"Perhaps I can make my case this way—" and he leaned against one of the dryers that wasn't running and crossed his arms over his chest. "The lady who had the place before you started with one cat. By the time she was done, she had six. I'm no expert, but it seems to me it all starts with one cat."

Faye returned to the bench against the back wall and pushed her coat out of the way to sit down. "I'm a one cat girl, if that abates your worry."

Norman sat down next to her and lifted his eyebrows. "That's what you say now. What good will that do me when I've got a whole pack of pussycats clawing at my door wanting milk because you're working late and they're hungry?"

Faye swallowed a laugh. "If that ever happens, I give you permission to contact my father and inform him that his only child has cracked under the pressure of being overworked...resulting in an excess of furry friends. Trust me, he'll know what to do."

"Speaking of being overworked, how are the preparations going for the Van Gogh exhibit?"

Norman watched the Asian woman fold her clean clothes and place them in a wicker laundry basket while her daughter made a game of running from the door to her mother's leg at top speed, back and forth several times.

Faye turned to look at him. "Everything's falling into place. This acquisition will let our little gallery rub noses with the big art powerhouses in New York City. The Metropolitan and the MOMA will have to see us as a force to be reckoned with."

Norman screwed up his face, which made his nose appear larger, his mouth nestled underneath it as a small wavy line. "Raising thirty grand to rent the space is flat out unfair. But if anyone can do it, you can."

"Bobby's barely on board with delaying the renovations for me to show these works. But if I don't show them, my efforts will have gone to waste, and the community will be worse off for not having seen these amazing pieces."

Norman looked at Faye—about to add something serious—but in the next moment he decided against it. "How does brunch sound?" he said. "I'm buying."

She raised one eyebrow. "Have you forgotten I put tabasco sauce on my eggs?"

"Hey, it's your eyes that are going to water, not mine."

She smiled at him and began to arrange her clean, dry clothes in the laundry cart.

Chapter Six

In return for having Sunday off, Faye talked Zoe into hanging ornaments and garlands on the tree for the front lobby after her shift. Open six days a week, except for Saturdays, the gallery benefited everyone who wanted a bit of culture. The flower shop around the corner would have a couple of wreathes for the entrance doors that Faye could pick up on her lunch hour. She entrusted the unearthing of the artificial Christmas tree from the storage room to Isaac.

The fake Douglas fir spent all but one month of its existence boxed up in the storage room, and Faye felt bad hearing Isaac sneeze repeatedly when he opened the long, narrow, dusty box and lifted out the stiff branches. But as he carried the tree over his shoulder toward the front entrance, she heard him mutter something about the ugliest trees transforming into the prettiest ones as soon as they were decked out with silver balls.

Isaac set the branches down and tested the half red, half green tree stand to determine its sturdiness. "A listing tree can topple over on someone," he said to no one in particular, "and I'm not about to risk my job or Faye's by letting that happen." He used a piece of string to anchor the tree from its narrow top portion to a hook in the wall.

"Making progress, I see." Faye stood at the top of three wide stairs that led down to the double doors at the gallery's entrance. The tree fit in its usual corner, but she realized how small it looked in comparison to the high ceiling. "It needs a grander appearance," she said, tapping one finger on her chin. "What about raising it off the ground two feet or so? There's an extra plinth in the back we could make use of."

Isaac was bent over tightening the screws on the stand, but when he stood up to his full height, Faye could see the dismay on his face. "Miss Faye, you've got great ideas, only I wish you'd think of them sooner."

She descended the steps and stood on her tiptoes to give him a hug and a kiss on the cheek. "This year's different. With the gallery in jeopardy, we need to make it the best Christmas ever."

"I'm all for that," he said and slid a wrench into his back pocket. Then he gave Faye one of his big smiles, his white teeth gleaming against his dark skin. "You know I'm a good listener. Heck, with my big ears"—he touched them on either side of his head—"I can listen enough for two people. So whenever you feel like unburdening yourself, I'm here."

She sighed. "Everything will work out. You'll see."

Isaac looked her up and down. "If anyone can save this place, it's you."

"I've been hearing that a lot lately. I'd better get back to work, then." She darted through an archway and then into a small foyer that led to the gallery door.

She found Zoe cleaning the information cards next to each piece of artwork with a mild spray solution and a rag. Patrons touched these surfaces and left smudges. The small cards were covered in Plexiglas and could be rubbed clean quickly. Faye believed a pristine gallery allowed the artwork to stand out.

Although it wasn't his job, Isaac had buffed the wood floors earlier and they gleamed in the well-lit space. According to him, it was in his blood to make things look nice, and he was damned if he could get it out after thirty years in the janitorial business. Dull floors seemed to whisper his name until he did something about them.

Zoe must have heard the sound of Faye's heeled boots on the

hardwood floor because she turned around. "I could only find one box of ornaments where you told me to look. Are there any more?"

Dressed in an olive-green shirtdress with an ivory cardigan and black dress boots, Faye put one hand on her hip. "Ah ha, the question of the day. Let me see what I can do."

In her office she turned around in a circle. "Now where would the rest of those ornaments be?" A box on the far edge of the shelf looked promising, so she peeled back the tape, opened the flaps, and found rumpled drop cloths.

A step ladder leaned against the block wall near her desk. She undid the lower buttons on her dress to have more range of motion as she climbed up. It took her a while to rummage through half a dozen boxes, but eventually she noticed glitter on the outside of one box. It had twine wrapped around its width to keep the lid securely closed. She peered through the oblong cut-out for the handle. From what she could tell, glass ornaments, surrounded by massive amounts of tissue paper, were inside. Either Zoe would be ecstatic with Faye's discovery or visibly disappointed; she wasn't sure which.

Faye set the ornaments by the door and then sat down at her desk. She fingered an envelope and stared at the address:

> Mevr. Anouk De Ven
> Van Gogh Museum
> Paulus Potterstraat 7
> 1071 CX Amsterdam
> The Netherlands

The thank you note to Anouk for allowing the Van Gogh drawings and letters to journey to America in three months would either have to be mailed or torn up. It hinged on Faye's ability to raise the money to keep the gallery open for the duration of the show.

A quick knock on the door, followed by Zoe poking her head in, startled Faye, but only because she was intently concentrating on the envelope. "I was going to ask if you'd found the rest of the Christmas balls, but I'm guessing that this"—she pointed to the box on the floor wrapped in twine—"is what I'm after." She bent down to pick it up. "I'll sort through it in case some are broken. As soon as my shift ends, I'll be ready to decorate the tree."

"Zoe," Faye said before the door closed, "how'd your art history test go? Did you ace it?"

"Not quite. But you'll be happy to know I got the one right about St. Peter's Basilica."

Zoe put her knee up to steady the box as she closed the door with one hand.

Faye returned her gaze to the letter and recalled her excitement in writing it. Of course, that had been prior to Mrs. DuPont's visit. A quick jog to the flower shop up the street for two wreathes to hang on the gallery doors would keep her mind off the letter, off the gallery's fate, off the need to raise thirty grand.

Of all the choices, she picked ones with oversized red-velvet ribbons and holly berries interspersed with the greens. Both wreathes were looped through her arm when she pulled the letter out of her pocket again. If she mailed the note, it meant she believed she could raise the money that would allow the show to occur.

Isaac seemed to be anxiously awaiting Faye's return. The moment she appeared on the other side of the glass doors, two wreathes dangling from her elbow, he waved her inside.

She eased open the door but didn't step in. "What is it?"

"We've got a problem."

"Is there any chance it can wait until after I hang these up?"

"No chance at all, Miss Faye. This is going to need your full attention."

Isaac came around the small security desk positioned at the top of the three wide stairs and rested one thigh on it, his other leg outstretched, arms crossed over his chest. "Might be best if I just say it outright." He adjusted his footing on his outstretched leg and then continued. "We've got ourselves a vagrant inside.

He slipped past me, Miss Faye, when I left my post to grab that pedestal in the back." He paused and looked down at the steps. "Real polite, I asked him to leave, but he's got a right to see the art. That's what he told me." Isaac stood up. "The police'll march over here, if you want me to put in the call."

Faye ascended the stairs and placed the wreathes on the desk, the small surface being dwarfed by the greenery overhanging on all sides. "Officers will be our last resort. I want to try something first."

Isaac reached for Faye's arm. "Best if I come with you. I won't have you being hurt or bullied by some vagrant."

Faye smiled. "Okay, but wait by the interior door. We don't want to spook him."

As if it were an ordinary Monday afternoon, Faye strolled into the gallery and looked around. The majority of the space was open, except for two partitions in the far corner that created the backdrop for a modest sculpture. Several paces from the smooth, ivory sculpture that resembled a top-heavy figure eight, she spotted a man with tattered clothing peering up at a large oil painting. His hands were clasped behind his back. Even in side profile Faye could see he had a scraggly beard.

"This one's a favorite of mine," Faye said as she slowly walked toward him. She stopped a few feet away, her gaze mirroring his.

The man said nothing.

"I wonder if any two viewers see the same things in a work of art," she said and hoped to sound nonchalant.

After a long silence he replied, "Are you going to try to get me to leave, too?"

"This gallery is open to everyone. So the answer to your question is no."

He glanced at her for a split second. "Sure it is."

Faye pointed to the middle of the painting. "Do you see that?" she asked and then moved closer to the canvas, slightly in front of the man. "The way the brushwork overlaps here...it reminds me of something very fragile exploding."

The man tilted his head, as if to investigate the spot from a different angle. After a moment, he confirmed, "I just don't see it."

Faye appreciated that he'd even bothered to look and wondered if he was feigning interest just to get out of the cold weather for a while. "I'm Faye, by the way." She stuck out her hand which was met with a wary look on the man's face.

He made no move to shake hands with her, and seemed anxious for her to retract her fingers. "Alan," he stammered, and pulled on his beard. "I go by Alan."

"Well, Alan, it's wonderful to chat with you about art."

"Is it?" he said cynically. "Were you hoping for some sob story about how I used to be successful and now I'm down on my luck?" He wiggled his lips to show his teeth, only technically he wasn't smiling. "Get a good look," he said in an even tone. "They're not rotten yet. I've still got some dignity left."

Although Faye was taken aback by his straightforwardness, she wasn't afraid of him. He hadn't made any moves to harm her. "Please understand," she said slowly, "I'm not judging you. I would talk to anyone about art because I love it so much. My only reason for engaging you in a conversation was to learn how you felt about this painting. As I said, it's one of my favorites. Anyway, I'm sorry to have bothered you. Please feel free to look around."

Faye strode off and nodded to Isaac who stood in the doorway with a hardened look on his face, which was probably meant to intimidate Alan in case he tried anything. It was preposterous for Faye to even think of Isaac in a bad mood, much less glaring at anybody. No sweeter man existed on the planet, and she knew that for a fact, especially since he'd made it his mission to look out for her.

Faye stopped at the attendant's desk, but at first Zoe was out of view, bent over in her seat to reach into the box of Christmas bulbs on the floor.

"Ten so far," she said, when she sat up. "I'm only halfway through the box, and already I've located ten broken bulbs."

Right at the moment Faye wasn't concerned about the bulbs. "Have you had a chance to speak with that man?" She gestured toward where he stood, but the jut of the wall didn't allow either one of them to see him. In a lowered voice, she added, "The homeless man."

"Oh yeah, he's phenomenal. He borrowed a piece of paper from me. I gave him a pencil with the gallery's name on it too. And look—" From under her notebook she pulled out a rough sketch and showed it to Faye. "I swear it only took him five minutes. Don't you think it looks like me?"

Alan must be an artist, Faye thought, possibly self-taught. She stared down at the sketch of Zoe; it included all of her piercings. "He must've said something to you while he drew this?"

Zoe pushed the broken bulbs aside and put her elbows on the desk. "I don't know." She sighed. "...We both dislike the commercialism of Christmas, for one. And he loves music almost as much as I do. I mentioned my garage band in case he'd heard of us on the streets, but apparently we're still under the radar with our edgy sound."

Faye smiled, fully remembering what it was like to be twenty years old and attempting to make a creative dent in the world. "Well, he has every right to look around and he doesn't appear to be dangerous. However, I'd like you to keep your eyes open while he's here."

"Sure thing, Faye."

No sooner had she spoken than Alan walked diagonally across the space and out of the gallery, practically brushing shoulders with Isaac who appeared unwilling to vacate his post in the doorway. Deep down Faye hoped Alan had stored up enough warmth in his bones to brave the chilly temperatures outside. She had wanted to offer him some donuts left over from this morning, but somehow she was afraid it would offend him.

Isaac walked over to them. "Seems like we got away easy on that one," he said, and wiped his hand across his forehead. "I followed him into the lobby to make sure he exited the building. I'll be more careful next time; you can bet on that."

"It all worked out," Faye said and patted Isaac on the arm.

"I'll take a quick look around. Double-checking the building will put me at ease."

"Sometimes you're too thorough," Faye said with a laugh.

Isaac paced around the gallery while Faye and Zoe discussed the magic of decorating a Christmas tree during childhood. They both agreed the ritual of placing ornament after ornament on every branch created happy memories. Zoe was sharing a story about hiding her brother's favorite baseball ornament when Isaac shouted for them to come quickly.

Crouched down in the corner of the gallery, Isaac pointed to a messenger bag leaning against the wall. With Faye and Zoe standing behind him, he said, "This here's a bag with God knows what inside."

"Where did it come from?" Faye asked.

"Alan," Zoe replied. "I saw him wearing it under his coat. I remember seeing the strap going crosswise over his chest when he drew my portrait."

"Did he take it off and forget it here?" Faye said softly.

"Not likely," Isaac said and sniffed the air near the bag. "There don't seem to be any harmful odors coming from it." Then he put his ear close. "Why don't you two ladies stand back. I don't hear anything ticking...so I'm guessing there's no bomb inside...but something ugly could be just under that flap."

The women backed up and Faye told Isaac to be careful.

Almost with a surgical flare, Isaac wove his hands under the flap and ever so gently lifted it. Next came the zipper which required slow, steady movements and a great deal of patience. Isaac pulled a small flashlight out of his back pocket and aimed the light into the shadowy interior.

"Well huh, peculiar for sure," he said. "I don't quite know what to make of it."

Carefully, he lifted out the contents of the bag and set them on the floor. A tin of breath mints (which turned out to be empty), a notepad with a loop for an attached pen (the pen was missing), a hairbrush with a painting on the handle, and a stack of postcards for Hirsch gallery. Nothing else was in the bag. Isaac had unzipped an interior pocket, but it was empty.

Faye bent down to investigate the postcards. Someone had drawn pictures and patterns in the empty spaces on the fronts and backs. She turned each card over and marveled at the images. Then she fingered the notepad and folded back the leather cover. There, too, were beautiful drawings of birds, lampposts, storefronts, and people. Artistically, the renditions lacked proportional accuracy, which gave them an inexperienced crudeness, but the pencil-work was something Faye could admire.

Immediately recognizing that these items were the ones stolen from her purse gave Faye a shiver down her spine. Had Alan been the thief? Did his conscience dictate the return of things that didn't belong to him? Worse yet, was he disappointed there was no money in the purse, and by leaving the messenger bag in the gallery was he saying thanks for nothing, lady—here's your junk back? Maybe she would never know the answers, but her gut told her Alan had made amends in his own way. Perhaps the spirit of the season had spurred him to do it.

***

Long before the gallery was scheduled to open the next morning, Faye wiggled between the wall and the tree to plug in the colored lights. Decked out and looking festive, the gallery lobby, which had taken shape last night, looked even better this morning.

It had taken just under two hours to unravel the lights, string the garland, hang the bulbs, press the wrinkles out of the tree skirt, and change the defective batteries in the glittery star topper. They'd all cheered when all five points of the star lit up. After Isaac had stifled a yawn for the third time, he announced his plans to head home. Norman, who'd been hovering outside with the intent of walking Faye home, cheerfully stepped inside to take his place.

"Whatever gave you the idea I needed an escort to walk me home?" Faye had asked him, unsure if she would ever get used to it. His thoughtfulness didn't outweigh the fact that she was a big girl who could take care of herself.

"You can grumble all you want," he'd replied, and widened his stance, probably to show he wouldn't budge. "Just think of it as the neighborly thing to do. You're the source of my leftovers and I want to keep you safe." Lots of times Faye delivered a container full of goulash to Norman, and apparently he didn't want that to change. She only prepared it on weekends when she had more time to dice up the ingredients. Who knew it meant so much to him!

"Might be a while before I'm ready to get out of here," Faye had said, as she screwed up her mouth, slightly embarrassed that she'd given him a hard time, again. He'd already walked her home several times since he'd heard about the purse-snatching. A part of her figured he'd stop showing up one day.

Norman had glanced at Zoe who sat on the steps with a ball of tangled lights in her lap. "Let me work my magic," he said and sat down next to her to examine the mess. Because his striped tie got in the way he undid one of his shirt buttons and fed the pointed end through the gap.

If it hadn't been for Norman, they might never have gotten those lights untangled. She had him to thank for that, and now, as she prepared to open, she thought that it might take more than some spicy goulash to show her appreciation.

Faye set the bag with Isaac's muffin on the tiny security desk and walked through the archway to unlock the door to the gallery space. By the time she'd gotten to bed last night, it was late and now she felt as though she hadn't slept at all.

Chapter Seven

As the second set started, Isaac blew into his cupped hands. "I wish someone would explain to me why the younger generation has the sense to wear mittens but not to zip their coats," he said under his breath. A sea of Zoe's schoolmates swayed their hips in the driveway as the band banged out a mix of edgy songs from the garage. Since the Bowen family's home was an older ranch style, the narrow garage only accommodated a handful of them, mostly shivering females, who squeezed their bodies along the sides. Those nearest to the drums were probably deaf by now, and the others by the keyboard bobbed their heads like their necks were too loose. Everyone else stood out in the cold.

"Most of your body heat escapes through your head," Faye shouted above the music. She'd walked up behind Isaac wearing a red knit hat and matching scarf.

"Nobody dragged me out here," he shouted back, and shoved both hands into his pockets. "I came of my own free will."

"You'd never disappoint Zoe, and you know it."

Isaac hooked Faye's arm through his own and they moved beyond the crowd. "This is better," he said once they'd reached the end of the short driveway where it was quieter. "After you told her what Ray had done, collecting money from his friends like that, she thought up this idea."

"Her heart's in the right place," Faye agreed. "She believes it's a privilege to help save the gallery. That's what she calls this...singing to save the gallery."

He shook his head. "Our Zoe sure does have a smooth voice, heaven help her."

"With her talent and brains, she'll go far." Faye watched Zoe practically swallow the microphone when she opened her mouth wide to scream into it.

Isaac chuckled. "Those piercings of hers may be overkill, but I'm not her father, so it's none of my business."

The only illumination shattering the grayness of the night sky came from the garage's interior lights, under which Zoe's bright red hair stood out. From their vantage point at the end of the driveway, it looked like she wore a red hat like Faye's—only it was her hair.

Tugging the knit hat down over her ears, Faye said, "Despite the cold, this isn't a bad way to spend a Friday night."

Isaac started hooting and clapping when Zoe hit a high note. Then he bent his head toward Faye. "You think they know any soul or jazz?"

She rolled her eyes. "Don't push your luck."

A student with purple hair passed around a black top hat. "Please give what you can to save Hirsch Gallery!" she shouted. "Art matters! Save the gallery!" Faye watched her weave through the concert goers, occasionally pausing to tamp down the dollar bills into the bottom of the hat.

By the time purple-haired Amber headed toward Faye and Isaac, the hat overflowed with money. Twice she darted into the grass to chase after a few bills that had blown off the top.

"Looks like people are in a giving mood," Isaac said, and added his own bills to the haphazard pile of money, some of which was folded or crinkled.

"You two seem kind of old to jam. Is Zoe your niece or something?" Amber asked Faye.

"I'm her boss, actually. And this is Isaac, a dear friend of ours, who happens to work at the gallery also."

"Yeah...okay, cool. This belongs to you, then." She handed the top hat to Faye and walked back toward the crowd.

"Do I look like a dinosaur to you?" Isaac asked. He turned his hands over, maybe to see if they looked old.

"Tell me about it. I bet she thinks we escaped from an old age home."

He slapped his knee and laughed. "Probably she does."

"This next song is for my new friend Alan," Zoe said into the microphone. "He promised he'd come tonight, so I'm hoping he's out there somewhere." The redhead shielded her eyes with her hand to see into the darkness beyond the crowd. "Well, if you're out there, Alan, this one's for you."

Isaac rubbed his hand across his face and grumbled. "Oh my word, what'd she do that for? Inviting him here? The girl's too trusting."

Faye patted his arm. "I think we both know Zoe would rather give up singing or promise never to get another piercing again than judge someone based on their appearance or circumstances. The essence of what she stands for is admirable. Still, I wish she'd play it safer in the future."

Slowly, Isaac turned his head to the left and then to the right. "With all these people, it won't be easy to spot him. And I don't like the looks of those dark shadows over there—" He pointed to a row of hedges that lined one side of the driveway. "Who's to say he's not hiding behind them right now? We'd be none the wiser, that's for sure. He can make as much noise as he wants and nobody's going to hear it above those drums. It's a wonder the neighbors haven't called the cops to complain about the noise level." He paused.

"Maybe I should take a look around," he finally said, an octave lower than normal.

Faye recognized the deeper pitch of his security-guard voice and hoped there wasn't anything to be worried about. Isaac had excellent instincts about these things, she thought, and she would have to leave it to him to take care of any disturbance. In all likelihood, she decided, Alan had promised Zoe he would attend her performance but couldn't afford the bus fare to her house.

Isaac walked around the perimeter of the house using a tiny flashlight no bigger than his index finger—a practical gift from Norman that Faye had forgotten to remove from her coat pocket.

"Did you get your stuff back?"

Faye turned around to see Alan several feet behind her, practically in the street.

She couldn't help but notice he wore the same clothes as the last time she'd seen him. "My stuff?" she asked.

"I didn't take them. Your purse and the stuff inside, I mean." He paused, as if he thought about taking a step closer, but didn't dare. "I know the guy who did, though. I traded him a sandwich to get your things back."

Faye cleared her throat. "That was so kind of you." She could only imagine how much more important a sandwich would be to Alan than to ... well, herself ... but he'd sacrificed his needs to rectify a wrong, one that he hadn't even committed. "Why, though?" she asked him, and waved her hand for him to come closer.

"I saw those gallery cards inside. I always wanted to be an artist."

Now that Alan stood about two feet in front of her, the sadness in his eyes was plain to see. "Zoe showed me the portrait you drew of her. It was very good."

He raised an eyebrow. "You really think so? The thing of it is... I started drawing to keep my mind off my troubles ... and then I grew to like it."

"I thought maybe you'd had some schooling."

He shook his head no. "Studied literature. Ended up becoming a grant writer once I graduated. You must've gone to art school, though."

Faye's response was inaudible because the drums banged out a solo just then. After a moment, she repeated herself. "Yes, I did. I majored in art history, but I took quite a few drawing courses as well."

Alan fidgeted on his feet. Faye thought he might be uncomfortable carrying on a conversation with her, but then she re-minded herself that he'd approached her. No, there was some other reason why he was on edge suddenly.

He scratched his long, snarled beard and said, "I've got something to show you." Without removing his fingerless gloves, he pulled a folded piece of paper from his tattered coat pocket. "Zoe told me about the trouble the gallery's in. I thought I could help." He stretched out his arm with the paper in his hand.

She assumed it was a sketch, perhaps of the gallery's façade, but when she unfolded it, the entire page was handwritten. She couldn't quite make out what it said in the dimness, so she asked him to explain.

"You're holding a grant proposal. Turns out I still know how to write a good one. Anyway, the address for their website is on the back. Fill out the form, type in what I wrote in the proposal section. Send it to them if you want, or throw it away. It's up to you." He scratched his forehead, just under the fabric of his gray knit hat, which had several holes in it. "Back when I was working as a grant writer I used to send proposals to this place all the time. They were always responsive."

It had not occurred to Faye to write a grant to save the gallery, and now this man without a place to hang his hat had taken the reins and written one. She couldn't help but smile. "And how much is the grant for?"

"Twenty-five thou."

Hearing the amount weakened Faye's knees. "T-t-twenty-five thousand dollars?"

Alan nodded and then started to walk off toward the street.

"Wait!" she called after him.

He stopped but didn't turn around.

Faye jogged toward him. Since he didn't turn around, she stepped in front of him. So now Alan's back was to the concert instead of hers. "So you've worked with this grant-making agency before?" As soon as he nodded, she continued. "How long do they usually take to respond?"

"There should be a clause in the form indicating how quickly you need the money. Tick that box and your grant will be reviewed before some of the others that are pending but not urgent."

Faye's eyes softened, but she held back her tears. Then she dashed across the street while shouting over her shoulder, "Be right back. I've got something for you." She ducked inside her car, but left the door open to rummage around. The top hat with all the money in it was on the floor with a blanket over it. She grabbed something off the seat.

Alan hadn't moved.

Faye slammed the car door, tucked something under her arm, and crossed the street again. "I believe this is yours." She held out the messenger bag that had been left at the gallery with her things inside. "I've kept it in my car in case I saw you again."

For a moment, his eyes seemed to come alive, wrinkles showing around them, as he took the bag and hugged it to his body. "This means a lot to me."

It was easy to understand that an item as seemingly insignificant as a bag for most people was exceedingly useful for Alan to keep track of what little he had, a means of safeguarding it against his body.

In addition to returning the bag to him, Faye had stuffed five twenties from the top hat into the zippered pouch inside it. After all, Zoe's benefit concert was meant to help the gallery, and Alan had written a proposal that very well might save Hirsch. He should be paid for his efforts, but she didn't want to insult him by offering him the money directly. To hide it in the pouch would salvage Alan's pride, even if it was the chicken's way out on Faye's part.

Faye knew a thing or two about pride. For the first time in her life she'd had to accept charity—the five-hundred dollars from Ray and now the proceeds from Zoe's concert. It wasn't easy. But to let people down put a lump in her throat that she had difficulty swallowing.

A crash of cymbals announced the last song of the evening. Zoe dedicated it to Faye (the best boss ever) and Isaac (the best guard ever).

"Isaac!" Faye shout-whispered. Intrigued by the possibility of the grant and chatting with Alan about it had made her completely forget about Isaac. The moment the band finished playing, she would find out where he'd been for so long.

Faye's ears continued to ring even after the music stopped. Hopefully it didn't indicate permanent ear damage, she thought.

"You made it!" Zoe shouted as she rushed down the driveway toward Alan to give him a hug. The two of them started talking about art and music, so Faye slipped away to locate Isaac.

With her hands on either side of her head, Faye banged her open palms against her ears to revive them. Maybe if she'd bothered to take off her gloves first, the attempt would have been more successful. Nevertheless, she walked around the side of the house, which was even darker than the front, and realized rather quickly that both of her senses were impaired now, sight and hearing.

When she almost fell a second time, she reached in her pocket and pulled out her phone. Why it hadn't dawned on her to use the flashlight function before was beyond her, but at least now she could see her brown leather boots and the blades of grass in front of them. Much better, she thought.

"Isaac, are you back here? It's me, Faye."

Either Faye heard a groan or she felt the vibrations of one in her chest. She stood still and listened. ...There it was again, only louder. It didn't quite sound like an animal, but she couldn't tell for sure with her fuzzy hearing. To increase the coverage of the light, she swung her phone from side to side.

"Is anybody there? Hellooo...."

"Just about to give up on you," Isaac said.

Faye aimed the light toward the sound of his voice, and immediately Isaac shot one hand out to shield his eyes from the brightness.

He sat awkwardly in the grass where he'd fallen earlier, his body leaning forward over his legs, his arm reaching out to massage his ankle with one hand.

"What happened to you?" she asked, lowering her phone.

"Twisted my ankle pretty good."

One fingertip at a time, Faye removed her gloves and knelt down in the grass. She turned up Isaac's pant leg to get a better view of his ankle. With her phone between her teeth, the light showed a defined bruise above the ankle bone where she'd pushed down his sock. "Does it hurt when I do this?"

Isaac yelped. "Miss Faye, I love you like a daughter, but please...don't do that again."

She apologized and patted his knee. "Try moving it. We need to make sure it's not broken."

He wiggled his foot. "Darn thing hurts like the dickens, but it still wiggles."

"Glad you think so, but if you call that a wiggle, well then, I think we ought to have the doctor look at your eyes, too. Come on, let me see if I can help you to the car."

Isaac was thin but very tall, and no matter how Faye placed his arm over her shoulders, there was too much of a height difference for it to be of any use. "So this is how it's gonna be?" he asked, and eased his body back down in the grass. "My fingers and toes get nibbled off by wild animals in Zoe's backyard?"

"Stop that. I'll go around front. I'm sure Zoe has some muscular friends who can help."

Isaac moaned. "Bring the guy who was holding that girl on his shoulders all night. He ought to be good for this."

Faye poked her fingers into her gloves. "I'll see what I can do."

It took her less than a second to spot the tall guy with the broad shoulders and shout to him to follow her quickly. He'd been helping the drummer carry his equipment to the back corner of the garage when Faye nabbed him. She'd expected him to ask a lot of question but he said absolutely nothing as he kept pace with her going around back. It was as if he was used to people calling upon him for help because of his size.

When they got to Isaac, he was singing a gospel song in a low tone. "...And the Lord carries us h... Oh good, you brought him. Son, do you mind giving an old man a boost?"

Lyle scooped Isaac up effortlessly, as if he weighed no more than a child, and carried him all the way to Faye's car. It was clear the young man could've carried him all the way to the hospital on foot without breaking a sweat. More to the point, Faye would've bet money on his ability to hoist her entire car onto his shoulder and heft it to the hospital parking lot.

Before she pulled away from the curb, Faye rolled down Isaac's window. "Lyle, I can't thank you enough. You have the strength of ten men."

Lyle smiled, waved his thickly-muscled arm in the air, and loped toward the house.

"I'll swing by to pick up Norman at the brownstone," Faye said as she headed south toward Delaware Avenue. "After that we'll make our way to the hospital."

Isaac sighed. "My long legs seem to be incompatible with your small car. I'm getting a fairly good idea of what it feels like to be a pickle in a jar. Look at my knees. They're practically touching my chin. And oh, do you mind telling me how an accountant plans to mend my ankle?"

"My reasons have less to do with your ankle and more to do with Norman being good-natured. He won't mind being dragged out of bed to help me get you to the hospital. Once the doctor assesses the damage you've done, we'll go from there."

"Damage I've done," Isaac muttered. "City people never fix the ruts in their backyards. That's what got me into this mess. Maybe if that flashlight you'd lent me had any oomph to it, I could've seen the hole before I fell into it."

She turned down another street. "Stop being so grumpy. You'll be good as new; I'll make sure of that."

He tilted his head back. "This headrest is too low to support my neck. But it sure does pinch the tops of my shoulder blades nicely. You ever think about getting a bigger car? Dear Lord, this thing was made for dolls, not people."

Faye smiled. "Fits me just fine. Now relax and enjoy the ride."

Chapter Eight

Bobby Sterling stopped pacing and looked down at his wing-tips. They felt decidedly snug since he'd only bought them the other day, but he loved the impression they made. It was somewhere between highly successful and private-jet wealthy. Along with the shoes, he'd been fitted for a pin-striped suit by an impeccable tailor who said the stripes made him look several inches taller. So far, California was treating him well.

He looked out the window, a partial view of Petco Park in the distance. His meeting with Wellington Brooks had been going well until the architect was called away a short while ago. Sterling was encouraged to make himself comfortable and was offered coffee to ease the wait.

Oddly enough, this delay increased Bobby's confidence in the firm. Busy and important were the two qualifications he admired most in business associates and it proved to him that his interests would be well served on the west coast. Closing the deal with this team of distinguished architects gave Bobby a means of making a name for himself in these warmer climates.

"My apologies for keeping you waiting," Wellington said as he breezed into the office and sat down at his desk. He gestured for Bobby to take a seat across from him, the same one he'd sat in earlier. "We had an issue with a new building in the gaslight district that needed my immediate attention. An architect's head is always on the chopping block if something goes wrong."

Wellington removed his wire-framed glasses and set them on a stack of papers beside his elbow. Even when seated, his tall, thin physique made an imposing figure. It was obvious he kept in great shape, which led Sterling to believe the architect sitting across from him could outrun a man half his age.

Wellington appeared to have the calm demeanor of someone who was used to doing business amidst interruptions. His closely cropped white hair and neatly trimmed beard with white and gray flecks gave him an air of seniority over the younger partners whom Sterling had previously met with over the course of the week.

Wellington leaned forward with a steady gaze. "I've looked into the variance you requested. The city is willing to rezone that parcel of land to accommodate your café. It's a lengthy process which won't see its final stamp of approval for another few weeks. However, a trusted confidant of mine gave me the information privately."

Sterling approved of Wellington having inside connections. A man had to know how to play by the rules as well as how to get around them when necessary. "Excellent. This is excellent news. Should we take a few minutes to go over the plans once more? I'm still concerned about the facade. I'm seeing something different in my head."

The architect grabbed the tube behind his desk, extracted the plans, and spread them across his desk, upside-down to give Sterling a clear view. To prevent the plans from curling, he set a book on each side.

Although Wellington's face expressed a look of seriousness at all times, it was tempered with a great deal of wisdom. "Not much can be done unless we revisit putting a support beam here." He pointed to the spot.

Sterling pulled his chair closer. "How will that affect the ambiance?"

"The beam will drop the ceiling height in that area by a foot or so, which should provide your coffee nook with a cozy vibe. Truly,

I don't think it's out of the question. You'd be wise to consider the change."

"And adding that beam would allow us to have the front doors come forward a few feet?"

"Ideally, yes. Our aim is to make the structure as sound as possible. After that we can make it look pretty. But the load-bearing walls need the proper support and that's non-negotiable. This firm respects safety above all else. Cutting corners isn't how we earned our reputation."

"Certainly not," Sterling replied, glad to see his café was in good hands.

"Be advised, though...once the building process begins...any change orders could cause significant delays. Your deadline for the grand opening doesn't leave much room for crimps in the schedule. It would be in your best interest to finalize what you want and let us sort out the details."

They talked business for another thirty minutes, during which time the other two partners stepped away from their respective clients to share some private words with Wellington outside his office door. In low tones, they voiced their opinions about the proposed changes to the café and then stepped inside to offer Sterling handshakes for coming on board with the extra beam.

Wellington rolled the drawings up and shoved them into the canister.

The firm's secretary knocked twice and then poked her head around the door. "Your suitcases have arrived, sir." Blonde and stylish, with incredibly long legs, the young woman wheeled two bags into the far corner of the office and left them parked beside a bookcase.

"Are you off somewhere?" Bobby asked as the secretary closed the door.

"To see my daughter in New York." Wellington stood behind his desk and peered in the direction of the suitcases.

Bobby turned around to glance at them, too, only they were nothing special—black and hard-shelled with neon yellow luggage tags dangling from the handles. "You're cutting it a bit close, wouldn't you say? Christmas is in three days."

"Leaving at the last minute beats not going at all. That's how I look at it. Last year I didn't fly out to see her—and maybe I'm just getting to be an old man who can't understand his own child anymore—but I think it put a strain on our relationship. Grown daughters can be a handful when they don't have their mothers around to set things right."

Bobby waited for the sound of an airplane flying overhead to fade out. "Is your daughter in the same line of work as you?"

Wellington eased into his chair and picked up his glasses off the desk. "Oh she loves old buildings, that's for sure. An art history buff at her core, if nothing else. Spends most of her time wading through artwork for a little gallery she runs on State Street in Albany."

Bobby allowed for some silence and then remarked, "Is that right? Runs a gallery, of all things. How interesting." Clearly, Faye hadn't brought her father up to speed about the gallery's dismal fate, and right at this moment, Bobby wasn't sure if he wanted to either.

"Hirsch," Wellington said and leaned back in his chair to fix his gaze on Sterling. "Hirsch Gallery. I thought maybe you'd heard of it."

Bobby squirmed, his suit jacket nearly falling onto the floor where it hung over the back of his chair. Then he cleared his throat several times and remained still. He could feel perspiration staining the armpits of his good shirt. "Rings a bell possibly."

"Well, my daughter adores that gallery. If she had to choose between it and me, I'd hope to make second place. Not a single day goes by without her putting her heart and soul into making Hirsch a venue for extraordinary artwork. And honestly, she doesn't give the workload a second thought. Once she sets her mind on something, it usually turns out to her liking. I'm hoping I'm the one who taught her that hard work pays off, but you never know. Life's its own teacher sometimes."

Sterling eyed a mini Zen sandbox on the edge of Wellington's desk.

"Faye gave me that for Christmas one year. She said all the important people use them to create harmony at work. You're supposed to use the tiny rake to make waves in the sand. Like this—" Wellington stretched out his arm, took the little rake between his two fingers, and wiggled it through the grains of sand.

"Should I feel more enlightened by watching you do it?" Sterling asked and then shrugged his shoulders. "I may need to experience it for myself to get the full effect."

Wellington handed him the rake. "By all means."

"Ah, yes...I'm beginning to feel something." He made two passes with the rake and then set it down. "...If you don't mind my saying, your daughter sounds amazing. What would she ever do if the gallery closed?"

Wellington guffawed, and then took a sip from his water bottle. "No chance of that happening."

"No? You seem quite sure."

"Mrs. DuPont, the woman who owns the gallery, wouldn't have any reason to close it. After her husband passed, the building came into her possession to do with as she wished. Creating a gallery was her brainchild and Faye has turned it into something everyone can be proud of."

"If the gallery is as successful as you claim, it surprises me that a headhunter hasn't made Faye a suitable offer. All those highbrow galleries in New York City must be vying for her. That's where the art game is played best, isn't it?"

"Faye's not going anywhere. She's remarkably loyal. Hirsch may have been DuPont's brainchild, but Faye's the one who rears the child, so to speak. She'd no sooner leave that place than she would move to California to be closer to me."

"There have been offers, though? People in the art world who have requested Faye join them? Curatorial endeavors can go far in the right hands, I imagine."

"Well, I wouldn't be privy to who offers her what, but I get the feeling Faye's waiting for a big show to come her way, an exhibit that will make its mark. A higher paying directorship won't tantalize her to sell out Hirsch, not until she's made it shine like a jewel." He straightened his desk blotter with both hands. "Unequivocally, she loves that gallery because it's the right place for her."

Sterling got a wild look in his eyes. "Take me, for example. If I'd stopped at one café or two or even a dozen, I'd never have known the success I do now. Perhaps it's the same with Faye. Maybe she needs to expand her horizons. Leaving Hirsch could set her career on fire."

"You could be right, but I doubt she's looking to start a blaze just yet. The only way my daughter would leave Hirsch is by force. To her credit, she's resilient and never gives up." As if for emphasis, he tapped his pen on the shiny surface of the mahogany desk. "Just like her old man, I guess."

Sterling glanced at the little sand garden on the desk and then at Wellington. "Don't let me take up any more of your time. You've got a plane to catch in the near future and I've got more shopping to do. The quality of the textiles in this town amazes me."

"San Diego is a business hub, which means all these business folks need fine clothing. Half of the deals struck in this city are accomplished by individuals wearing impressive-looking suits that make the other guy feel unimportant. If you can't dress well here, it's your own doing."

Sterling laughed. "Well said." Then he stood up, pulled his handstitched suit jacket of the finest Italian wool off the back of the chair, and slid his arms into it. After he secured the button, he thrust out his hand.

Wellington shook it. "I've got plenty of time before my flight. Let me take you to lunch. On the firm, of course."

Sterling knitted his brows. "I suppose there is cause for celebration, but maybe I'll take you up on it another time."

"Nonsense. A good Brazilian steakhouse can make a man

rekindle his passion for meat." Wellington stuck his head out of the office door and told his secretary to make reservations for two at Rei Do Gado. "If you don't mind waiting for me in the lobby, I won't be long."

"Norman," Wellington said into the phone the moment Sterling exited the office. "It's Wellington here. I need some clarification on the things you told me during our chat the other day. The three-month rental price for Hirsch is thirty grand. Is that correct?"

"That is correct."

"And Sterling and my daughter have met in person?"

"They met at the gallery. Faye assumed one look at the artwork would convince Sterling to rescind his offer to buy the place. According to her, a latte-serving café was no match for a gallery of abstract art. But I'm afraid she miscalculated Sterling's gumption."

"That scoundrel," Wellington said, perhaps more to himself than to Norman. "I've just spent most of the morning with the man and he has pretended not to know Faye. What's more, he's trying to extract information from me to ease his own conscience."

"Such as...."

"Whether or not Faye can obtain other work if the gallery closes. That sort of thing."

"I see," Norman said, and sounded alarmed. "What do you plan to do?"

There was a long silence and then Wellington responded. "I'm going to make him sweat a little."

***

Sterling sucked in his breath as Wellington reached over and pressed several buttons on his treadmill. The belt accelerated to top speed. Bobby almost took off flying and had to triple the action of his legs to keep up. "Is it good to work out so soon after eating?" he asked, his voice shaky from the increased motion.

"Pshaw!" Wellington said. He jogged on the treadmill beside Sterling's.

The older man didn't seem out of breath at all, and Sterling thought he detected a smile on his lips.

"We just ate a lot of meat," Sterling managed to get out. "I'm pretty sure they recommend not exercising directly after eating a big meal."

"No you're wrong. That's swimming. Shouldn't swim right after you've eaten. Jogging on a treadmill is fine. Trust me."

Sterling didn't understand how Wellington wasn't on the verge of collapsing like he was, but then again, the man hadn't sampled quite as many meats. It'd been a while since Sterling had enjoyed his food so much, but now that lunch was over and this—he had no idea what to call this blinding flurry of exercise—was underway, he felt like he was being punished.

Had he done something to offend Wellington? Was the man testing him, and if so, for what reason?

Then again, he could be looking at it all wrong. The man didn't have a son. Maybe he wanted to bond with Bobby because he liked him, and the only way he knew how was through vigorous gym activities.

"I'll be sitting on a plane for six hours," Wellington said, and pumped his arms as he jogged. "Must get the heart revved up to endure all that sitting, right?"

Bobby thought about reminding the architect that he wasn't going to be flying back yet and perhaps he should watch from the bench. There was one located just beyond the row of treadmills, next to the rack of free weights. It looked so inviting when he glanced at it, only he couldn't envy the motionless bench for long. Concentration was key to outrunning the machine rather than being swept off it backwards. Since that would be too embarrassing, he hiked his knees up and kept running.

Wellington growled a few times, as if to spur himself to go faster.

The man was too fit, Sterling thought. And at the present moment it put the broad-shouldered Bobby "Bulldog" Sterling at a disadvantage. For one thing, Bobby preferred lifting weights to running in place. Raising something heavy over one's head was palpable; running in the same spot lacked imagination.

"Had enough yet?" Wellington asked.

Bobby thought he detected a rumble of laughter just under the surface as the man said it. Sweat poured off his face and soaked into the neckline of the tee-shirt that Wellington had lent him from his gym locker. As much as he wanted to say yes, he decided to distract himself from his throbbing quadriceps. So he glanced across the room at the elliptical machines, quickly pinning his gaze on a woman's ass; the left side of her buttocks went up as the right side went down. It was beautiful and it was all he needed to crush Wellington's hopes of breaking his spirit.

Even if it killed him, Bobby wouldn't quit until Wellington did, and not a minute sooner.

Wellington slowed down his machine and stepped off to towel his face. "So Bobby, tell me about your plans for the holidays?"

Bobby blinked a few times to clear his vision. Either the onset of dehydration had set in and he was seeing things that weren't there or Wellington was finally standing still. As miraculous as that was, it took Bobby a moment to command his legs to stop, and once they did, both thighs felt wobbly and incapable of holding him up. As nonchalantly as he could, he leaned one elbow on the display panel and grasped the handle. Then he took a few deep breaths to steady his racing heart.

"Your plans?" he repeated.

"My plans, yes. Looks like I'll stay around here and head back to New York the day after Christmas."

"You have family here, then?" Wellington squeezed his bottle and squirted water into his mouth.

"No actually. It's just me. I usually don't admit this to anyone, but I've been known to work on Christmas day. Being here in San Diego, though, I might treat myself to a day off."

Wellington handed Bobby his water bottle. "I've got a proposition for you. Hear me out before you say no."

Chapter Nine

Faye sat across the table from Lucinda Piedmont who made a show of correcting the position of the silverware. The coffee spoon didn't appear to the left of the soup spoon, a glaring error which probably bothered Lucinda's sense of decorum. In Faye's rush to add two more place settings to the table, she had inadvertently reversed them.

Not surprisingly, Wellington had neglected to mention he would be bringing Lucinda along for Christmas dinner at her place. The woman hadn't changed much from the last time Faye had seen her, but the shock of watching her waltz into the apartment in a long ivory gown still hadn't worn off. In Faye's opinion, the dress was more appropriate for a ball than for dinner at her boyfriend's daughter's apartment; but she knew Lucinda considered herself duty-bound to be elegant at all times. She looked as snooty as ever, Faye thought, especially with her light blond hair in a chignon.

It stood to reason that her father might be lonely, but Faye didn't consider that a viable excuse to rekindle a relationship with a woman who had exhibited unfaithfulness. Partly, she blamed herself. With all the turmoil at the gallery, she'd barely made time to speak with her father on the phone, much less ask about the status of his love life. Maybe Norman had been right to urge her to confide in him about the gallery's imminent closing. If nothing else, it might have prevented him from reconnecting with Lucinda.

As if it wasn't enough to have to put up with this woman who looked down her thin, birdlike nose at everyone and everything—including Faye's handmade centerpiece of pine cones and coiled twigs—she had to make small talk with Bobby Sterling. He sat beside her and requested she pass him the rolls. It still wasn't clear to her why her father had brought him along, but it was certainly turning out to be a flop of a Christmas.

"More wine?" Faye asked her father, who sat opposite Bobby. He accepted the bottle and topped off Lucinda's glass and then his own.

"Everything's delicious, Faye," Wellington said, his fork poised at his mouth.

Lucinda glared at him. "She didn't cook it herself, dear. You do realize that, don't you?"

"Who's to say I'm not applauding her excellent choice of dishes. Now I wouldn't have picked this lentil and bean concoction for a side dish, but I'm enjoying it immensely."

Lucinda patted her lips with the edge of the napkin and then looked at Faye. "Your father is impossible. I can hardly take him anywhere without some embarrassing faux pas on his part."

"I think it's sweet," Bobby piped up. "You know, for a father to care enough about his daughter to comment on the selection of foods. And I heartily agree, everything is spectacular."

Faye couldn't help but smile. "Actually, Norman's sister made that." She pointed to a fresh cranberry salad.

"Ah, how is old Norman boy?" Wellington asked as he picked up the plate of cranberry salad and scooped some into his dish. "Can't say I've seen him in quite some time. Perhaps later we could go knock on his door and say hello."

Faye put down her wine glass. "I'm afraid he's eating at Jacklyn's. His niece and nephew have been relentlessly pumping him for information about which toys Santa may bring."

"Kids are good at weaseling more loot out of Santa. If I remember correctly, you wrote out your list every year and mailed it off to the North Pole like clockwork. The top three things were always colored pencils, an assortment of markers, and a coloring book. I should've known right then and there you would wind up in the art field."

Faye tilted her head and remembered her letters to Santa. "I wish it were that simple now, just mailing off your wishes to someone."

Bobby used his fork to push the potatoes to one side, as if he knew the reason Faye was having a less than satisfactory Christmas was because of him and his plans to turn the gallery into his milestone café.

"The ham is overcooked," Lucinda said and stared down at the morsel on the tip of her fork. "Perhaps you should phone the caterer and demand your money back. They can't expect people to swallow this shoe leather and be happy about it."

"Nonsense," Wellington said, "it's just the way I like it." He cut himself another slice.

Lucinda shot him a look that could've melted wax. And instantly, the candle in the pinecone centerpiece flickered. "Some of us have discerning tastes," she said hotly. "Apparently, you wouldn't be one of them."

Wellington opened his mouth, as if to respond, and then closed it. He focused his gaze on his plate, not looking up until he'd consumed every crumb on it.

Nonchalantly, Bobby hung his arm over the back of Faye's chair. "Better save room for dessert," he told everyone, perhaps in an attempt to be upbeat. "I caught a glimpse of it earlier. It takes up an entire shelf in the fridge. At first, it distracted me from locating the wine. That's how delectable it is...so be warned."

"I couldn't decide between that and a chocolate pie," Faye said. She smiled that Bobby approved of her ultimate choice.

"I know what you mean," Bobby said, and pivoted in his chair to look at her. "I never met a pie I didn't like."

"Listen to the two of you," Lucinda chided, her eyebrows

raised. "It's as though neither one of you has heard of cholesterol."

For a woman in her mid-forties, Lucinda's slender body rivaled that of a thirty-year old, and the only way she'd managed it, Faye knew, was by watching what she ate, closely. "To
know there's a mega-desert in the kitchen," Lucinda began, "only
causes me to sigh at how shortsighted you can be, Faye. Obviously you want to be fat someday. You'll have absolutely no
hope of keeping your figure past forty if you continue to indulge
in desserts with such abandon. It's for your own good that you
should heed my advice."

Wellington looked over at Faye. "I'd like to hear about the
gallery. Usually I can't get you to stop talking about it. And yet
today, we haven't heard one word about the brilliant paintings
and sculptures that are gracing the walls and pedestals of Hirsch."

"Abstract art," she said, and took a sip of wine. "We've got
canvases with deep-rooted and alluring themes, all abstract. I
decided to do an open call for work this time, so in addition to
established artists sending their digital images to us, we got newcomers also. Quite a few of the pieces on display were created by
fresh new talent." Faye's face brightened considerably. "Before
you leave, I'd like you to check it out."

Her father broke a roll in half and reached for the butter knife.
"Wouldn't like anything better, darling."

"Even though I had to explain the meaning of several paintings to her, I believe Mrs. DuPont appreciated the selection I
chose. Abstract work can be difficult to cull, but I managed to
pull together a cohesive grouping."

He paused from buttering the roll. "Am I to understand Mrs.
DuPont visited the gallery in person? Recently?"

Perhaps Faye had said too much. "Ah well...yes, you could say
that."

Faye could feel Lucinda's piercing gaze on her.

"My boss," Faye said slowly, "plans to make some changes to
the gallery in the near future. She wished to alert me of those

changes, that's all."

Lucinda gave a shrill laugh. "Let's not mince words, Faye. You've been let go, isn't that so?"

Wellington turned to his girlfriend and patted her hand. "Lucinda, please." He pushed his plate forward and clasped his hands on the tabletop. Then he softened his eyes as he looked at Faye. "I'm sure that's not the case. Tell us, Faye, what is going on?"

"I might be the best person to answer that," Bobby said. He looked as though he'd just swallowed a pinecone from the centerpiece. "I may be the reason Faye is having a less than satisfactory Christmas, what with the gallery being in jeopardy."

His handsome face twisted. "I may not have been as upfront with you as I should have been." He steadied his eyes on Wellington. "When we first met I should've told you I knew Faye. I suppose I didn't because I figured you wouldn't appreciate my part in the gallery's closing." He paused to run one hand over his face. "I should tell you that I'm feeling pressure to lower the rental rate."

"Go on," Wellington said as he rested his chin on his fists, both elbows on the table.

"Wait a second," Faye said, startled. "Who's pressuring you? Has someone spoken to you on my behalf?"

"No one has approached me, but"—Bobby removed the cloth napkin off his lap and balled it up on the edge of the table—"it makes sense to allow the Van Gogh show to proceed. In the interest of doing that, I will reduce the rent."

"Just like that?" Faye said, her palms up in question.

"It's Christmas," Bobby replied.

Lucinda's eyes were narrowed and Wellington's lips curled into a grin.

"So it is," Faye said, unmoved by the sentiment. "Perhaps you'd like to relinquish your claim to the gallery altogether, then. Why not find a new location for the café?"

Bobby grunted. "My offer is to reduce the rent. Let's be clear about that."

Lucinda waved her hand in the air. "Back up a minute. You're going to close the gallery and use the space for a café, is that what I'm hearing?"

Bobby and Faye nodded at the same time.

"And what's all this talk about Van Gogh?" Lucinda asked.

"I've spent months getting a museum in Holland to loan us some drawings and letters of Van Gogh's. However, the exhibit will take place after the renovations are set to begin. Bobby has offered me the option of renting out the space to accommodate the show."

"This reduced rate," Wellington began, "what would it be?"

Sterling pushed his chair closer to the table. "I've got to be honest with you. I'm not in a position to go any lower than seven." His dark eyes turned to Faye. "Twenty-one in total."

If Bobby was willing to kiss nine thousand dollars goodbye, Faye had to wonder what had occurred between him and her father to allow for this sort of compromise.

"Excuse me," Bobby said, awkwardly getting up from the table. "I need to stretch my legs."

Bobby moved into the kitchen on legs that didn't seem to work. By the looks of things, he was stiff and perhaps experiencing sore muscles, which prevented his knees from bending in the logical way for forward propulsion. His robotic movements were a dead giveaway to Faye. Now she knew how her father had done it.

"Could I speak to you in the other room?" Faye asked.

Wellington rose from the table and followed his daughter into her bedroom, the only private space where they could talk. "Anything you have to say to me can be said in front of Lucinda. If you'd just give her a chance. She's not as bad as you think."

Faye sat down on the edge of the bed. "I'll keep that in mind, but this has nothing to do with her. I'm more interested in why Bobby is hobbling around. It appears that sitting at the dinner table for so long locked up both his legs. You wouldn't know anything about that, would you?"

"The man has short legs," Wellington responded drolly and

pulled out the stool from Faye's makeup table. Once he sat down, his knees thrusted upward from the lowness of the stool. "Maybe it has something to do with that."

"I don't think the length of his legs is the issue here. How could you?"

He adjusted himself on the stool. "Darling, I really don't see why you're getting so upset."

"Danny Filbert," she said and looked directly at her father. "And Stanley Green. Oh and Jason Nelson." She tilted her head. "You should remember those names. Boys I tried to date in high school. Boys you brought to the gym ... and after that they were deathly afraid of you ... and had no intention of getting near me. My God, Dad, this has gone too far."

Wellington leaned forward and reached out his hand to her. "What are you getting at, Faye? Inviting someone to the gym isn't a crime."

Faye pulled away from his hand. "It is when you work the person to within an inch of their fitness capabilities. And for what? Some sort of preparedness training to see if they're worthy of your daughter? Or in this case, to get them to lower the rental fee for the gallery."

Faye urged him with a tilt of her head to explain his actions.

"Sterling is a client with my firm. As such, I took him out to lunch. After that we wanted to work off our food. It was strictly a way to bond with a client, nothing more."

"This amazing reduction in the rental price is purely coincidental, then? You had nothing to do with it?"

Wellington raised his hands up in surrender. Then he shrugged his shoulders and hung his head. "I should've heard it from you. Why didn't you come to me with this? If Norman hadn't informed me that my daughter was about to go down with a sinking ship, I would never have known. Do you think I want to see my little girl this unhappy?"

Faye's jaw dropped. "Norman snitched on me?"

"He's a good man, Faye. He knew you were too proud to ask

for help yourself. I give him a lot of credit for keeping me in the loop. And don't think for one minute that he was going behind your back for any other reason than pure concern."

Different emotions played across her face.

"It is obvious to me," he added, "that Norman thinks the world of you."

"He betrayed my trust," she shot back.

Wellington eased himself onto the bed to sit next to her. "Sometimes a man has to do things to protect a woman that she may not like. But he's willing to risk her disapproval for the bigger picture."

Faye didn't know what to think. Anger had taken over. If her father weren't in the room she might have thrown a few punches at her pillow to blow off steam, followed by a good cry. What else had Norman told her father?

Gently, Wellington lowered Faye's head onto his shoulder. "Perhaps I haven't completely forgotten how to comfort my daughter after all. Maybe you still need me to make things better; at least I hope so."

"This is all such a mess. In three months I won't have a job. I'll never get to see the gallery reach its full potential. Why is this happening?"

He patted the side of her head. "First off, you need to have a means of paying the rent. I would suggest taking a loan from me, but somehow I know that's not an option. Once you have the rent money squared away, we can tackle a way to save Hirsch from a café's fate."

Faye lifted her head to look at her father. "There's the possibility of a grant coming through, which would cover the rent. But to save the gallery outright, well, I don't have a clue as to how to go about that."

"Leave that to me. Buying time isn't as hard as it sounds."

She knitted her brows. "No more workouts at the gym with Bobby. Promise me."

"Of course not, darling. I'll be going about Phase II in a completely different way."

The door flew open and Lucinda's eyes flashed. "Is it too much to ask for my boyfriend to entertain me for a while? I haven't traveled all this way to sit with that man at a table that needs to be cleared. The food, if you could call it that, should be refrigerated. Unless, of course, you plan on throwing it out, Faye, which is what I would recommend."

Faye kissed her father's cheek and walked out of the room. She would let the two of them chat or argue, whichever came first.

She found Bobby cleaning off the plates at the sink and then lowering them into the dishwasher.

"What a fantastic sight." Faye stopped in the middle of the kitchen with her arms folded across her chest and stared at him. "To see a man scraping food off a plate."

He turned around and smiled. "Looks like I had to earn my supper tonight."

"What if I give you a hand? I suppose there'd be no harm in helping someone who had the good sense to lower my rent." She took a plate from him. "Can I ask you something?"

As he smiled yes, Faye noticed a dimple form in his cheek and wondered why she'd never taken note of it before. With his black hair and dark eyes, he really did have a handsome face, she thought.

"When my father invited you to Christmas dinner, what went through your mind?"

"Overwhelming panic accompanied by looming fear." He rinsed another dish. "Since saying no wasn't an option—I knew that right off the bat—I decided to make the best of it. On the plane I contemplated a couple of scenarios. In one, you clawed my eyes out the moment you laid eyes on me. And in the other, we sat beside one another at the dinner table like two grownups."

Playfully, she swatted at his arm with the dishtowel. "I rather prefer the first one."

He barely shifted his torso out of the way in time. "I thought you might. You've got a dark side that I'm just beginning to see come out."

"That would be my artistic side. And it's not dark. It's indefinable."

Chapter Ten

Spencer Adler wore a fistful of keys at his belt. They jangled enough to wake the dead as he trudged toward Faye's door. He raised his hand to knock at the exact moment she opened the door to leave the apartment for work. "Oh!" she said, startled.

He simply stood there looking at her. "Do you see this?" He showed her a tennis ball in his hand before releasing it to bounce on the floor.

The ball rolled toward the toe of Faye's shoe. She bent to pick it up, stared at it, and then handed it back to her landlord.

"The exact same thing happened with your rent check," he said, his mouth a straight line.

Faye began to speak, but Adler put his hand up. "Your excuses are no good here. I told you when you moved in...no bounced checks. I won't stand for it."

She didn't see her landlord in person often enough to charm him with a cup of tea and an invitation inside to discuss the weather, and no other ideas popped into her head that might work to appease him. Sure enough, she had been setting money aside for when the gallery's rent was due, and perhaps she had transferred too much out of her account into the Hirsch fund without realizing it. She should've been more careful.

"Twenty-five dollars," he said flatly, in reference to the canceled check fee. "On top of that you'll owe me an additional ten percent of the rent, plus the rent itself. Are we clear?"

As Adler spoke, Faye noticed the ruddiness of his complexion and the crisscrossing strands of hair hovering over his balding head. Because he never smiled, the muscles around his mouth seemed slack and contributed to the downturn of his lips.

Faye nodded to show she understood the terms and conditions of her punishment.

"I'll leave it to you to make sure this doesn't happen again. Eviction will be my only course of action if it does." He started to walk away and then stopped and looked back at her standing in the doorway. "A pretty face can't solve everything, Ms. Brooks. Remember that."

Faye wondered what he meant by that remark, but if she stood there any longer pondering it, she would be late for work.

There was a light dusting of snow on the ground which made Faye thankful she wore boots and carried her high heels in a bag. She walked briskly because she wanted to get to the gallery as fast as possible to check on the status of the grant application. There was an online recipient portal that gave basic information on pending requests. It had been two weeks since she'd completed the forms, which made it all the more likely that a decision would be forthcoming.

Less than half a block from work, it started to snow. Faye watched the white flakes fall to the ground and disappear. On the sidewalk and roadway, the snow melted on contact, but on the small patches of dull green grass along the curb it stuck. For January, it was cold but bearable. Men and women dressed in work uniforms or business suits descended the wide steps of their brownstones and passed in front of her; some beeped their key fobs and ducked into vehicles at the curb, while others trotted toward the bus stop further down the street.

If she failed to save the gallery, her daily routine of watching these fellow brownstone-dwellers go their separate ways to the various professions they held would come to a screeching halt. She would no longer belong to this early-bird club of employed professionals.

"Morning, Miss Faye," Isaac said. He sat at the security desk reading the newspaper, which he lowered when she came up the stairs.

It still felt odd for Faye not to hand him a small bag when she entered in the morning. Isaac, however, had forbidden her to waste money on muffins. Put it in the Hirsch fund, he'd told her, and every day after that he brought an orange in his pocket, and a thermos of strong black coffee to leave by his desk.

A lot of people loved the gallery and were willing to sacrifice all manner of things for it, which put Faye in their debt. When she thought about Isaac's muffin strike, Zoe's benefit concert, Alan's ingenious grant proposal, and the contribution of Ray's friends, she knew she had a tight-knit group of supporters who would rally around her to the end.

Faye pointed to Isaac's foot under the desk. "How's the ankle?" He had it propped up on a box. A single crutch leaned against the wall.

"Hardly hurts anymore, but the doc wants me to go easy on it for a while longer."

"Sprains take time. Listen to him." Faye patted his shoulder and walked through the archway toward the gallery door.

When she sat down at her desk, she hurriedly pushed a stack of mail aside, repositioned her laptop in the center, and logged into her account on the grant-making agency's website. She watched the circle spin as the computer pulled up the information on Hirsch. Then she scrolled down to the bottom of the page. There were two boxes on either side of the screen.

In very large letters, the box on the left read: DENIED.

Faye gasped. As she lowered her hand from her mouth slowly, her shoulders slumped and a knot formed in her stomach. This couldn't be happening. She blinked her eyes to refocus them, and then looked at the screen again—DENIED. It wasn't a mistake.

She scanned the page for a reason, something that would tell her why it was denied. When she found the passage detailing the committee's review of the proposal, she put her hand over her mouth again, another small gasp escaping. It read: As much as we consider this proposal to be an exceptional example of good grant writing, we cannot condone the use of valuable grant dollars for such a short reprieve. If the requested total of twenty-five thousand dollars would allow Hirsch Gallery to remain open permanently, our determination would be different. But as it stands, we cannot allocate funds in the amount of twenty-five thousand dollars for a mere three months. Our decision is final in so far as you may not resubmit this proposal a second time. However, you have the right to an appeal. The appeals process is quite thorough and taken very seriously. The necessary forms can be found at the end of this document. Best of luck to Hirsch and its employees. We regret our response lacked the positive answer you required.

The devastating news dampened Faye's resolve for an instant. The weight of the world felt like it had descended upon her shoulders. Once she absorbed the shock, she decided that the best thing to do was start the appeals process, not because she thought the effort would meet with success, but because she had an obligation to at least try; people were counting on her.

For now, the primary focus was to raise the rest of that twenty-one thousand dollars to keep the gallery open for the Van Gogh exhibit. After that, she would tackle the long term goal of keeping the gallery open permanently. One step at a time, she told herself.

Her head sunk into her hands, and she saw herself sitting on her bed next to her father on Christmas day, a week ago already. Wellington had offered his daughter a blank check, which she had summarily refused. Regrettably, the means she'd used to solve this problem up to this point hadn't panned out. To run to her father now and admit defeat was more than she could bear. The longer she sat there thinking, the less likely she was to pick up the phone and call him.

But then she remembered something Norman had asked her the other day. Apparently, he'd promised his niece a special Christmas gift that required Faye's help, something about private art lesson for a few months. Faye knew it was Norman's way of giving her money without offending her. And as much as she'd rather teach Lily about art at no cost, the extra cash would go toward the Hirsch fund.

Doing a quick calculation in her head, there was five hundred from Ray, three hundred from Zoe's concert, and the two-thousand she'd pulled from her own savings. Combined with the reduction Bobby had agreed to...the remaining balance for the February rent would be four thousand two hundred dollars.

That number would be reduced further by Norman's generosity. Typical Norman, he'd put his foot down during the negotiations for the art lessons. Faye knew better than anyone that the going rate was between fifty and seventy-five dollars per session, but Norman insisted on one-hundred. Plus, he increased the frequency of the lessons to twice per week and explained it would benefit Lily's retention of the material. That would total another eight-hundred dollars per month.

The February payment was a month away, and she would only needed another three-thousand-four-hundred dollars. By breaking it down in this manner Faye believed she could make this work, and even though the situation was far from ideal, she decided it was doable, as long as she kept a clear head. At this point, she didn't want to leave anything more to chance than she absolutely had to. Her biggest mistake had been believing the grant would be issued, but that fairytale hadn't happened. This time, she would do something she should have done before—something that was guaranteed to work.

Faye popped the hood. "Runs great. Never had a day of trouble with it. And I think you'll find its compact size is a real plus in the city. You can park it anywhere. It was made for wiggling in and out of those tiny spaces that the big SUVs have to pass up." Faye stood on the curb, rubbed the roof of her car, and smiled.

The man bent his head to peer at the engine and all the hoses. "Looks like everything that's supposed to be under the hood is here. Not that I'm a mechanic or anything."

"Will you be driving long distances with it? I only ask because you're fairly tall, and as you can see, the car is small. It's a great vehicle, though, for driving around the city—to and from work—that sort of thing."

"I'll be driving it to work," he said and stood up straighter, as though he was proud of what he'd just said. Then he tilted his head and stared at Faye. "I realize I've changed, but I thought you'd still recognize me."

Faye squinted her eyes. "Your voice sounds familiar. But no, sorry. Have we met?"

"A couple of times." He looked up and down the street and then added, "Once at the gallery. Then on the night of Zoe's garage-band concert."

Her eye widened. "No way! Alan? What a transformation! But how?"

With his clean shaven face and respectable tan trousers paired with a blue button down shirt, he looked like anybody else. The light windbreaker he wore instead of a winter coat may have suggested he was low on funds, but it did nothing to mar his new look as an upstanding citizen.

"That night when I gave you the grant proposal," he began and glanced at Faye, "I half expected you to crumple it up and throw it in my face. The fact that you didn't made me wonder if I wasn't as useless as I felt. Maybe other people would take me seriously again if I did something about my appearance.

"And then when I found that money in my bag, it meant somebody believed in me. Funny thing is, I couldn't seem to stop myself from old habits. I marched straight to a liquor store to buy some booze. Without any kind of plan, I just did the same thing I was used to. I'm no drunk, but a bottle keeps a body warm on a cold night. Anyway, just as I was handing the guy behind the counter the money, I changed my mind. The next thing I knew I was walking into a little shop to buy some nice clothes. They threw me out, of course, for being a bum, but I can't blame them for that.

"So basically, I had to decide if I really wanted to change. I thought about going back to the liquor store...but I ended up at a shelter instead. I got somebody to listen to me. I told him I wanted to get cleaned up and buy some clothes. I showed him the money I had balled up in my fist."

He paused and grinned, almost to himself. "Long story short, underneath that mangy beard that obscured most of my face, I still had a good jawline. And once I washed the grime off my body and pulled on those trousers, I felt like a human being again. I was able to apply for a job with the help of my case coordinator, and the interview went well." He shifted his feet and then crossed his arms over his chest. "You're looking at an employed man...and I have you to thank."

"Me? From what I've just heard, you did it all on your own. You made the right choices, which is what second chances are all about. So tell me, what type of work will you be doing?"

"Research mostly. A local law firm has hired me to do research for some of their minor cases. The job may require a bit of travel, so I was given an advance to buy a used car." He turned away from Faye to smile at the car. "When I saw the For Sale sign in the back window, and the cheap price tag, I called the number." He took an old flip phone out of his pocket and showed her. "Another perk. It's not as fancy as the smartphones the lawyers have, but I'm grateful for it."

"This is the best news I've had all day," Faye said and gestured that she'd like to hug him if he didn't mind.

They embraced awkwardly and then separated. "You haven't told me about the grant. Have they made a decision?"

"Oh, the grant," she said with a little laugh. "No, we haven't heard anything yet."

"I'll just have to do this a while longer, then." He raised up his hand to show that his fingers were crossed. Then he planted both hands on his hips. "Should we trade cash for keys? I'm anxious to drive somewhere...anywhere really."

"Right, of course. I've got the seller's forms you'll need to register the vehicle. If you give me a minute, I'll go grab them."

She left Alan to look over the car some more as she jogged up the brownstone's steps and disappeared inside.

"May I help you?"

Alan stopped pressing the buttons on the dash and looked in the direction of the voice. A man stood on the sidewalk with a little girl by his side. "I don't think so," Alan said.

"I'm going to have to ask you to step away from that car. You see, it's my friend's car and you're not her."

Alan's face twisted up. "You know Faye?" He stepped out of the car. "I'm buying this from her."

Norman looked at him suspiciously. "It's not for sale."

Alan walked around the car and pointed at the back window. "See."

The For Sale sign taped there didn't satisfy Norman. Why would Faye sell her car? She needed it for grocery shopping and...he couldn't think of any other reasons at the moment. Faye walked most places, but that wasn't the point. This man, whoever he was, shouldn't be taking Faye up on any offers to sell her car. "Where is she, then? Faye, I mean. If she's selling you this car, why isn't she here?"

Alan scratched his jaw. "I still can't get used to my beard being gone. Anyway, she went inside to get the papers to complete the transaction."

"What's a trans-ac-shin?" Lily asked as she tilted her head to look up at Alan.

Norman squatted down to her level. "It's something grownups do."

She clapped her mittens together. "When can I do it? When I'm seven?"

He patted her head and stood up. "We'll see, Lily. Tell me, how much is she asking for it?"

"Thirty-four hundred."

"Auntie Faye is giving me art lessons," Lily volunteered. "That's why I'm here. To have my first art lesson with Auntie Faye. Is she giving you art lessons, too?"

"Art lessons?" Alan asked and shook his head. "I'm too old for art lessons, but you're just the right age for them. I bet you'll have lots of fun. My name's Alan, by the way."

Norman looked this Alan fellow up and down. He appeared to be in his fifties, clean shaven, respectable looking. Priding himself on his ability to spot a con-artist a mile away, Norman didn't think Alan was a threat. It did bother him, however, that Faye was selling her car to obtain money for the gallery. Her passion for saving the place was beginning to cost her dearly, and what if her car was only the first of several private possessions she was willing to sell?

Lily twirled in a circle on the sidewalk. "Do you know how to draw?" she asked Alan, looking a bit dizzy when she came to a stop.

"Sure do. I like to draw people and buildings, mostly. How about you? What do you like to draw?"

Lily scratched her head under her pink beret. "Teddy bears, I think ... and unicorns, too."

"Oh, those are good choices," Alan said. "They'll sit still while you draw them."

"No they won't. My stupid brother hides my stuffed animals all the time. His name is Ben and he's a pest. Look—" She pushed up her coat sleeve and showed Alan a scratch on her wrist, just below the edge of her mitten. "My brother did that. He got sent to his room for ten whole minutes. Mommy says he wasn't being nice and she was sad about it."

"Okay, Lily," Norman said and tried to quiet her down so he could find out a little more about Alan. "So how do you know Faye?"

Alan leaned against the car by resting his elbow on the roof. It took him a long time to answer. "Faye gave me a fair shake, you could say. She didn't judge me, and her belief in me gave me a new start. That's really the only way I can describe it."

Norman didn't know what to make of what he'd said. Was he

a former convict or something? Was Faye letting a criminal buy her car? "What you're telling me is that Faye gave you the benefit of the doubt? So my next question is...in what regard? Are you connected with the gallery?"

"I wrote a grant proposal for the gallery, yes, but other than that I'm not employed by Hirsch."

Lily tugged on her uncle's arm to get going, so he picked her up. "Faye mentioned a friend writing a proposal, only I didn't know it was you. Too bad it didn't pan out, though."

Alan's eyes narrowed. "What do you mean?"

"Didn't Faye tell you? The grant fell through. It was denied."

Chapter Eleven

Because it was her father's fault that she was forced to abandon the gallery for several days in order to fly west to California for his engagement party, Faye allowed him to pay the airfare. The fact that he hadn't mentioned anything about marrying Lucinda when they'd visited her at Christmas only meant he hadn't been roped into it yet. This turn of events proved to Faye that her life was in a downward spiral.

For the second time in less than two weeks, Bobby Sterling sat next to her. First it had been at her dining table at the brownstone on Christmas day and now it was on a jetliner to the west coast.

"Are you going to eat those?" He pointed to her little bag of pretzels laying on the fold-down tray.

"Go ahead." She rolled her eyes and contemplated the use of earbuds to alleviate any further conversation, but she doubted Bobby would take the hint.

A handful of their fellow passengers were destined to share in the engagement festivities also. Wellington had booked the same flight for all of his east coast clients, an expense that made Faye question her own lofty ideals, the very ones that had prevented her from accepting his blank check for the gallery. Obviously, her father was in the mood to relinquish thousands of dollars to schmooze his clients and make a big show for his bride-to-be.

"What hotel are you staying at?" Bobby asked her as he eased his seat back.

"My father's insisting I stay with him. The last time I counted, he had ten bedrooms in that palace of his up on the big rise. You need to leave a trail of breadcrumbs when you venture out of your room just to find your way back."

"You're his daughter. He wants you close." He stretched out his legs, which Faye noticed weren't long enough to impede the aisle like the legs of the taller men on the opposite side. "Isn't it an architect's prerogative to design a palatial house for himself anyway?"

"I suppose you're right." She turned her head to look out the window. The clouds were so thick they choked out the blue sky.

"Did you leave your car at the airport?" Bobby asked her.

"My car?" She chuckled. "We've parted ways, I'm afraid. I didn't see the value in keeping something I wasn't using often enough. Sold it to a friend, and it couldn't be in better hands. Turns out he needed a car at the very same time I didn't need one. It all worked out for the best."

"I only asked because I chose to take a taxi this morning. The ride to the airport was very enlightening. The driver's name was Ray and I do believe he's a friend of yours."

Faye pushed the tray up and secured it in place on the back of the seat in front of her. "So you've met Ray?"

"The two of us got to talking, but when I mentioned my name was Bobby Sterling he pulled the car over and said, 'You're the dumb-ass who plans to build a café in Faye's gallery, aren't you? I should—' but luckily for me he didn't finish his thought. I explained how sorry I was that he didn't share my vision for the space. That's when he twisted around and rested one of his big arm muscles on top of the seat."

"Ray's a good guy," Faye said, and wondered if she wanted to hear any more of the story.

"Good guy? I thought he was going to clobber me ... toss me onto the side of the road ... and drive off."

Faye suppressed the urge to laugh. "Ray's a big teddy bear and you can't tell me otherwise. You were never in any real danger.

He was just looking out for me."

"Easy for you to say. You weren't there. You didn't see his eyes get all squinty. There was a look of venom in them." Bobby knitted his brows, as if to show her what he meant.

Not in the least bit did she feel sorry for him. He had it coming. Yes, he had reduced the rent, and yes they had enjoyed themselves at Christmas dinner, but Faye was beginning to agonize over making the second and third payments. Alan's purchase of her car had taken care of the first month's rent, but after that she was almost back to square one.

"Maybe we should talk about something else," she finally suggested. "Like how I'm going to feign happiness for my father when I think he should be running in the opposite direction from that woman who has her claws in him."

Bobby raised one eyebrow. "So you don't like your new step-mother?"

"You saw how she acted at Christmas dinner. The woman is two steps away from being intolerable. Nothing is to her liking, at least if I'm the one doing it. She can't say a kind word to spare her own life, at least not to me. Her superior attitude grates on my nerves, which makes me hard pressed not to scream. And if all that weren't enough"—Faye lowered her voice—"I think she may have a lover."

"Well," Bobby said gravely, his attention momentarily focused on the flight attendant who advanced up the aisle toward their seats. "No thank you," he told her when she offered to refresh his drink. "But I wouldn't mind another bag of pretzels if it isn't too much trouble."

"I just don't understand what my father sees in her," Faye continued. "I know her beauty attracts men, but her personality is substandard."

Bobby got a goofy smile on his face. "Your dad seems to like her."

"No kidding." She shifted in her seat. "He's lost all objectivity when it comes to her. I doubt he'd see the truth if it bit him on the ass."

"You could always expose Lucinda for who she really is—unfaithful and unkind. Find some guy to seduce her and then arrange for your father to find out." He shrugged his shoulders. "It's worth a shot."

Faye looked him in the eyes. "You're not hearing me. Even if he found her with one of the firm's partners, he'd think he was lucky to be next in line."

"Honestly? Your father seems smarter than that."

"Like I said, he just can't see straight when it comes to Lucinda."

For a moment the plane experienced some turbulence and since Bobby and Faye were sharing the same armrest, their hands touched briefly.

"You shouldn't work yourself up over this, Faye. Your dad's a big boy. If he's making a mistake, he'll know soon enough."

"Like after he's already married to her and it's too late? Is that what you mean?"

"I sense a bit of sarcasm in your voice. Perhaps I should let you cool off a bit," and with that he put his head back and closed his eyes.

Faye threw her hands up. "You're going to take a nap now?"

He opened one eye. "Yup."

As much as it annoyed Faye to have him depart from the conversation like this, she used the quiet time to finish a crossword puzzle on Norman's tablet. He'd insisted she take it on the flight to have something to do, and now she was glad she hadn't fought him on it.

Every so often she nudged Bobby's arm until it flopped off the armrest; then she moved hers into position. He would grumble without opening his eyes and then settle down.

Maybe this was what she needed after all—a chance to get away for a few days, to distance herself from the gallery and all its problems. The further westward they got, the more at ease she felt. On the one hand, she was merely trading one sticky situation for another—the issues with the gallery for her father's unwise, impromptu engagement. On the other hand, maybe she could wrangle a way out of both dilemmas if she gave herself a moment to relax.

After a long while, Bobby stretched his arms over his head and then slapped his own cheeks a few time. "Did you sleep at all?" he asked her.

She angled the tablet toward him. "Crossword puzzle, see."

"What about that one?" He pointed to 33 down, which was left blank.

"The only one I couldn't get."

Bobby stared at the clue. "That is a tough one."

She straightened the tablet on her lap, and then told him matter-of-factly, "You sleep with your mouth open."

He smiled at her. "You're lying."

"Now why would I do that?"

Bobby remained silent. He picked some lint off his pants from the airline blanket.

After a while he said, "You've never told me about your mother. Are the two of you close?"

Faye got a distant look in her eyes. "She died when I was little."

Bobby lowered his head. "I didn't mean to pry."

Faye smiled weakly. "I rarely talk about her if you want to know the truth. Every time I bring up the subject of my mother, my dad changes the topic and we end up discussing his latest architectural plans. I've been hearing about cantilevers, I-beams, and decking materials since I was old enough to sit on his lap while he worked at his drawing board. He'd let me slide the T-square up and down the board as he pointed out the different means of egress in the building." She rested her head against the back of the seat before she continued. "I know why he does it...why he doesn't talk about her...."

She paused to collect her thoughts. "My memories of her aren't as clear as they once were. It feels like she's slipping away."

"Have you thought about explaining that to your father? Maybe he'll open up."

"I think he's buried everything too deep for that. It wasn't easy on him to raise me. To watch his wife die from a tumor that doctors couldn't remove and then have a little girl to bring up." She rubbed the corner of her eye. "If I had to guess...my mother was his one true love."

He rested his hand on Faye's knee. "That's why this is so hard on you, isn't it? To see your father with someone like Lucinda. To know that your mother was a far better person."

She felt the warmth of his hand on her knee and for the first time on this flight, she was glad he was beside her; it was a relief to share these feelings with someone. "I believe he picked Lucinda because she's nothing like my mother. He doesn't want to be re-minded of what he lost. It's one explanation. That and loneliness, I suppose."

"Does she make him happy at all? I mean, maybe they're com-patible on some other level that you and I don't see."

Faye put her hand up. "I don't want to think about that."

Bobby laughed. "I didn't mean that. I was thinking maybe Lucinda comes on a little strong when she's around other people. She could be a different person when she's with your dad, just the two of them."

Faye watched a mother carry a toddler over her shoulder up the aisle toward the bathroom. "It's possible, but my gut tells me Lucinda's not a keeper."

"Doesn't this party we're going to tell you that your father's unlikely to throw her back?"

Someone sneezed in the row behind them, and Faye said Bless you through the seat crack.

"An engagement ring," Faye said and turned back around, "can slide off someone's finger just as easily as it can slide onto it."

Bobby shook his head. "Oh, I agree they're not glued on, but let's face it, your father is going to marry Lucinda. Whether or not you accept that has nothing to do with it."

He was right, of course, but Faye still held out hope that something would change to make her father see the light. She didn't mind sharing him with another woman, as long as that woman was an improvement on Lucinda Piedmont.

***

Faye accepted another glass of champagne. She took consolation in the number of business associates wishing her father well, even though the occasion, in her estimation, was falsely happy. Across the room, she watched him shake hands with men and then lean in to kiss their wives. Every time he did so, Lucinda clung to his side, most likely to indicate that Wellington belonged to her.

Waiters with starched collars and silver trays walked up to guests who stood in small groups chatting. Mouth-watering appetizers were lowered for their view. Faye hadn't begun to mingle, so she swiped a couple of jumbo shrimp off the tray as the waiter walked by.

"Excuse me, Miss. I didn't see you there," he said, and held out the tray.

Faye had been hiding behind a large marble pillar in the enormous hall that her father called a dining room. The deliciousness of the seafood had dulled her reflexes, so that she'd failed to dart behind the pillar quickly enough to escape Bobby's notice. He headed directly toward her.

"Is it your job to hold this up?" he asked and stopped inches in front of her. Then he stretched out his arm to lean against the marble pillar. "Or maybe you were hiding behind it." He gave a low chuckle. "You'd make a lousy spy if that's the case."

"I've been in this room for ten minutes, I'll have you know. If I was such a lousy spy, why didn't you find me sooner?"

Smiling, he looked her up and down. "You look nice, by the way. That outfit isn't one I would've imagined you wearing, but I like it."

The short black dress had red, embroidered flowers across the bodice, the upraised texture of the petals providing an artsy flare. Her chunky black heels had a single embroidered flower on each toe.

"I hesitate to admit this," she began and smoothed her hand over the dress, "but I borrowed it from my gallery attendant, Zoe. She's shorter than I am and a good twelve years younger, which is why I'm exposing more leg than usual. I only hope I'm pulling it off."

"More leg isn't a bad thing," Bobby commented, a wicked grin on his face.

Faye ignored him but felt flattered all the same. Honestly, she couldn't justify buying a new dress for her father's engagement party. The ones she had in her closet didn't seem right for the occasion, so when Zoe offered this little black number, Faye took a chance.

"I don't look like I'm in a garage band, do I?"

Bobby shook his head. "Oh I don't know. Show me how you'd look playing a guitar."

Faye held one hand out to the side and used the other one to strum against her belly. "Well? What do you think?"

"Nah. I don't see it. The dress may be a little punk rock, but with you in it...it's just sexy."

Faye blushed. "That's it. I'm going upstairs to change."

He caught her arm. "No, don't. I'll behave."

Her face softened. "I happen to have a very lovely dress hanging upstairs, brand new. The tags are still on it. Norman's sister, Jacklyn, lent it to me as a backup. It's a stunning dress by all standards, which is why I was afraid to wear it. I had a vision of myself spilling cocktail sauce down the front."

"Let's go mingle," he finally said. He stuck out his elbow, and Faye hooked her arm through his. "All of these guests are your father's clients?"

"A few of them must be acquaintances of Lucinda's, I would imagine, but the majority appear to be dad's cronies. He has a knack for getting his friends to fund the structures he creates on paper. He twists their arms after a brandy or two, and it always seems to work."

"Commendable tactics that I completely agree with. A man has to know how to make the most out of his friendships." Bobby released Faye's arm to grab two glasses of champagne from the waiter. "I think we've both earned this."

She raised one eyebrow. "Walking halfway across a mammoth dining hall has earned us some bubbly? How do you figure?"

He tilted his head. "I'm directing us toward the happy couple. Consider this champagne the courage you'll need to show how delighted you are for them."

"Very clever, but an entire vat of champagne couldn't make that happen. Perhaps I should let you do most of the talking."

He twisted his lips as he looked at her. "Is that right? You'll be the pretty thing on my arm while I carry the whole conversation? That's not the Faye Brooks I know."

"The Faye Brooks you know is a product of complicated circumstances, but I'm not about to bring up the gallery now. I've got enough on my plate with—"

"Faye, darling," her father bellowed as he rushed toward them. "We've been looking for you." He hugged and kissed her. "Are you having a nice time?"

"Truly exquisite," Bobby interjected.

Lucinda stood just beyond the three of them with a plastic smile on her face.

"Lucinda," Wellington said and waved her over, "come say hello to Faye."

As though the path leading to them was covered with hot coals, Lucinda slowly advanced two steps closer. "Isn't it nice that you could take time away from your job at that little gallery to come join us. I suppose a free vacation at your father's expense didn't give you too much pause."

"Lucinda, congratulations," Faye said without smiling.

"Isn't it marvelous?" She thrust out her hand to display a diamond ring that covered most of her finger.

The brilliance of the diamond made Faye wonder if the cost of it could buy ten galleries and half a dozen authentic Van Gogh masterpieces. What a waste, she thought.

Lucinda gave a shrill laugh. "This ring bears the mark of true good taste, which is why I can honestly say I picked it out myself. I, for one, was not willing to leave such an important decision to a man who thinks more about concrete and steel than he does diamonds."

"Well, we hope you'll be very happy together," Bobby said.

Chapter Twelve

From the expansive portico that framed his mansion on a hill, Wellington Brooks waved to his guests who drove off in their Mercedes and Land Rovers, pleased that the evening had been successful, devoid of any scandalous behavior on the part of his fiancée.

Because it would precipitate a quarrel, he refused to point out that he'd been right to invite Faye, his only child, to the festivities. Lucinda had argued vehemently against it by citing Faye's impending unemployment as a reason to just let her be, but in the end Wellington had won. Through his fatherly eyes the evening had been made worthwhile by his daughter's presence.

Something about that dress she'd worn reminded him of when she was a little girl; perhaps it was the embroidered flowers—he couldn't be sure—but it made him realize in a split second, as if for the first time, that she was all grown up. The vulnerability and the need for protection that he felt compelled to notice in her were minimized by the transformation of his little girl into such a lovely woman.

Faye was capable of living her own life; Wellington could see that now, and it confirmed for him that he was doing the right thing in moving on with his own. His marriage to Lucinda would affect Faye, no doubt about that, but he couldn't dwell on it because seeking a bit of happiness for himself was long overdue. Full steam ahead, he thought.

Lucinda walked over to Wellington and pivoted in front of him. He eased down her zipper, and she climbed out of her dress. She wore a silk slip underneath and strutted across the room with the dress dangling over her arm.

"What on earth was that atrocity Faye was wearing tonight?" she said, her voice growing fainter as she entered the depths of the walk-in closet.

Wellington pretended not to hear her and veered into the bathroom for his nightly routine of trimming his beard. He held the clippers alongside his jawline and snipped an errant hair every so often.

"Did you hear what I said?" Lucinda asked as she poked her head into the bathroom.

"Something about how nice my daughter looked tonight? I didn't catch the rest." He glanced at her through the mirror.

"Oh Wellington, you're such a diplomat." She disappeared into the bedroom.

"One of us has to be," he said under his breath.

Lucinda settled herself on the bed—king-sized with a massive tufted headboard—and flipped through a glamour magazine. She called into the other room, "The picnic tomorrow should be fun."

Wellington had decided that their engagement party should extend over two days' time, the best way for everyone to feel included. A few of his top clients weren't arriving until tomorrow anyway, so the picnic would be their first glimpse of Lucinda.

"I've always said a pig roast is a crowd-pleaser," he said. The idea of a midsized animal roasting in his backyard satisfied his need to impress their guests.

"Wellie, will there be an apple in its mouth? Promise me you'll see to it."

"An apple it is...." He came around the corner toward the bed, snatched the magazine out of her hands, tossed it over the side, and lowered himself on top of her. They kissed fiercely.

"If this is what an engagement party does to you," she said, breathlessly, "then I can't wait until the wedding night."

An hour later, around midnight, Wellington went downstairs to grab a drink and maybe a snack. He knew he shouldn't be eating this late, but he'd missed the opportunity to sample the tiny meats on skewers that he'd seen pass by him all evening. The task of making his guests feel welcome had done nothing to fill his belly, which was the primary downfall of hosting a soiree, he wouldn't doubt. He only hoped the caterer had placed the leftovers in the refrigerator like he'd asked.

The gourmet kitchen had lights under the cabinets that made the milky green subway tile glisten behind the state-of-the-art cooktop. Two ovens were ensconced, one above the other, in a nearby wall jog. If Lucinda had liked to cook, this kind of setup would be desirable, but Wellington knew she thought cooking was something other people did.

A long marble island with tall leather bar stools on one side separated the cooking area from a lengthy table that could seat fourteen. The redwood had been hand hewn by a friend of his, and Wellington never got tired of running his hand across the smooth surface. The thing was beautiful, impeccably made, a work of art.

Wellington found what he wanted on the second shelf. He used his hip to close the refrigerator door before he set the plastic containers on the marble countertop and sat down on a bar stool. "I'll have one of these...and one of those," he whispered to himself as he popped the morsels into his mouth.

As each one melted on his tongue, he wondered if this heavenly food didn't trump the sex he'd just had, but whose fault would that be?

He thought about setting a limit for himself, a method not to overeat, but he kept extending the max when he reached it, which led to three more scallops wrapped in bacon going down his hatch. Purely sinful, he thought, and reached for his glass of water to wash them down. He anticipated the roast pig tomorrow—it would be outstanding also, possibly topping tonight's delicacies, if the caterers were on point.

Wellington stood up, pushed in the bar stool, and rubbed his belly. He would take the long way back to the master bedroom to give his stomach a chance to settle before he got into bed.

As he shuffled past the den—which housed his drawing board, a carved antique desk, an enormous flat screen television recessed in the wall ledge, and a bear hide stretched out on the floor in front of a leather sofa—he saw a strip of light beneath the door. It was unlikely that one of his guests had strayed to this side of the house from the dining area during the party and had forgotten to turn off the light. He turned the doorknob and stepped inside.

Faye sat at his drawing board, the banker's desk lamp with the green shade casting light on her arms and hands, which rested on the slanted surface.

"This looks like the gallery," she said and hunched over the drawing, "but what is this area on top of it?"

Wellington rushed over and rolled up the drawing. "Not yet," he said, more calmly than he thought he could. "You'll have to wait, Faye...until I'm ready to show you."

He secured the drawing with a rubber band and slid it into one of the cubbyholes. Hundreds of rolled up blueprints peeked out of wooden nooks that ran halfway up the wall, an architect's dream storage system.

"I'm sorry," she said and followed her father to the sofa. "I couldn't sleep and somehow I ended up here."

He patted her wrist. "Those drawings are still in the preliminary stages. You'll be the first to see them when they're completed." He lowered his head and rubbed his jaw. "One of the first, I should say. If what I'm planning is to be of any use to you, I'll have to run it by some other people first. But again, that's a few weeks off, if not longer."

"I'll let you tell me about it another time, then." She smiled at him.

"Are you hungry?" he asked her. "I happen to be one of the few who knows where the leftovers are kept. Second shelf, way in the back. Don't tell anybody."

Faye laughed. "I'm finding out you have quite a few secrets, Mr. Brooks."

"I'd call them handy bits of knowledge. Case in point, there are approximately five scallops wrapped in bacon remaining in a plastic container. Basically, I'm willing to give you my blessing to gobble them up. Not many fathers would do that, you know. At least not the ones who really like bacon."

Faye shook her head. "You're impossible sometimes. And of all the fathers I know, you're the only one who watches his caloric intake so precisely, which makes me wonder if you want me to eat those scallops so you don't."

Now Wellington was the one who smiled. "Perhaps you know me too well, darling." He took a deep breath in. "I must've done something right because you turned out so well."

She leaned her head against the leather sofa. "Tell me about tomorrow. Will the same guests be attending?"

"Some of the same faces, for sure, but new ones also. Brace yourself. I'll be introducing you left and right."

Wellington glanced at Faye who peered up at the shadowy coffered ceiling. "Most of the people I met tonight seemed lovely. Your clients must really like working with you. Either that or they love free champagne and out-of-this-world appetizers."

He kept a straight face. "In my opinion, a caterer can make or break a party. Always choose one wisely."

"Your engagement party will be the first pig roast I've ever attended."

"You're in for a treat, then." He paused and looked around the room. A part of him wanted to ask her something that he wasn't sure was any of his business. "Lucinda and I noticed how much time you spent on Sterling's arm tonight. Is there anything I should know about the two of you? I mean, is it safe to assume you've both laid down your weapons and have become friends?"

Her gaze broke from the ceiling and seemed to focus on the bear rug at their feet. "Well gee, I didn't have much choice, now did I? You invited him. We flew here together. In such close quarters we had to come to an arrangement or die trying."

"I'm proud of you, Faye. If I didn't think it was in your best interest to play nicely with Sterling, I would've seen fit to pummel him with my bare hands a long time ago. Life is a delicate balance. It's best to know when to strike."

"You've lost me. How exactly are we going to strike?"

"Not to worry. Fortunately, I extended an offer to Sterling that he couldn't refuse. You'll see what it is shortly." He patted her knee. "I'm off to bed, sweetheart, good night." Then he kissed her cheek and left the room.

She really hated when her father was cryptic, which was why she remained in the den for another hour to mull over what he had said. The worst part was not wanting any surprises where Bobby was concerned. Unfortunately, all she could do was go up to bed and ask more questions in the morning.

The long staircase that wound up to the second floor from a grand foyer covered in travertine suggested Wellington believed a man could live comfortably surrounded by beautiful things. The bronze statue at the base of the staircase was worthy of placement in a national gallery, and Faye snapped a few pictures of it to show Lily during her next art lesson.

Once at the top, her slippers padded along the handwoven Persian rug that extended down the long hallway. There were five doors on either side and a handful of evenly-spaced wall sconces that provided a candlelit ambiance. A pair of suitcases sat outside the door closest to her bedroom. They weren't hers—she knew that much—and they hadn't been there prior to her going downstairs.

"You're up late," came a voice from behind her.

She turned around slowly as she closed her robe over her nightgown. "Shouldn't you be at your hotel?"

"Your father assured me I'd be more comfortable here. I thought it might be rude to decline." Bobby's eyes sparkled, which proved to Faye how much he enjoyed her discomfort.

"Every square foot of this place is spectacular," he continued. "The four poster bed in my room is carved out of the darkest Italian wood I've ever seen. Unfortunately, it's too big to fit in my suitcase." He reached out for her hand. "Come take a look."

"That's really not necessary." Her father had promised to take her on a tour of the estate tomorrow, and she'd rather see everything with him. The last time she'd visited California this house hadn't been built yet, which meant her father would provide commentary about how he'd come up with the design and layout, just to wow her.

Bobby gently squeezed her hand and led her toward the door where the suitcases sat. He turned the knob. "After you. It's guaranteed to take your breath away."

She entered his room, which was similar to hers, only more masculine as far as bed linens and draperies were concerned. Off to one side, a stone fireplace took up a portion of the wall, and two wing back chairs in blue and ivory toile fabric sat in front of the hearth. A knitted throw was draped over the armrest of one chair.

With its European flare, the magnificent four poster bed resembled something from a period movie set, she thought. And to that end, she half expected two actors, one dressed as a king and one as a queen, to reveal themselves from underneath the covers. The richness of the wood surpassed anything she had ever seen.

"It's very nice," she said, still thinking about how her father should have discussed it with her before he invited Bobby to stay at the house.

"Your dad has amazing taste." He glanced in the direction of the door. "Your turn. Show me where you're staying."

"I don't have a fireplace," she said quickly. A part of her didn't want him to know she was right next door.

He looked up and down the hallway. "Which door is yours?"

When she opened the one nearest to his room, he mumbled, "My God, we're neighbors. How fantastic!"

Faye stood just inside the door to her room and watched Bobby walk around the space with his head tilted back. The ceiling fresco that wrapped around the circular dome above her bed had obviously caught his eye.

"I think you got the better room," he finally said, still staring up at the ceiling, his mouth gaping open.

"Every room has its own charm, I suppose."

"They look so real." He pointed to the fruit-laden vines in the fresco.

"I know. It's amazing. I was told a local artist hand painted the entire thing."

He shook his head, as if to break his gaze away, and walked over to her. "It's obvious W. Brooks spared no expense. I may have to move in here permanently, just so all of these extra rooms don't go to waste."

Faye laughed. "I'm guessing Lucinda would have a problem with that."

The dimple showed in his cheek. "You're probably right."

Whether it was due to the lateness of the hour or the particular way he'd just smiled, Faye thought about the first time they'd met. That Saturday afternoon he'd walked into the gallery wearing an expensive suit and a cocky grin, so self-assured that he could appease her and get his own way.... She remembered thinking he was handsome, and that she had her work cut out for her.

"Tell me what you thought of me when we first met," she asked, and invited him to sit down on a sofa at the front of the bedroom. The small sitting area had two sofas, a wooden trunk for a coffee table, and a television mounted to the wall. A hand-hooked wool rug with a gigantic flower pattern grounded the space.

He leaned back against the cushions. "A die-hard art lover. Someone who would risk everything to save a painting from a burning building. That sort of thing. It crossed my mind you might locate the perfect tree and then chain yourself to it. Anything to get me to alter my plans for the gallery."

She sat on the adjacent sofa and raised her eyebrows. "A burning building, huh? How creative of you. And if I did chain myself to a tree...what would you do then?"

He rubbed his hands together before answering, "Unchain you, of course."

Her jaw went slack. "That defeats the purpose. How could I stand up for my principles if you did that?"

"All along I imagined you sitting beneath the tree, not standing. I don't think your principles would be offended either way."

She made sure her robe was overlapped before tucking her feet up under her buttocks; she hugged a pillow to her chest. "Am I the first woman to challenge your plans for a café?"

He leaned forward and planted both elbows on his knees. "I do believe you are."

"Consider yourself lucky I haven't unleashed more of my wrath on you, Bobby Sterling." To show him she meant it, she didn't allow herself to smile this time.

The lamp's yellow glow made the right side of Faye's hair appear golden.

"Faye Brooks," he said, "I'm thinking a lot of things right now, but none of them have to do with you being angry at me. Now could we please see what other options are available at this time of night?"

Faye recognized the look in his eyes and hoped her own weren't betraying her. As physically gratifying as it might be to indulge in a bit of male company, she had other things to consider. Her self-respect, for one. Being under her father's roof, for another.

Get rid of him, she told herself. Push him out the door and close it quickly.

Bobby must have sensed that she was conflicted because he said in a deep, unsteady voice, "I'll go if you want me to."

Chapter Thirteen

"You'll stay here and that's all there is to it," Norman said as he observed the panicked look in Faye's eyes. She stood in his doorway with a suitcase in each hand. Suddenly, she dropped the bags and hugged him fiercely. Then she glanced across the hall once more before Norman ushered her inside.

"How can this be happening?" she asked and shoved aside a teddy bear on the sofa cushion to make room for herself to sit down.

"We'll get to the bottom of it. You can count on that." He sat down across from her. "Why don't you tell me what Adler said to you, word for word."

She fingered the teddy bear's face. "He and I spoke before I left for California." Slowly, her face scrunched up. "My rent check bounced."

Norman sighed. "Oh, Faye. As an accountant, I'm not liking the sound of this. And as your friend, I distinctly remember telling you never to let that happen. Our landlord equates a bounced check with that first shove in a fist fight. Considering I've never known him to back down, we're going to have to be very smart about this."

"I can't lose my apartment, Norman."

He tapped his fingers on his knee as he tried to think. "There must have been some sort of agreement between you two. Did he give you a timeline to get the money to him? He tacked on a penalty fee, I'd imagine."

Faye set the bear aside. "Ten percent. I owe him my rent, plus ten percent, and twenty-five dollars for the bounced check." She paused and looked everywhere but at him. "With the news of my father's engagement, I completely forgot about making the payment. Adler promised he would serve me with an eviction notice if that happened."

Norman grimaced. "At least the man is true to his word."

"It was foolish of me to forget to pay Adler before I left. The last thing I need is for more pieces of my life to crash down on my head. I stand to lose the gallery, now my apartment, and maybe even my father."

A fresh look of distress entered Faye's eyes, which compelled Norman to sit next to her on the other sofa. As he squeezed her to his side, her body felt listless; its only movement was the shaking of her head against his chest. "I've made a mess of things," she said, her tears soaking into his shirt.

He patted her head and had a feeling one of his shirt buttons was poking into her cheek. "We're going to fix this."

"But how? He changed the locks already. I can't even get my things."

Norman's arm was draped across her. He gave her a little squeeze. "You have what's in your suitcases. That's a start."

She rested one hand on his thigh. "The day before yesterday I was sitting on a terrace eating roast pork in my father's backyard, chatting with all sorts of people who have interesting lives. Now today I come home to find I've been evicted. Turns out, I'm officially the most uninteresting person I know."

"You're someone who has a lot on her mind...which makes you very interesting. This could've happened to anyone. What we have to focus on now is paying Adler."

She spoke quietly, "Paying him?"

Norman shifted his torso so he could see her face. "You don't have the money, do you?"

Faye sat up, but Norman kept his arm around her. "Not exactly."

Even though Norman planned to rectify the situation with Adler in the morning, he wanted to be able to do it with the cash in hand. If it came down to it, he would cite code after code of renter's rights to get his point across. And if that didn't work he would attribute the late payment to a big misunderstanding. The landlord would grumble, no doubt, but it would be an opportunity to save face and give Faye another chance. With any luck, Adler would shake his finger in Norman's face, accept an extra fifty dollars on top of what he was owed, and things would return to normal.

Although Norman had a fair idea of what post-bounced-check life would be like on the second floor of the brownstone from now on, he was willing to get on Adler's bad side if it would help Faye keep her apartment. The more he thought about it ... what would he do if she no longer lived across the hall? The 'cat lady' who had occupied 2A before Faye hadn't been the type of woman to befriend, much less fall in love with.

This had to work. He kissed her forehead before getting up to fix them something to eat.

Faye followed him into the kitchen. "If only I'd thought to pack some pork meat in my suitcase, you could see how the other half lives."

He took carrots out of the refrigerator and looked over his shoulder at her. "I'm sure it meant a lot to your father to have you there. Did you two get a chance to talk?"

"After he toured me around the estate, he sat me down by the pool. I almost gave up hope that he'd say anything; he stared at the water for a long time before he spoke. Then he patted my knee and told me I'd always be the number one woman in his life. 'Don't worry,' he said, 'about coming second to Lucinda because you never will.'"

Norman peeled the carrots at the table. "That must've made you feel better."

She reached over to grab one off the plate and bit into it. "He knows I don't agree with his decision to marry her. That being said, it's very difficult to pretend I'll eventually get used to it."

"A distance of three thousand miles is pretty far. That alone ought to help." He moved the plate back so Faye couldn't reach for more carrots before he was done peeling them. "Think about it ... Lucinda can't visit you on a daily basis."

Faye eased open the refrigerator door. "You should've seen the way she looked at me in Zoe's dress. I thought she was going to have an attack of some sort."

"It probably helped to have other guests around." He eyed her as she took the lid off the container of vegetable dip. "She couldn't very well insult you in front of your father's clients."

She dipped a carrot and then pulled it out with a glob of white on the end that she licked off. "Bobby turned out to be a good buffer. He never let me out of his sight, and every time Lucinda looked like she was about to say something unpleasant, he spoke first. It seemed to do the trick."

This was the first time she'd mentioned that Bobby had attended the party. At least he would've stayed in a hotel while Faye slept at her father's, Norman thought—a satisfactory way to minimize opportunities for Sterling to get too close to her. Norman didn't want Faye to get tangled up with someone who seemed to respect coffee grinds more than a culturally-sound experience at a gallery. It was not difficult to think of Sterling as a café-owning jerk, even though he'd never met the man in person.

"So Wellington invited Sterling?" Norman pushed the plate into the center of the table so they could share the carrot sticks.

She nudged the container of vegetable dip toward him. "I was surprised, too. But I have a feeling my father's up to something. The night of the cocktail party I had trouble sleeping, so I wandered around. The door to the den was open and I went in and sat down at his drawing board. Right in front of me were these plans, rough sketches really, that involved the gallery. I can't be sure what he's attempting to do." She paused to dip a carrot. "Probably wouldn't like it if I knew."

"These plans showed the existing gallery?"

"Seemed to. There was something extending up from the roof that I couldn't figure out. And when I asked my father about it, he clammed up. Apparently, he's not ready to tell me yet. The most unsettling part is the next day I saw him and Bobby go in there and close the door. I'd never wanted to be a fly on the wall more than at that moment, let me tell you."

Norman stopped chewing his carrot and looked at her. "The Faye Brooks I know wouldn't let a little thing like a door stop her."

Faye hung her head and then lifted it slowly. "Well...I may have tiptoed to the door to listen, but solid oak isn't very forgiving. I only caught every other word. Something about merging two things into one, they were saying."

"That's it? You didn't hear anything else? And this relates to the gallery how?"

She shook her head. "I don't know. They kept their voices low."

Norman went over to the sink to wash his hands. "I may have better luck finding something out over the phone. A quick call to Wellington...a simple chat to hammer this out."

She pressed the lid onto the container of dip. "My inclination is to wait and see how this plays out."

Norman thought she was joking and continued to rub the dishtowel over his hands past the point of them being dried. "You're the least patient person I know, and you want to wait and see?"

"My father promised to assist the gallery according to my wishes—strictly in a non-monetary way—and I have to assume he's doing just that."

"Then we wait." He crumpled up the dishtowel and tossed it onto the counter.

Faye got up and stretched her arms over her head. "If the spare bedroom is still in the same spot, I think I'll unpack my suitcases and take a bath."

He leaned his buttocks against the countertop and crossed his arms over his chest. "Plenty of extra blankets in the closet."

Faye spent over an hour in the tub. Then she tossed one suitcase onto the bed and then the other, the mattress jiggling both times; she pressed down on it with her open palm to find it wasn't very firm. It hardly concerned her because she would be back across the hall shortly, at her own place, as soon as this business with Adler got ironed out.

She pinched the little switch under the shade to turn on the lamp. A box wrapped in Christmas paper lay on the nightstand, and the tag had her name on it. There was space to wiggle her thighs between the two suitcases on the bed. In one motion she peeled back the paper and opened the box to find a silver picture frame inside. Upon looking closely at the document under the glass, she realized it was the last page of the procurement papers for the Van Gogh exhibit. Several signatures were on it, including her own, as well as a description of the acquisition, plus an embossed seal in the bottom corner.

How sweet of Norman to do this for her! The keychain she'd purchased for him at the San Diego airport paled by comparison. When she thought about all the steps he must have taken to accomplish this, she shook her head in amazement. To get his hands on that piece of paper showed Faye—once again—how even a straight-laced guy like Norman could be sneaky if the circumstances called for it.

With the frame positioned on the nightstand, Faye decided to unpack her suitcases before thanking him. Prior to leaving her father's place, she'd laundered all her clothes, one less thing she had to worry about doing now. Everything smelled liked California, she thought, a combination of sunshine and grapevines; she sniffed one of her folded shirts, placed it in an empty dresser drawer, and hung her pants in the closet. The slinky dress Jacklyn had lent her was at the bottom of the suitcase, rolled up to prevent wrinkles, the best she could do without an official garment bag. Since Jacklyn and she were about the same size, Faye hadn't even tried it on.

"Well?" She found Norman on the sofa watching television.

"How do I look?"

Faye stood in front of him in a shimmering sequined gown, her bare feet peeking out at the bottom. The dress clung to her slender waist and to her buttocks when she spun around.

"Like my apartment isn't glamorous enough for you," he finally said.

The price tag dangled from one of the sleeveless arm holes, so Faye tucked it inside the fabric. "Jacklyn has excellent taste. I wonder when she plans on wearing this."

"If I know my sister, she'd walk the dog in it just to get a rise out of the neighbors."

Faye touched the neckline and smiled. "It was really nice of her to let me borrow it. Personally, I wouldn't let a dress like this out of my sight."

She gathered her hair in both hands, twisted it up, and left one hand behind her head to hold it in place. "A dress like this calls for a woman's hair to be up," she explained.

Norman had gotten awfully quiet, which made Faye wonder if she didn't look half as good as she thought she did all decked out. But after a moment she realized he was probably waiting for her to mention his extraordinary gift. Mindful of the pretty dress, she carefully sat down next to him. "I've got to tell you how amazed I am"—she leaned her head on his shoulder—"about my gift; whatever gave you the idea to frame one of the procurement papers?"

With the way his head was angled toward hers, Faye felt the edge of his smile touch her forehead. "Accountants are known for their good ideas," he said. "I thought you knew that."

"Bear with me," she said with a laugh. "Every so often I forget." She felt his warm breath on the top of her head. "Was it Zoe who helped you find the document?"

"Couldn't have pulled it off without her. The way she tells it...you went looking for the papers one day...and she had to act fast."

Faye sat up. "I remember that. We were in my office and she

was behaving strangely. In fact, she insisted I sit down at my desk while she rummaged around in the filing cabinet. When I said I could do it myself, she told me to go make a cup of tea, two if I didn't mind getting her one."

"I have little doubt that I could've asked Zoe to help me rob a bank for you and she would've asked 'with ski masks or without.'"

The dress had a slit up the side that parted when she shifted her position on the sofa. Not noticing that her thigh was exposed, Faye returned her head to rest on his shoulder, more heavily this time...until she caught herself falling asleep.

"Let me get you to bed." He eased off the sofa and twisted around to scoop her into his arms. The multitude of sequins sewn on the dress scratched his wrists. "Ouch!" he whispered, and in an even softer voice added...a small price to pay for holding you against my chest.

She rubbed her eyes. "I'm not Lily. I'm perfectly capable of walking to the bedroom."

Norman bent his head and kissed her forehead. "Hush, you're sleeping."

***

Adler stood his ground. "Tell me why I should care?"

Norman clasped his hands behind his back and resisted an urge to sock Adler squarely in the jaw. "There are so many reasons. Where should I start?"

The landlord snickered, "Just as I thought. You haven't got one."

Norman had already explained how Faye thought she had another week to make the payment. Misunderstandings were a part of life, Norman had argued, and hoped to see a glimmer of compassion on Adler's face. When there was none, the accountant slid the checkbook out of his back pocket. He scribbled down a number, signed the bottom, and handed the check across the desk to Adler. "Take it," Norman had said, but to his surprise, Adler slowly ripped it up and let the pieces fall on the scarred surface of the metal desk.

He'd never been in Adler's office before. It was the size of a small elevator with one desk, two chairs and a calendar on the gray block wall. The no-frills aspect of the space matched Alder's personality. There was nothing to look at except Adler, whose downturned mouth reminded Norman of the time his nephew had accidentally swallowed a ladybug. If the man refused to take his overly-generous check to cover Faye's rent, then he was almost out of options. He could try one last thing, and pray it worked.

"Mr. Adler, will you excuse me for a moment?" Norman walked into the hallway and made a phone call.

Less than five minutes later, he reentered the office and stretched out his arm to hand Adler his phone.

His eyes got squinty. "What am I supposed to do with this?"

"The person on the other end would like to speak with you. I suggest you hear what he has to say."

"Spencer Alder here. Who's this?"

To hear only one side of the conversation put Norman at a disadvantage, but not too much because the things he overhead sounded positive. Adler was saying yes sir left and right and I don't doubt what you're telling me, sir, and I'll change the locks back this afternoon, sir.

After Norman returned his phone to his suit jacket pocket, he waited for Adler to say something.

"Had yourself an ace in the hole all along, didn't you Maynard?" Adler shook his head. "Well, I don't care too much for being bamboozled, but you one-upped me this time, that's for damn sure. Tell Faye she can move back into 2A real soon. I'll see to the locks myself."

Norman stuck out his hand, but Alder didn't shake it. "No hard feelings, Mr. Adler."

"Oh there are plenty of hard feelings—you can be sure of that—but I'm going to keep them to myself for the time being."

Chapter Fourteen

The train pulled away from the station. Faye believed Norman's vigorous wave from the platform was meant to encourage her, only when she twisted around in her seat to watch him grow smaller as the engine picked up speed, she wished he'd agreed to come with them to New York City.

"Your father wants you to get to know Lucinda," he'd reminded her an hour earlier as they'd rushed toward the ticket booth. "Give it a chance." Next, they'd tried to spot Lucinda in the crowd of people waiting to board.

Leave it to her father to come up with an idea and then carry it through—a last ditch effort to gain her approval of his impending marriage. Apparently, he'd tossed an unwilling Lucinda on a plane headed for Albany. The plan was for her and Faye to ride the train from Rensselaer to New York City for two days of shopping and girl talk. No doubt, her father considered this a brilliant idea—a girls' weekend—a way to solve all of his problems. If the two of them could bond over a pretty blouse in the garment district or a Broadway play or a slice of phenomenal pizza, then his peace of mind would be restored. She knew that's how he was looking at this.

On the face of things, Faye only had to give up her time, because all other expenses were being sent directly to her father's tab. It was a free vacation, if she wanted to look at it that way.

"This could backfire," Norman had told Wellington when he'd

run the idea past him a week ago. "You could start a war without even knowing it."

"I prefer to think of it as a battle. And if it can be won, it has the potential to stop the war from ever happening."

The conductor walked down the aisle to collect the tickets. Lucinda held hers out as though she expected him to kiss her hand. Faye smiled weakly at the man and then leaned her head against the window.

"So how does it feel to be back in your own apartment?" Lucinda asked after a long silence.

Faye turned from the window with knitted brows. "Excuse me?"

"From what Wellie told me, I got the impression you'd been evicted, living with Norman, I think he said, until it could be straightened out."

Faye practically spat out the words: "Oh it's been straightened out."

"Well yes, of course it has. Your father won't stand for that kind of thing, dear. No one has the right to inconvenience his precious little girl, now do they?" Lucinda stretched out her legs. She wore peach cashmere pants and a matching cashmere sweater. "Code violations. That's how Wellie did it. And your landlord ate up every bite. Wellie relayed to him several code violations he saw while we visited you at Christmas. Either that Adler fellow let you back into your apartment or the proper building officials were to be informed."

Faye didn't recall Norman discussing the exact methods he'd used to get Adler to relinquish apartment 2A, but if what Lucinda said was true, he'd had her father's help.

"So it was my father who paid my rent?"

"Norman tried to," she began, "but your lowlife landlord tore up his check. Wellie had no choice but to wire the money over."

In light of the fact that she was on a train to the city with someone she loathed, this revelation about who had paid her rent did less to unsettle her than being able to walk across the hall to Norman's apartment to give him a piece of her mind would have. It seemed like everyone butted into her affairs and she was the last one to find out about it.

"Facials," Lucinda said bluntly. "Shall we get facials first or did you have something else in mind?"

That depended on whether the esthetician would cover Lucinda's face in mud or with a carrot scrub, Faye thought. To have her traveling companion's face blackened out by muddy goop, only her blue eyes showing, would be something worth seeing. "Sure, why not," she said, suddenly feeling that making friends with the enemy might keep her informed about the events of her own life.

Lucinda turned to her, and looked like she'd swallowed a button off her designer coat. "If I promise not to tell your father, will you answer my next question with a yes or no?" Her eyes bored into Faye's. "It's regarding Bobby Sterling."

Ah, Bobby, the man who could toss a jumbo shrimp into the air and catch it in his mouth. Out of all of his attempts, she'd only seen him miss once. Far from a cultured thing to do, it proved Bobby had tried to impress her, which she thought was sweet. A few days had gone by without her thinking about him, which was why she didn't mind fielding a few questions now, especially since she had nothing better to do. "I'm not sure there's anything to say, but you can ask."

Lucinda lowered her voice and positioned her face close to Faye's. "Did you sleep with him?"

Faye's eyes widened. It looked like Lucinda took this 'girl-talk' weekend a little too seriously. "Did I sleep with him?" Repeating the question gave Faye a chance to think of the correct answer. She couldn't very well say yes, and she figured saying no might make her look dull and boring, so she smiled and rolled her eyes. "What gave you that idea?"

"You and he were in such great moods at the pig roast. It was a natural assumption."

Her good mood had not been a product of Bobby's prowess in

bed, but rather of meeting some of her father's eclectic clients who believed the art world would someday save humanity. Faye didn't know if that would ever happen, but she liked the sound of it.

"Fine, you don't want to tell me," Lucinda said and held out her hand to admire her engagement ring yet again.

Actually, Faye longed to discuss Bobby with another female, only she had too many misgivings about the one sitting next to her to take a chance on it.

"I saw him feed you a piece of meat," Lucinda said, as if it proved her point.

Across the aisle a man in a bomber jacket with a fur collar reached into a worn leather bag at his feet and pulled out a book. The cover had a picture of a 1950's car on it with a woman in a dress in the foreground. If Faye had been sitting in Lucinda's seat, she would've struck up a conversation with the guy.

"You promised me a yes or no answer," Lucinda reminded her as she adjusted her Louis Vuitton handbag on her lap.

Faye pushed a strand of hair behind her ear. "We came very close."

Lucinda unzipped the bag and poked her hand inside it. "What stopped you?"

"I'm not exactly sure."

Lucinda slid a pair of white Gucci sunglasses over her eyes. "Some juicy details would be nice."

This side of Lucinda was new to Faye—the general interest she was showing in her life—and the assurance that she wouldn't tattle to 'Wellie' meant a lot to her. Maybe this weekend wouldn't be a complete waste of time after all.

"Let's just say we were partially undressed but it went no further than that. We kissed mostly."

"Ah ha, I've spotted the flaw in your tryst," Lucinda said, the darkness of her sunglasses making it difficult to tell if she was looking at Faye or just past her out the window. "Never underestimate the power of kissing." She lowered the sunglasses down her nose. "I presume he's good at it?"

"Quite."

"So the man is a good kisser...good looking...wealthy...and you thought twice about sleeping with him?"

Faye took two granola bars out of her pocket and handed one to Lucinda. "When you put it that way it sounds ridiculous, but yes."

Her mouth twisted. "What am I supposed to do with this?"

"I brought an orange if you'd prefer that."

"As if an orange squirting all over my cashmere outfit is a viable option." She took the granola bar and sighed. "Subconsciously, you must resent him for taking your baby."

"My baby?"

"The gallery."

Lucinda peeled back the foil on the granola bar. "Speaking of which, after our facials and some light shopping, I'd like to take you to an art emporium I know. It's a hole in the wall, really, but the owner and I have become quite close over the years. I think she'd be interested to meet you."

Was Lucinda attempting to add something to the weekend's itinerary that Faye would actually enjoy doing? If that was the case, the woman didn't deserve every bad thing Faye had ever said about her, only some of it.

"I'd like nothing better." Faye peeled the orange for herself, but only after Lucinda had spread out a fashion magazine on her own lap to avoid any spray from the peeling process. That was the Lucinda Faye knew—the one who thought about herself first.

Lucinda ignored Faye's suggestion that they take the subway to their hotel. "Penniless thugs with minds emptier than their pockets use the subway," Lucinda told her, "and the last thing that belongs underground is cashmere knitwear, accessorized by an oversized Louis Vuitton handbag. There are classier ways to arrive at a hotel than with the grime of the subway station in one's hair and a pink wad of gum stuck to the bottom of one's shoe."

Faye watched as Lucinda set her jaw and pinned her eyes on an approaching yellow cab. Abruptly, she stepped into the roadway and thrust out her arm. The cab swerved and came to a stop. "That wasn't so hard," she said over her shoulder to Faye, who had a suitcase in each hand; the plainer one was hers, the designer one Lucinda's. Why someone needed three heavy suitcases for a two-day trip was beyond Faye, but at least Lucinda carried the other two herself.

"We're in a bit of hurry," Lucinda told the cabby, "so don't hesitate to step on the gas when necessary."

"Aye, aye, lady," he said, his big belly scraping the rim of the trunk as he leaned forward to set the luggage inside.

Faye settled herself in the back seat, which smelled like cigars and cooked cabbage, just two of the odors that immediately met her nose. Lucinda got in on the other side and must've smelled it too because she reached into her bag, extracted a perfume bottle, and spritzed the air in front of her face. She breathed in. "Ah, much better."

The two-bedroom suite Wellington had booked for them erased the smelly cab ride from Faye's mind the instant she opened the door. And while Faye found the penthouse suite to be modern and luxurious in white tones with bright yellow accents, Lucinda pointed her nose in the air as she looked about. "Who in their right mind considers this a premier suite?" Lucinda asked as she threw herself onto the white leather sofa and kicked off her heels.

Curious to have a look around, Faye poked her head in each of the rooms and then stopped in the bathroom to splash cold water on her face. Elaborately tiled, the room was triple the size of her loo at home, and she wondered why anyone would need this much space for bathing and toiletries. Until she twisted the faucet handle to stop the running water, she couldn't hear Lucinda moaning in the other room.

"You sound like an artist whose work has been rejected," Faye said as she strolled into the big room. The center part of the space had white leather furniture, a fluffy white rug, and a yellow lacquered coffee table. Beyond that, the full length of the back wall was a kitchen area. "It's really very lovely, and we could cook our own meals."

Lucinda rolled her eyes. "In case you haven't noticed, dear, we're on a weekend getaway. Cooking just isn't done."

Of course it wasn't. Faye kept sticking her foot in her mouth, it seemed. First with the subway and now with the audacious suggestion of cooking their own fare. With the gallery in peril, her whole world had turned into a series of cost comparisons. It was cheaper to ride the subway than take a taxi, for example. Cooking their meals at the hotel instead of going to a restaurant was also cheaper, but Lucinda probably knew that and didn't care. Faye could have taken money from her father to make the gallery nightmare go away, but she hadn't. Either she was an overly-confident fool or just simply a fool.

"I need a bubble bath," Lucinda said. She glided the back of her hand over her forehead. "Please tell me they had the good sense to put a claw foot tub in this underwhelming penthouse."

Faye nodded and wondered if it was the foul-smelling cab ride that had worn Lucinda out or her sheer disappointment with the suite. Either way, Faye had a few moments to herself and decided to call Norman.

Lily picked up the phone and told Auntie Faye that Uncle Norman was acting very strangely and couldn't come to the phone. When Faye asked her to explain, she described her uncle waving his arms wildly at her and saying he wasn't home. Lily said, "Silly Uncle Norman, of course you're home. You're standing in your own kitchen."

"That's okay, Lily. He doesn't want to talk to me. Please tell him I'll try back later."

Clearly, Norman must've guessed that Lucinda's loose lips would've revealed his part in the rent-check matter during the course of the long train ride. How very clever of him to use Lily as a buffer. "When's my next art lesson, Auntie Faye?" she'd asked before they hung up.

By the time Lucinda had bathed herself and put on a fresh cashmere outfit, this one in burgundy with a chevron-patterned sweater, Faye was anxious to head out to the art emporium, only she didn't know if it was within walking distance.

"We won't be walking," Lucinda said as she arranged her blonde hair at the nape of her neck. She punched a number into her cell phone and waited for someone to answer. "Yes, this is Lucinda Piedmont. I'll need a limo within the hour. That's right. The address is...."

Lucinda could be overbearing and abrasive at times, but Faye admired the way she took charge of a situation until it turned out to her liking.

Large prints of well-known masterpieces flooded the central space of the emporium. Stacked five inches high on top of crates that reached knee level, they were meant to be sifted through by patient art lovers. Faye walked down one lane to get to the next set of prints. Back and forth, her head swung to view the display on both sides. She bent down and lifted the edge of one print. Marked in pencil in the lower corner was a price of forty-five dollars.

Sample frames clung to the back wall. Only the top corner of each partial frame was nailed in place to create a massive pattern from floor to ceiling, a bunch of upside down v's. The selections came in gold, silver, varying shades of brown, bright red, lime green, and every color in between.

In front of the wall, a circular rack of artist postcards spun as Lucinda set them in motion.

A woman scurried out of the back wearing an apron covered in little dabs of paint. Short and blue-eyed, she darted toward Lucinda and kissed her on both cheeks. Stiff, wavy blonde hair stuck out around her face. "About time you made a trip here to see me," she said and stood back to look at Lucinda who towered above her.

"What's three thousand miles between friends?" Lucinda said, as she diverted her gaze. "Wouldn't you know...I've brought my stepdaughter with me. See there, she's the one trying to view the very last picture in the pile."

Angie tilted her head, the thick hair around her face not budging. "This wouldn't be the gallery director from Albany, would it?"

"For now." Lucinda sighed and then scowled. "A wealthy heiress by the name of DuPont has given Faye the heave-ho, only the poor dear refuses to accept what that means. She's holding onto the gallery with both fists, and quite frankly her father and I are worried about the consequences. Faye plans to fight to the very end."

The small-statured woman pulled a postcard from the rack, glanced at it absently, and then put it back. "What exactly is she fighting? Does this DuPont lady plan to keep her on in another capacity?"

"Like sweeping floors, you mean? I only wish, but no. The building is being sold. A café is slated to take its place. No more paintings and sculptures, just tall lattes with extra foam."

Angie adjusted the apron's strap around her neck, which momentarily fluffed out her hair even more. "And Wellington...how is he taking the news?"

Lucinda twirled one hand in the air. "As one would expect. My Wellie wants to scribble his signature on a check and save the day, only his daughter won't hear of it. She gives new meaning to the word headstrong. It's put a damper on our lives, I can tell you that. With a wedding to plan, this little mess with the gallery is pulling me in more directions than I care to think about. It's the reason I've brought Faye here, in fact. Wellie thinks I can talk some sense into her privately, woman to woman."

"If anybody can, you can, Luc."

"Well I thank you for that vote of confidence, but I may need your help to pull it off."

Eyes squinted, Angie looked up at Lucinda. "Something tells

me I may not like what you're about to say."

"We need bait, and since I don't have any of my own, I thought you could provide some. You own an art emporium, after all. Clearly, you must need an extra set of hands around here."

Angie looked out, perhaps watching Faye stroll down an aisle. "So I'm being asked to give Wellie's kid a job? Budgets are tight, Luc. I can't just hire another employee without considering my bank account."

Lucinda dug into the purse that dangled from her arm. "I thought you might need a little coaxing." She handed her a check. "Will that cover the costs of hiring a washed-up gallery director?"

Angie held the check in both hands. For a long while she remained silent and stared down at it. "I'm not sure I can be bought, but then again, no one has ever tried."

Faye wove through the piles of prints and came toward them. "Are you the owner?"

"I'd better be because I pay all the bills around here."

They shook hands. "It looks like you've got"—Faye turned around to eye the rows of prints once more—"thousands of reproductions under one roof. How do you manage to keep the prices low?"

"Customers prefer art they can afford. And I prefer the ones willing to buy over lookie loos. If that hurts my pocket a little, then so be it."

Faye crossed her arms over her chest. "Either it's my imagination or I've never seen so many Klimt's in one place. It's a thing of beauty if you ask me."

Angie patted Faye's arm. "The secret's out. He's one of my favorites."

Lucinda held up her hand. "Before you two start drooling over these art posters, I'd like a tour of the gallery. Angie, would you be so kind?"

Large and square, the room had a high warehouse ceiling and miles of inventory. Faye hadn't known a gallery existed on the premises. "What types of artwork do you show?"

Angie led the way across the vast emporium space toward a side door that said EXIT. "Whatever I can get my hands on," she answered as they entered a small room with a dozen modest canvases on the walls.

Chapter Fifteen

Two cucumber slices rested on Faye's eyelids, but the moment she wiggled her nose one of them fell off. In an attempt to locate it she ran her hand along the edge of the pillow. The narrow massage table didn't leave much room for her, which made it very possible the cucumber had rolled onto the floor.

On the adjacent massage table, Lucinda laid completely still, wrapped in seaweed, her cucumbers perfectly positioned over both eyes. The idea that some women found it rejuvenating to be swaddled in algae for a solid hour prompted Faye to choose a daisy scrub that slowly hardened on her limbs. At least she wasn't green.

"Things are looking up," Lucinda said without moving her head. "Don't you agree?"

"We're both flat on our backs covered in goop."

"I mean you've been offered a job. A fresh start is exactly what you need—a new beginning for your career."

Faye removed the cucumber from her left eye. "The art emporium was massive and remarkable—don't get me wrong—and Angie was great, but I haven't given up on Hirsch."

"Well you had better. Understand this...the place is finished. Neither you nor I can change that."

"The first month's rent is taken care of. That's a start. And if the appeal for the grant comes through...who knows.... Who's to say Bobby won't focus all of his energies on the west coast from now on and drop his interests here?"

"Is there no getting through to you? That's never going to happen." She paused. "Oh dear, I have an itch on my nose." Encased in seaweed, her arms firmly tucked against her sides, she sighed several times.

"I'd advise against wiggling. But don't ask me how I know that."

A veteran spa-goer, Lucinda jutted out her lower lip and blew her breath upward until the force of hot air must have relieved the itch on her nose. "You have a job lined up for when the gallery closes. That's a step in the right direction. I suggest we call your father and tell him the good news as soon as we're done here."

Faye had no intention of reporting this potential job offer to her father. Firstly, it was several notches down from her current position. At the emporium, she would oversee the tiny gallery attached to the main space, but it was nothing compared to Hirsch. The low ceiling wouldn't allow for large canvases, and the narrow configuration created poor traffic flow if sculptures were placed in the center. No better than showing artwork in her apartment bathroom, she thought.

Secondly, a move to New York City would put miles between her and Norman. His company and friendship were too important to her to take lightly.

"Ladies, how are we doing?" The esthetician, dressed all in white, walked into the room to check on them. She scanned each of their bodies and then gasped when she saw Faye's arm. "You've been moving, I see." The pale yellow scrub had cracked along Faye's forearm when she'd reached up to remove the cucumber. "And what do we have here?" The woman crouched down to retrieve something from under her shoe. With the cucumber pinched between her fingers, she held it up for Faye to see. "If you didn't want the puffiness under your eyes reduced you could have told me."

Faye opened her mouth to apologize, but in the next moment, the woman left the room.

"I've never been so embarrassed," Lucinda muttered. "Good God, Faye, it's a wonder they don't throw us out."

In the dim light, Faye surveyed the shadowy ceiling. "It was an accident. Cucumbers can be slippery."

Lucinda pursed her lips. "If it's all the same to you, I'd prefer we discuss something other than your inability to keep a couple of vegetables over your eyes. Honestly, I think you hurt her feelings. Also, since we're supposed to be on a ladies' weekend, I believe the gallery should be off limits from now on, too."

No more talking about the gallery? Perhaps the bright green seaweed was wrapped too tightly. What else could explain Lucinda's sudden renunciation of Hirsch?

"While we're in the city, we must scour the garment district for a suitable dress for you. The wedding will be here before you know it, and I won't have you showing up in God knows what."

Terrific, the gallery was nixed as a topic of conversation only to have it replaced with talk of the wedding. Things were definitely in a downward spiral. The alarming part was that Faye had decided to play along. She would submit to endless hours of shopping for a dress if it would get Lucinda off her back.

***

Surrounded by dresses that sparkled with sequins or other glamorous embellishments, Faye dragged two more of Lucinda's choices into the dressing room.

"Try the pale blue one first," Lucinda shouted to her from the other side of the curtain. "If nothing else, at least we've established that you don't look good in teal, mauve, lavender or fuchsia."

Faye shimmied into the dress and twisted her arms behind her back to zipper it halfway. She twirled in front of the mirror, the pleated bottom flaring out, but then she stopped abruptly. Lucinda had pulled the curtain back and stared at her blankly. "If it came in plaid you'd look like a Catholic school girl."

Faye glanced at herself in the mirror again. "What does this make it? Strike twelve?"

Lucinda fluttered her eyelashes. "Well, my goodness, I'm certainly not keeping count. You have a challenging figure, to be sure, which requires our patience until we find what suits you best."

Faye hadn't a clue what she meant by challenging, but she supposed it was Lucinda's way of saying they had different body types, with hers being one of average height with slender curves and Lucinda's being tall and pleasantly bony.

The curtain swooshed closed as Lucinda yanked on the fabric. "While you try the next one on, I'll search the only rack we haven't tried."

Lime-green chiffon slid up Faye's body and the massive green rose attached to the belted waist flopped over until she tied the two pieces of ribbon at the back. Clownish was the only term she could use to describe her own appearance in this dress. "I know, I know," she said to Lucinda once the curtain opened several minutes later, "I look like a Jell-O cup exploded all over me."

Lucinda waved her hand in the air. "Take it off! I don't want to burn that image into my memory, thank you very much." She held a dress over her arm and pushed it toward Faye. "Whether or not you can pull off a dress of this stature, I don't know, but at this point, we must try."

Unlike all of the others, this dress, in a soft rose color with thin layers of overlapping silk, exuded sophistication and elegance. Faye slipped it over her hips and only had it partway on when her breath caught—the dress was perfect. She slid one arm through and then the other. It may have taken fourteen tries, but there was no way Lucinda could turn her nose up at this one.

The curtain swung open, but instead of Lucinda's face on the other side of it, the boutique's bridal attendant stared back at Faye with wide eyes and an open mouth. "Come quickly," she said. "Your mother has collapsed."

Faye dashed out of the dressing room to follow the young

woman in a diagonal line through the stacks of dresses. In order to see around the attendant, she dodged her head from side to side and caught a glimpse of Lucinda stretched out on a settee, the store's manager beside her.

"What happened?" Faye asked as she glanced down at her father's fiancée.

Slightly propped up, Lucinda sipped water from a paper cup. The wobbly look in her eyes and the pale cast to her face intensified when her hand started shaking and Faye had to take the cup from her. "Is that you, Faye?" she said weakly.

"Yes, Lucinda. It's me. It appears you've fainted, but we'll get to the bottom of this. Just lie still." Faye turned to the manager. "Has someone called 911?"

The manager wiggled her finger in the air. "Yes, of course. But there's no telling how long it will take them to arrive."

Faye bent over Lucinda. "Does anything hurt? Can you tell us what you're feeling?"

"A bad batch of sushi," she said in a soft tone. "I'm guessing that."

"Does your stomach feel upset?"

She closed her eyes and didn't answer. After a moment, she opened and closed her mouth several times as if it was dry. Finally, she said, "You mustn't bother Wellie with this. He has too much on his plate right now. But promise me if anything happens you are to tell him how much I adore him. Do that for me, won't you?"

Faye gave a partial smile. Lucinda was full of surprises. Did she love her father after all? Was there something genuine to their relationship that she'd overlooked?

A manikin with a netted hoop skirt and no top sat directly beside the settee. Someone must have been dressing it when Lucinda collapsed. "Could you give us a minute?" Faye asked the attendant and manager. The younger woman in high heels walked off, but the manager peered at Lucinda first, raised an eyebrow, and then paced toward a round, tufted ottoman in the center of the boutique.

"We shouldn't keep my father in the dark about this. He would want to know."

Lucinda poked her elbow into the short rolled arm of the settee to leverage herself higher, but she was not fully sitting up. "I've told you. Wellie must not know. He's overwrought with your situation and the gallery's. I will not add myself to his list of burdens. So, let me make myself clear...he is not to be informed about this silly little incident. Understood?"

So as to not jostle Lucinda, Faye eased herself down onto the edge of the settee with the utmost care. She patted the older woman's hand which rested on top of the fringed edge of her cashmere shawl. "There's no need to get worked up. I won't say anything. After we get you checked out by a doctor, we'll do what we should have done long before now, which is to cut this weekend short."

In slow motion, Lucinda returned her head to rest on the rolled arm of the settee. "Not on your life. I'll be fine. We mustn't let this spoil our fun. And you look amazing, by the way."

Either Lucinda had just complimented her or the nearby manikin with the graceful, outstretched arms had learned to speak. "Uh, oh, thanks. So we're in agreement, then. This dress is the one?"

"Of course it's the one, but I haven't the energy to go on about it now. For heaven's sake, there are mirrors around every corner of this place. Go look for yourself."

Faye stood up. "Let me call for the manager to come sit with you while I take this off." She waved her hand down her body to indicate the dress. "Then I'll ride with you to the hospital."

"Stop making a fuss and go. I don't plan to expire on the east coast, if that's what you're thinking. No, no, Wellie needs me and I won't let him down." Without raising her arm, she flicked her fingers forward, as if to spur Faye along. "I'll still be here when you get back."

Faye took a few steps, turned back to eye her, and then continued to the dressing room.

***

"We'll order room service," Faye said once she got Lucinda settled on the couch.

"I'm not an invalid, dear. The doctor couldn't find anything wrong with me, remember? If it wasn't the sushi than it was surely the dry air in that boutique. But that's neither here nor there. We are duty-bound to carry on with our weekend. And by that I mean we ought to experience the night life."

Faye sat on the edge of the coffee table and faced Lucinda. "Come up with another idea. Something along the lines of playing gin rummy right here in the room."

"I've come all this way to spend time with you. Sitting in a hotel room does not qualify as heaps of fun. Besides, what will I tell my girlfriends when I get back? Oh yes, Faye and I sat around playing cards. I'll be laughed at and perhaps ridiculed, if that's a comfort to you."

Faye twisted to push the floral centerpiece back, and then adjusted herself more fully on the low tabletop. "Rest—that's what the doctor advised. You didn't hear him prescribe a nightclub and umbrella drinks, did you?"

"Well, my goodness. Look who's being a stick in the mud. I suggest a little fun and you drop the hammer to squash my enthusiasm. I can honestly tell you that a few plates of food from room service is not the way to spend the time we have left in this city." She draped one arm over the back of the couch, her shawl fanning out.

Faye stifled a groan. "A nightclub is not going to happen. Think of something else."

"Coffee and scones," Lucinda said flatly.

"At this time of night?"

"It's eight o'clock. That's hardly midnight. And I have a craving." She flashed Faye a smile. "Call a cab, won't you?"

***

Now Faye knew what the next generation of illuminated coffee bars looked like close up. Rays of royal blue light streamed down the rare wood grain of the bar, probably Costa Rican rainforest lumber harvested without permission, and the thick stainless steel top surface held dozens of deep blue coffee mugs. Patrons perched on high bamboo and leather stools in front of it as they sipped their lattes. The atmosphere was that of a nightclub, but without the alcohol.

Faye had to hand it to Bobby—the man knew the formula for making high-end coffee drinkers content. The place was packed, and almost immediately the ambiance had sucked Lucinda in; Faye noticed the sparkle in her eyes long before Lucinda said, "Do you see this place? I'm struggling not to fall completely in love."

It had been Faye who'd insisted the cabby drop them at a Sterling-owned café on Lexington. She'd spotted one earlier and considered it research to have a look inside. "It certainly is nice," she said in a stilted tone, "but it's not gallery-replacing nice."

"Oh, I don't know," Lucinda said as she leaned back in her chair. "The trendy vibe is palpable if you ask me. People need coffee and this place lets them grab a cup in style."

The dark lighting made the white tips of Faye's fingernail polish glow. "Very soon you'll have one of these in San Diego."

"That we will. Oh Faye—" Lucinda reached out her hand to cover Faye's. "You mustn't be so down about all of this. Life moves on, doesn't it? Of course it does. And your father and I are of the opinion that a little change will do you good."

A woman with deep eye shadow, burgundy lipstick, and a turquoise necklace brought their coffees and scones to the table. "Here we are," she said and set down the mugs and plates. Then she lifted her chin to add, "Please allow me," and snapped out each of their cloth napkins with a flick of her wrist before placing the blue rectangles that matched the cups on their laps. "Enjoy."

Lucinda leaned in. "Quite possibly this café exceeds all of my expectations. I feel as pampered here as I did at the spa." She raised the scone to her lips and nibbled on it.

Faye studied the foam in her cup as she raised it toward her mouth, but then set it back down on the table without taking a sip. "Lucinda," she said, and pushed the cup toward the electronic list of specialty coffees in the center of the table, "what do you know about some architectural plans that involve the gallery?"

Lucinda cocked her head and sighed. "Well, you've caught me off guard, I must say." She placed the scone back on her plate. "Wellie has sworn me to secrecy about the whole thing."

The honey-colored waves of Faye's hair climbed over her shoulders when she pitched forward. "So you do know something, then?"

Briefly, Lucinda rubbed the tip of her narrow nose. "I know a handful of select details."

"Details are just what I'm after. Tell me everything and go slowly, please."

"That hopeful look in your eyes is about to be crushed. I haven't the luxury of breaking Wellie's trust to satisfy your need to know what comes next with those plans."

Faye pasted a silly grin on her face and jiggled her shoulders to show she was loosening up. "But we're on a girl's weekend. Come on, now, we should talk about everything. No subject is off limits, right?"

"Well I'm afraid this one will have to be. I'm not about to let the chickens out of the coop."

"I would've staked my life on you considering this enemy territory." Bobby walked up behind Faye and stopped at their table, an intrigued look on his face. "What are you doing here?"

"Isn't it obvious?" Lucinda interjected. "We're sampling the coffee. And these scones, by the way, are thigh-thickening, which is precisely why I won't be finishing mine."

Bobby eyed Faye. "Well, Faye, to what do I owe the pleasure? I never imagined you'd set foot in one of my cafés, least of all the one on my home turf."

She pushed her hair back over her shoulders and parted her

lips. "It's just as Lucinda said. We've come to sample your brew."

He stepped closer to her. "If my recollection serves me, there are a great many cafés in this city. The fact that you've chosen mine is...well...a bit out of the ordinary, considering the circumstances."

"Do join us," Lucinda offered and waved her hand at the empty chair in between them.

Bobby looked down at it, perhaps weighing his options, but finally pulled it out and sat down. "I'm wondering what would bring the two of you to New York City. You—" and he gazed at Faye, "don't seem the type to leave the gallery, and Lucinda"—he glanced at her—"lives on the other side of the country."

"A girl's weekend," Lucinda said as she rested one elbow on the table and a hand under her chin. "Does that meet with your approval, hmm?"

Bobby leaned his head toward one of the coffee attendants who paused at their table to whisper something in his ear. "Yes, thank you, Carla. I'll take care of it in a minute." He clasped his hands on the table. "So, tell me what you think of the place." First he swung his head in Faye's direction and then in Lucinda's. "The scones are too fattening, I get that, but what about the ambiance. It's calorie-free, I assure you."

Faye adjusted the napkin on her lap. "You've captured a nightclub vibe for coffee drinkers, which is an excellent niche market. And let me guess, this place stays open until three in the morning, just like a traditional bar."

He tipped his head. "Four actually."

"I'll leave you two to chat while I powder my nose," Lucinda said and stood up.

Bobby looked intently at Faye. "You despise that woman," he whispered. "What on earth are you doing with her here? And please don't tell me you plan to off her and leave the body on my doorstep."

"We've been dress shopping and to the spa. My father wants us to bond."

Bobby laughed. "Is it working?"

"Let's just say I'm beginning to see another side to her."

"Is that so?" He scratched his chin. "That leads me to believe you're willing to look past the unspeakable things people do to you in order to give them a second chance. Perhaps someday you'll do the same for me." He winked at her. "I'm not a bad guy, you know. And we've hit it off before. It's the momentum we can't seem to get right. You like me, and then you seem to stop liking me, and then we start all over again. Do I have it right?"

Faye watched a crowd of people leave and a larger group of men and women take their place. "Is it always this bustling?"

"On most nights the traffic flow is comparable, but then again, I'm not a fixture here. It could only qualify as good fortune that I decided to check in on things tonight—the very same night that you and your stepmother show up. Kismet at its best, wouldn't you say?" He wrinkled his brow. "But at the moment, I'm not interested in the volume of customers all around us. Tell me when you head back to Albany. And most importantly, is there a chance I can see you tomorrow?"

Chapter Sixteen

"Why is it a funny color?" Lily asked as she held Faye's phone in her hands, a picture of a statue on the screen.

"It's made of bronze." Faye sat down next to her at the kitchen table. "That's a type of metal commonly used for statues."

Lily scrunched up her face. "I don't like it. There's no pink in it. And why doesn't it have arms?"

"It's a bust, which means it only includes the head and torso. And if it was pink, it wouldn't be made of bronze. You may not like the brownish color, but that's how bronze looks."

The child handed her the phone and then flipped through her sketchbook until she came to a blank page. "If you hold still, I'll draw your bust Auntie Faye." She selected a red crayon from the box.

Faye angled herself toward Lily. "Remember what I said about how far apart a person's eyes should be. If you make them too close, it'll make me look silly. The same goes if you make them too far apart."

After creating a wobbly oval, Lily bit her lower lip as a concentration tactic, switched to a green crayon, leaned her head closer to the paper, and formed two enormous eyes on the page. "There," she said. "You look pretty already."

"Gee," Faye said, "those eyes look like they've seen everything from here to Kalamazoo!"

"Next I'm going to make your nose. I'm not very good at

noses."

Norman walked into the kitchen. "Ah, ha—you're in the midst of a Picasso moment. How utterly mesmerizing." He patted Faye's shoulder, but looked at Lily. "Just remember to put lots and lots of details on there. We want Auntie Faye to keep this pose for a while."

"You're not helping," Faye told him without moving a muscle.

Norman grabbed a bowl out of the refrigerator. Then he stood behind his niece. "Give her a bigger nose," he said and put a strawberry in his mouth. "Use your yellow and tan for her hair. The yellow will show the highlights." He walked out of the room laughing.

She stopped drawing for a moment and looked up. "Auntie Faye, when are you and Uncle Norman going to get married?"

Faye shifted in her seat. "Married? Where is this coming from?"

"See that," Lily said and pointed to the spice rack on her uncle's countertop. "My mommy bought it to help Uncle Norman find a lady. Ladies like spices, I think. Anyway, do you like spices, Auntie Faye?"

Faye looked blankly at the jars. "Lily, a spice rack is just an item in a kitchen. It can't make someone like your uncle, I'm afraid."

The child twirled a crayon between her fingers until it dropped onto the table. "But you like my Uncle Norman, right? You want to kiss him all the time, don't you? And after you get married, you can live here and have babies. Only girl babies, though. Boys are yucky."

"Lily, I want you to understand your uncle and I are friends. You know what friends means. Friends care about one another but they usually don't get married."

She bent both knees and sat on her heels in the chair. "But I want you to be my aunt for real instead of pretend."

"How about we take a little break." Faye stood up and stretched her arms behind her back. "A nice walk down to the gallery to look at the paintings might be in order. Would you like that?"

Lily shook her head. "Okay, Auntie Faye, but I still think you should let my uncle be your husband. You'll thank me someday."

"Go get your coat and hat. I'll tell Uncle Norman we're going on a field trip."

***

"Is it that time already?" Faye asked Jacklyn when she strode through the gallery door to pick up Lily.

"Mommy, Mommy, you have to come see this," Lily said. She grabbed her mother's hand and pulled her toward a large canvas at the back of the space.

Faye watched Jacklyn—who wore high-heeled leather boots and a tan wool coat with fur at the collar—jog to keep up with her daughter. In her opinion, Norman and Jacklyn didn't resemble one another. Both owned extensive wardrobes, but otherwise, Norman was the boy next door and his sister was beauty-pageant-queen material.

"These art lessons are really bringing out her creativity," Jacklyn said as she walked back toward Faye a few moments later. "Slow down and please be careful," she shouted to her daughter who was running in big circles around one of the partitions. "The last thing I need," she told Faye, is for her to break something valuable."

"Most young children connect with art, but not all, so I'm glad you've noticed a positive response in her. Bringing her here today was my way of getting out of a tricky situation."

Parted behind her neck, Jacklyn's long dark hair rested on her chest. She pushed half of it onto her back. "Oh?"

"Lily was halfway through drawing me when she wanted to know when Norman and I are getting married."

Jacklyn shot one hand to her mouth. "Oh Faye, I'm sorry. She has a mind of her own. I never know what she's going to say."

Faye spied Lily moving her nose and fingers closer to a sculpture. "Artwork is for looking and not touching Lil', so take two steps backward, please." She turned back to Jacklyn. "Anyway, I explained to her that Norman and I are just friends. So I hope that will take care it."

"Oh, I'm sure it will. But tell me, are you seeing anyone? I thought Norman mentioned a Bobby somebody or other."

Faye evened out the gray knit scarf hanging around her neck. "Bobby and I are rivals more than we are suitable to date one another. I mean he's attractive and intelligent...and a surprisingly good listener, but he's the reason I'm scrambling to save this place." She looked past Jacklyn to the large canvas behind her. "When Lucinda and I were in the city last weekend, we actually ran into him at one of his cafés."

Jacklyn crossed her arms over her chest and tapped her fingers above her elbow. "Awkward, I presume, meeting him like that."

"You could say so. At the time, it seemed harmless enough to go into enemy territory—until we got caught, that is. The way that man gets under my skin is maddening. One minute I want to strangle him and the next he says or does something nice that makes me wonder where all this hatred came from."

Lily slammed into her mother's leg, tugged on it, and looked up at her. "I'm ready to go, Mommy. Can we get ice cream on the way home?"

"This one loves her ice cream, even in the wintertime. Can you thank Aunt Faye for taking the time to give you an art lesson?"

In two strides, she hugged Faye across her hip bones. "Thanks Auntie Faye. Maybe next time we could play tic tac toe before we start drawing. Bye."

As mother and daughter walked off, Faye could've sworn she heard Lily say, I told her to marry Uncle Norman just like you said but she wouldn't listen. I don't think she likes spices.

Less than five minutes after they'd left, as Faye reached behind Zoe's desk to grab her purse, she heard footsteps. She swung around and sighed. "Oh Alan, it's you. The gallery's closed. I wasn't expecting anyone."

"I noticed a woman with a little girl leave just now and I hoped you'd be inside. I've got some news I need to share with you."

Faye put down her purse and closed the distance between them. "Is everything all right?" Alan's blank expression didn't leave her any room to judge if the news was good or bad.

Finally, the corners of his mouth turned up. "We've got the grant," he said.

Staggering backward, Faye clutched her cheeks in her hands and searched Alan's face for more details. "How can this possibly be? I checked the website on Friday and nothing had come through."

Alan widened his stance. "I'm sure that's true, which is why I took matters into my own hands. One of the lawyers I work for is familiar with the grant-making agency. Apparently, he saved their necks not too far back in a suit of some sort. Anyway, he offered to contact a guy in the appeals division. One thing led to another, and although it's not exactly what we asked for, the agency has approved half of the requested amount to be forwarded to the gallery." He looked down at his feet and then at Faye. "Twelve-thousand-five-hundred is better than nothing, wouldn't you say?"

Faye squealed as she stepped forward to hug him, the ends of her long scarf swaying in front of her kneecaps. "This is unbelievable!" Perhaps her luck was changing. With news like this, the Van Gogh show was definitely within reach now. She released him from her grasp and stood back. "What made you look into the appeals case?"

In one fluid motion, Alan put both hands on his hips. "That day I bought your car—that's when I decided I had to do something more to help. If your boyfriend hadn't told me the original grant was denied, I might've just waited to hear something from you about the outcome."

She cocked her head. "My boyfriend? Oh you mean Norman told you the grant fell through?"

Alan nodded. "And a good thing, too. It's taken me weeks to

get half of the results we wanted. A lot of phone calls had to be made and a lot of wheels had to be greased, but thankfully, my boss respects me and he was willing to go the extra mile. I'm just grateful to be able to pay part of the debt I owe you."

Faye reached out for his hand, and held it briefly. "The good direction your life has taken is all due to you taking the initiative. You can lead a horse to water, right? So please, consider us even. And because of you, it looks like the Van Gogh show will be happening next month. Twelve grand will cover March and the majority of April's rent. How can I ever thank you?"

Alan turned and started walking toward the door. Over his shoulder he said, "Glad I could help. No need to thank me."

Faye stepped onto the sidewalk a short while after Alan had left, only to hear a car honking at her. A few feet away at the curb sat Jacklyn's white Land Rover with Lily waving out the back window. Faye stepped up to the passenger's window.

"We saw a man go inside," Jacklyn said, "so we waited around to make sure you were okay."

"Is he your boyfriend, Auntie Faye?"

"Alan, no, just a friend."

"Boy, you sure do have a lot of friends but no husbands."

Jacklyn twisted around. "Lily, let the grownups talk, please." She turned to Faye. "Get in. We're going for ice cream and you can tell us all about it on the way."

Faye wrapped the scarf around her neck a few times and hopped in. "I have the best news. Alan just told me. You won't believe it."

"I'm really good at guessing," Lily said. "I'm the best guesser in my whole class." She remained silent for a few moments. "It wouldn't be cheating if you gave me a hint, Auntie Faye. Just one, please?"

"It has to do with the gallery."

"Hmm.... Okay...I think I know. Is it that brownish color we talked about today, the one I didn't like very much?"

Faye laughed. "Bronze is a good guess, Lily, and you're very close, sort of. It turns out that Alan, the man you both saw just now, convinced some members on the Appeals Review Board to reconsider our grant proposal. They've decided to allocate twelve-thousand-five-hundred dollars to the gallery, which means we only need fifteen hundred for April's rent."

Jacklyn turned onto Madison Avenue. "That's fantastic. You must be thrilled. Triple scoops, then. We'll celebrate with ice cream cones as tall as the ceiling!"

"Yeah!" Lily squealed.

The light turned from orange to red and the car stopped. Up on a hill to the right was Washington Park. Several people in overcoats walked their dogs in front of the tennis courts, through the grass, and down the slope.

"Do you mind pulling over at that mail box up ahead?" Faye asked. "I have something that's long overdue to be mailed." She removed a folded, wrinkled envelope from her purse.

Jacklyn signaled and pulled part way into the street, the mailbox being positioned on the corner. Faye jumped out and fingered the address before she opened the little door and watched the envelope disappear. By mailing the thank you note to Anouk De Ven in Amsterdam, she could finally confirm to herself that she might actually save the gallery. The Van Gogh show was only the beginning.

"What did that Alan fellow do," Jacklyn asked once they'd ordered their cones and sat down at a table, "to convince the review board to reexamine your proposal?"

"His boss was owed a favor and he saw fit to spend it on Hirsch."

"Eh, Eh, don't tip it too much or you'll lose it," Jacklyn said to her daughter, who was licking her cone at an angle. Lily had insisted on sitting next to Auntie Faye, so Jacklyn reached across the table to wipe her daughter's lips. "Well, it couldn't have happened to a nicer person. Really, Faye, I'm so pleased for you. Norman has told me some of the hardships you've had in trying to raise the money, and I'm glad it's finally starting to work out."

"You and me both." Faye licked the strawberry ice cream and then the chocolate scoop above it. "It's just in the nick of time, too. I paid Bobby February's rent when I saw him in New York City, and I got the feeling he couldn't believe I'd come up with the total amount—on time, no less. But after I handed him the check, my heart sank because it put me back to zero dollars for next month's payment. That's a different story now that the appeal's come through."

Jacklyn's long eyelashes fluttered. "I've been thinking about Valentine's Day which is coming up. Do you have any plans? I mean now that the gallery's finances are a bit under control, you should seriously think about cupid's arrow."

Faye caught the top scoop from Lily's ice cream cone in her hand before it hit the table. She stuck it back on top and twisted it slightly to make sure it would stay in place. Then she used three small napkins from the dispenser on the table to wipe her sticky fingers.

Lily turned her head and smiled. "Thanks, Auntie Faye."

"So?" Jacklyn persisted. "Any plans?"

"Bobby invited me to his home for dinner. I haven't accepted yet, but I'm tempted to make him wine and dine me."

The surprised look on Jacklyn's face confirmed for Faye something she already knew—it was a big step to accept an invitation from a man she felt unsure about. Good looking or not, Bobby might always be an enemy in the recesses of her heart.

***

"Would the lady like more wine?" Bobby asked her.

"I should say no, but I'm not going to." Faye raised her glass from where it rested on her thigh to higher in the air for him to fill. He stood above her seated position on the sofa, and immediately returned to the kitchen to check on the roasted rack of lamb.

"Please don't get the impression that I know the first thing about cooking," he shouted to her from across his long Manhattan apartment. "I had the food delivered by a catering service before you arrived. The head chef was kind enough to give me explicit directions about warming up the meat and vegetables. But you know, by the look in his eyes when he handed over the food, I half expected him to camp out on my doorstep to make sure I didn't spoil his exquisite cuisine."

"Is that right?" Faye said and set her wine glass on the coffee table.

The apartment's floor-to-ceiling windows on the southern side appeared black with the dark nighttime sky. A whitewashed brick wall extended down the length of the interior side, tasteful metal artwork hanging on it. Wooden beams overhead gave a rustic feel to an otherwise modern and chic space. The kitchen end of the flat glistened with a subway-tile backsplash, an elaborate hood over the stove, stainless steel appliances, and black granite countertops; the other end of the apartment, Bobby told her, held the bedroom, bathroom, and a small office.

"Perhaps I'm out of my mind to think I can heat up this lamb to the perfect temperature, but at this point, my aim is to make it edible, even if it falls short of delectable. I suppose I'm out of my element in my own kitchen, sad to say."

"If it makes you feel any better, I'm starving, which means I'll eat anything right now, even undercooked meat."

"I am a lucky man, indeed. Not only because you agreed to spend Valentine's Day with me, but also for your kindness in overlooking my cooking flaws."

Faye sat down on a stool in front of the massive granite island. "It smells incredible."

He ducked into the oven and pulled out a rectangular pan. Steam rose above the meat as he lowered it onto a marble hotplate. Colorful roasted vegetables, heaped in a bowl, were passed to Faye to bring to the long, elegant table behind her.

With her index finger moving in the air, she counted the seats.

"Wow, this thing holds twelve. I'm glad you didn't put us on either end."

Bobby came up behind her to light the candles. "According to my interior designer, the table's length and that of the island balance each other out. And yes, I thought we should sit as close as possible."

Faye glanced at the coffee table. "It seems I've left something very important over there." She strolled in that direction, picked up her wine glass, and planted it beside her plate at the table.

Bobby extracted two large salad forks from a drawer. "I plan to ply you with mucho vino this evening, so you needn't worry about that."

She raised an eyebrow. "Did I look worried?"

"To me you did. But please—" he came toward the table and gestured with his hand. "Have a seat. We might as well dig in while this beast is hot."

Delicately, he lifted three pieces of lamb onto her plate, the bones sticking straight up. "Beautiful presentation," she said. "Almost too pretty to eat."

He filled his own plate with less precision. "The fancier the food, the more you have to consume to feel full—but what do I know?" He gave her a lopsided smile. Then he clinked his glass with hers. "To us. May this evening prove that bygones are just that."

Faye tipped her head back. "Hear, hear."

They ate the first few bites in relative silence. But soon, Bobby glanced at her, angled his fork on the side of his plate, and clasped his hands under his chin. "Good to see you're enjoying it. Perhaps I know my way around the kitchen after all."

She smiled with a mouthful of food and held up her hand until she finished chewing. "Give credit where credit is due; I'm all for that."

"Try the vegetables," he said and pointed toward her plate. "Leave it to a New York City chef to put sweet potatoes, eggplant, and carrots in the same pot."

"Mmm...divine...."

The way her lips curled and her eyes closed with satisfaction from the savory flavors did not escape Bobby's notice. "It seems like you're having a private experience with the meat I cooked, not to mention that carrot concoction."

"Heated up," she corrected, and slowly opened her eyes to gaze at him.

"Semantics." He reached for the wine bottle and poured more into her glass. "Maybe if you drink up, we won't have these points of clarification to contend with."

"Getting me drunk...is that your plan? Well, I assure you it won't solve anything. I can hold my vino very well. Everything"—she waved her hand across the table—"is superb, however." She paused and then chuckled. "Remember Christmas dinner? Lucinda's reaction to the food was not what I'd been going for. No doubt she'd love this meal."

Bobby shook his head. "It still boggles my mind that the two of you survived a girls' weekend without an ounce of bloodshed. Truly amazing, if not heroic on your part. And I admit to watching the nightly news after I saw you at my café, just in case they reported a homicide near Lexington."

"What little faith you seem to have in me." She tucked her honey-colored hair behind one ear and then proceeded to push a potato across her plate. "An appeal for a grant has been approved," she muttered, "which means I only need fifteen-hundred dollars to keep the gallery open through the end of April."

Bobby reached up to loosen his tie, only he wasn't wearing one, so he dropped his hand into his lap. "So you've singlehandedly orchestrated a coup? When will I learn not to underestimate you?"

She looked up. "I'm full of surprises, but I had a lot of help this time. A great many people are rallying to save Hirsch. I can't let them down...and I won't."

"That kind of determination can move mountains." He picked a cherry tomato out of the salad bowl, tossed it above his head, which he'd tilted back, and caught it in his mouth. "You're an impressive lady, Faye. A part of me thought you would've given up long before now. The fact that you didn't means I'm a fool."

Eventually, when neither of them could eat a bite more, Bobby steered Faye toward the sofa. "Let's relax and let our food digest," he said. "And if you don't mind, I'm leaning toward pouring myself a brandy to aid the process."

"Pour away," she said and leaned her head back.

The lights of the city dotted the distance beyond the row of windows. High-rises stood out in the night sky, the haphazard pattern of brightly-lit office windows creating more flare against the blackness.

Bobby eased onto the sofa and set his brandy in front of his knee on the coffee table. "There's no place I'd rather be," he said and turned toward Faye. "I can't remember a better Valentine's day than this one."

He followed the soft lines of her profile, the curve of her nose, the jut of her lips, before she turned to look at him. That time they'd traveled west to Wellington's engagement party came to his mind. He remembered thinking that if they were somewhere private instead of on a plane flying over the Midwest he would make a move to kiss her. Well, now she sat beside him on his sofa, looking completely at ease—if he hadn't misinterpreted the soft look in her eyes. At the moment, it didn't matter to him that the beautiful lady clung to the gallery and seemed to be saving it slowly, piece by piece.

To experience the taste of her lips again, as he had on the night Wellington invited him to stay at the house, he nudged his mouth toward hers. The way she accepted his lips encouraged him to crawl one hand along her thigh. A perfect opportunity to go beyond the kissing phase—it was a day invented for lovers after all—made him deepen the pressure on her mouth.

She pulled away and seemed to study his features. "I thought you'd be upset with me."

Gently, he touched his forehead to hers, the softness of her hair skimming his cheek. "Why...because you didn't eat all of your vegetables?"

"No, because I'm committed to saving Hirsch on an even grander scale now that some funds have come through. How can that not come between us?"

"I'll tell you how—" and he paused to kiss the tip of her nose. "For tonight we're going to think of nothing but this—" He rained kisses along her neck, the scent of her hair impairing his ability to think clearly.

She dipped her head and connected with his mouth. "You're right. Let's not think tonight."

Chapter Seventeen

Variously-sized wooden crates crowded the storage room. Jam-packed, they obscured Faye's desk and made it impossible to walk toward the row of windows at the back. Zoe rested an elbow on the tallest one, her tattoo of a paint palette visible when she jammed her hand under her chin. Meanwhile, Faye grabbed a pry bar off the shelf to loosen the largest crate's lid. "Everything that's here," she said and applied leverage to the bar, "should be listed on the inventory sheet. We'll need to cross-reference the identification numbers. If anything's missing, I want to alert Anouk right away."

Each upward thrust on the tool brought her closer to unearthing Van Gogh's sketches and letters. Almost like a first kiss, it made her knees weaken. "Today is February fifteenth. We have just two weeks to take down the current exhibit, unpack everything here, and get it hung in the gallery space. By the beginning of next week, the frames have to be hung, the letters arranged in the display cases, the cards attached to the walls, and the publicity work done. We should be set to open on March first."

Zoe peeked through the sliver of space between the lid and the crate's side. "Lots of bubble wrap," she said. "And it smells like an old shoe. But I can't see anything else. It's too dark."

Faye grunted and raised the lid another inch. "Get the flashlight."

Aimed downward, Zoe pointed the light into the depths of the crate. "I think I see the edge of a frame. Here—" She handed her boss the light while she held the lid open.

"Yep, I see it, too. Help me ease this off, so we can get a clearer view."

"Hold on one second," Isaac said, his voice raised as he walked into the storage room, a wild look in his eyes. Faye hadn't seen that look since Zoe's concert, when the idea of Alan showing up had forced Isaac around the back of the house. "A man takes two minutes to use the facilities and he comes back to find the two of you busting into this here crate. Was the Lord not clear when he said patience is a virtue? Oh, I think He was clear, but perhaps you both need reminding."

Zoe bowed her head while Faye put one hand over her heart. "We got ahead of ourselves, Isaac. And besides, you were taking too long." She smiled at him to soften her words.

"Is that right? Excuse me if I didn't know there was a time limit on taking a tinkle. Seems like I'm learning a lot of new things today." He took the pry bar out of her hand, sank it into the corner of the crate, and lifted his elbow toward the ceiling. "Eh, oh, there she goes, nice and easy." The lid rose up as Zoe and Faye squeezed beside the crate on opposite ends to grab the sheet of wood off the top. "It'd be best if I got the hand drill and unscrewed the front panel," he said and walked over to the shelves near the door for the tool.

Faye peered down into the crate. Interior braces wrapped with protective cushioning held the frames firmly in place. International, climate-controlled shipments left nothing to chance. The priceless artwork's flight across the ocean probably rivaled the majority of travelers experiences in the first-class cabin section. The crate itself had been custom built for these pieces. The cost to ship all of this to the United States had been absorbed by Mrs. DuPont, who had agreed to the exhibit expenses and insurance fees back before she'd sold the building.

The whir of the screw gun in reverse punctuated the silence. Isaac put each screw he removed between his teeth and then spit them all into his hand when he'd undone the last one. "Stand back," he said and spread his arms out to grab the sides of the panel. He hauled it a few feet to lean it against the shelving. "Have at it, Miss Faye. I know you're dying to get in there."

Faye stared into the open crate—a veritable womb to protect the delicate artwork—and took a deep breath in and out.... What a surreal moment! To have genuine Van Gogh pieces on the premises, within arm's reach, filled her with satisfaction. The long process to achieve this goal had been worth the months of preparation and all the endeavors to raise rent money. Would she ever accomplish anything greater than this? Saving the gallery—that would be her ultimate achievement, if she could do it. But she'd made a mess of things yesterday, on Valentine's day...and some mistakes were unfixable.

***

Norman rarely took a day off from work, clear proof that this day trip to New York City was of high importance. He had a fairly reasonable idea of what could be brought about by this meeting, but a part of him wondered if running it by Wellington first would have been wise. The man had so much experience when it came to deal-making and settling disputes. And yet, he'd decided against it because of the nature of the discussion.

"I'm not about to sit down," Norman responded gruffly when Bobby Sterling offered him a seat in his office. "You can bet I didn't come all this way to make myself comfortable."

Sterling eased into the chair behind his desk, and joined his hands in his lap. "Very well, but at least tell me what this is all about."

"Isn't it obvious?" Norman couldn't believe the audacity of this man. Sure, he was handsome and wealthy, but that didn't make up for the way he'd treated Faye. "I heard you shared a meal with Faye recently. Do you deny it?"

Sterling gave a brief smile. "So you're here about Faye? I can't imagine how that's any of your business."

"You can't imagine how that's—" Norman broke off, his eyebrows at sharp angles above his eyes. "Faye and I are close friends, but I believe I already mentioned that to get this appointment with you. The nature of my business here is not complicated, just delicate." Norman rested his knuckles on the high back of the chair he stood behind. "The way you're using Faye to get what you want appalls me."

Sterling seemed to study Norman's face for a moment. "If you're referring to the gallery, I already own the building. I've already gotten what I want and then some. As for Faye, don't you trust her to know which men to date and which to throw back?"

Somehow Norman's large nose gave him a measure of authority, so he poked it forward and said, "I'll be damned if you think I'll let Faye crumble in your clutches. She and the gallery deserve better."

"Shouldn't you be having this discussion with her? The whole thing seems rather pointless—you railing on about Faye, who isn't even here to tell her side of the story."

Now the accountant bent forward slightly and gripped the back of the chair, his fingertips pressing into the soft leather. "None of that changes the fact that you invited her to your home for a romantic dinner under false pretenses. It's clear that you want her to back off this pursuit of saving the gallery, which currently puts your café in jeopardy."

"I like her," Sterling said flatly, his eyes fixed on Norman. "That's why I invited her for dinner on the most romantic day of the year. That alone makes my intentions perfectly clear." He reached forward to straighten his nameplate, a wedge of metal at the tip of his desk. "And if I didn't know better, I might think your being here is a product of your own love for her instead of anything to do with the gallery."

Norman's mouth contorted and he gave a low chuckle. "Wouldn't you like to think that."

"Seems to me you wouldn't be this worked up otherwise."

Uncharitable thoughts ran through Norman's mind—ones he

didn't dare act upon. Who did Bobby Sterling think he was? The consequences for wining and dining Faye were steep, especially since the evening had ended in the millionaire's betrayal of her trust. "So the formal agreement you got Faye to sign," Norman began, "the one which states she'll make no further claims on the gallery once the Van Gogh show is over, had nothing to do with you getting her drunk and placing a pen in her hand?"

Sterling's face looked pinched as he stammered, "Well, eh, huh oh, I don't think you quite understand."

The hot look in Norman's eyes decreased as he snorted. "My god, you're a comedian, right? All these funny things you keep saying are meant to make me laugh, aren't they?" He stopped laughing abruptly. "Only I don't find any of it amusing." He took two steps closer to the desk. "I want answers, Sterling, and I want them now."

For a moment, Sterling closed his eyes, as if he hoped Norman would disappear by the time he reopened them. "You drive a hard bargain, Maynard, and Faye's lucky to have you as a friend. However, I have a business to run, and in order to do that, I have to open new stores. It comes with the territory. Expansion makes the world spin 'round."

Norman picked up the nameplate off the desk and waved it at Sterling. "I want to see those papers. Show me the agreement."

A bewildered look came across the businessman's face. "What makes you think I have the document here?"

"Oh I don't mind looking for it myself, if that's what it'll take." Norman spun around and peered at the row of filing cabinets along the back wall. "Should I start there?" He didn't wait for a response but walked toward them. "Good a place as any," he said over his shoulder.

"Stop, wait," Sterling said, and walked around his desk with a set of papers in his hand, ones he'd pulled from the middle drawer. He shoved them toward Norman. "See for yourself. She didn't sign her life away, if that's what you're thinking. But she did agree not to hinder my renovations when the time comes. It's a solid agreement. And binding."

They faced one another. Norman was a foot taller than Sterling and made use of every inch. He stepped forward to tower over him. "Let's say I rip this up—accidentally, of course. Do you have copies?"

Instead of looking up, Bobby seemed to stare at the knot in Norman's tie. "What kind of a businessman would I be if I didn't have copies?"

Without another word, Norman shot to the chair he'd stood behind earlier and pored over the papers. He tucked the ones he'd read behind the stack and continued to scan each page for the damnable clause. "Ah ha," he said finally. "I, Faye Brooks, formally agree not to hinder the renovations of Mr. Robert Sterling's café in Albany, New York upon termination of a gallery showing of Vincent Van Gogh's works. By signing this agreement, I realize I will be required to leave the premises on State Street in the hands of its owner, Mr. Sterling. At no point in time after that may I seek to disrupt his establishment by pursuing a means to retain functionality of said gallery." Norman swiped his hand across his face. "I can't read anymore."

Sterling leaned his buttocks against his desk and dipped his head to look at Norman. "As you can see, it's all there in black and white. And honestly, the formality of it is more for Faye's benefit than mine."

Norman tapped the stack of papers on his knee. "How do you figure that?"

"This agreement lets her off the hook. She's free to move on with her life and everybody will consider her a hero just the same. She tried her best to go down with the ship, but the captain said no. It's out of her control. Nobody can fault her for that."

He shrugged. "Your metaphor sickens me as much as these papers do." In one thrust he laid them on the seat next to him.

"Sorry to have wasted your time," Sterling said as he crossed his arms over his chest. "But nothing is going to stop things from moving forward very quickly, very soon. If you ask me, Margaret

DuPont is the bad guy in all of this for agreeing to sell me the building in the first place. Why don't you take your anger out on her?"

His lower lip quivered as he answered, "Because I'm not done taking my anger out on you!"

Sterling went behind his desk. "Calm down, Maynard. Like I said, it's all for the best. You ought to be thankful I allowed Faye to proceed with her precious show. That means I did my part for the gallery. Surely, you can appreciate that."

"Oh, I don't know. I think I'd appreciate your signature on a document of my choosing more than anything else." Norman reached for his briefcase in between the two chairs and lifted it onto his lap. He snapped open the cover and withdrew a manila folder. "I'm sure you're wondering what I've got here. Unlike what you had Faye sign, this"—he tossed the folder onto the desk over the open lid of his briefcase—"is very short. It states that if Faye finds a way to save the gallery prior to the start of your renovations, then you will freely entertain her thoughts on the matter. That's all."

Sterling looked up from the papers. "I don't like this Maynard. I never pegged you as the kind to strong-arm me, but I'm starting to see you accountant types are a bit less stuffy than I'd thought. Kicking you out of my office right about now is starting to appeal to me, only I wouldn't want to be rude."

He gave Sterling a rough stare. "I'm not leaving until you sign those papers."

***

Wellington had tried to contact Norman several times that morning, but without any luck. The lengthy flight from San Diego to Florida had provided chunks of layover time, a perfect opportunity to bring Norman up to speed on his upcoming meeting with an influential woman. Now that he was in her home, their discussion would have to wait until Norman saw fit to answer his phone.

"I trust your flight was as pleasant as most," the silver-haired woman said as she waved a handkerchief in the air, which brought the housekeeper with a tea tray and cookies through the doorway and onto the back porch where they were sitting.

Wellington gazed at a palm tree several yards from the porch; the light breeze made its fronds sway. "Yes of course. It's gotten so that I barely notice these flights anymore. In my opinion, flying is a heck of a lot better than the 405 during rush hour." The housekeeper, who wore a gray uniform with a white apron, lowered the tray in front of him. He lifted off his cup and nodded to her.

"That will be all, Rosa," Mrs. Du Pont said. Then she gestured toward the cookies which were on a low table between them. "Please help yourself. Everyone must indulge once in a while, right?"

Her smile seemed a bit forced to him, but then again, she'd probably figured out his reason for showing up out of the blue. He'd deliberately left out the details over the phone, but now that they were face-to-face, the woman in the form-fitting dress with the large blue flowers on it appeared to be reading him. "I don't suppose there's a good gym around here to work these off?" he asked, reaching for a cookie.

Mrs. DuPont crossed her legs. "For a man of your age, you're quite trim. A little cookie can't undo that."

Wellington wedged the cookie between the curve of his cup and the saucer. "Perhaps I should alleviate your curiosity about my intentions. After all, I'm Faye's father and you're her employer, for a little while longer, anyway. That alone leaves us with a common denominator."

"Does it?" she replied and took a sip of her tea.

"I would like to think so." He watched her eyes flutter above the cup's rim. "You started Hirsch and now Faye's pulling out all the stops to continue it. Isn't it reasonable for me to assume you have some regret about leaving that nice little gallery in the lurch?"

She set her teacup on the table. "You mean your daughter in a lurch, don't you? Well, perhaps you think of me as a sellout and I can understand why, but a villa like this one can get pricey. Boca Raton has an outrageous real estate market, if you didn't know that already. With the windfall from Bobby's purchase of the building, I no longer have to rent this magnificent home as I've done in the past. It's mine." She parted her lips and sighed. "But you're right. I will miss owning a gallery very much. That little place means a great deal to me, and I'm dreadfully sorry Faye is taking it so hard."

Wellington removed his eyeglasses from his shirt pocket and put them on. He brought the tube beside his chair onto his lap and pulled out a rolled set of blueprints. "I've got something to show you. And if I'm not mistaken, I think you're going to respond favorably. How about over there—" He pointed to a long granite countertop just beyond the porch. It was part of an outdoor kitchen surrounded by flowers and perfectly-maintained shrubbery. The deluxe barbeque grill and fire pit were twice the size of his back in California. "Bet that thing cooks up a juicy steak," he said of the grill.

"Red meat is no longer a part of my diet, so I honestly wouldn't know. Rosa, however, does prepare a wonderful swordfish steak seared on both sides. It's absolutely heavenly." She followed him toward the counter.

Once he spread out the drawings, he plucked a heavy copper ladle and a pair of tongs dangling from the side of the grill, a means to weigh down the curling edges of the blueprints. "This is the existing gallery," he said and pointed to a square on the front page. Next, he raised the tongs at one end to allow the drawing to roll in on itself. Then he set them down again to hold the second sheet flat. "Here we have the upper level."

"There is no upper level," she said blankly.

"Not yet. I've devised a way—and it's completely structurally sound—to reinforce the existing roof with the necessary support beams. Shoring that up will allow for a second-story addition. It solves all of our problems. The gallery can reside upstairs and the café downstairs."

Mrs. DuPont smoothed out the front of her dress. "Clearly, you've put a lot of thought into this. And it does seem like a workable solution, only I don't quite see where I fit in."

With a slack jaw, he searched her face. "You, my dear Mrs. DuPont, would own the second floor. This way you can watch your vision for Hirsch come to fruition."

Reading glasses dangled from a chain at Mrs. DuPont's chest and she swung them up to her eyes. Not bothering to unfold them, she merely looked through the blue frames while keeping them a good distance from her face. "The drawing is quite lovely," she remarked and stared down at it, now and then repositioning the glasses, "but I believe my days of owning a gallery are over. Unless, of course, you'd like to create some sketches for a place we could build here in Boca."

Aside from the fact that he had no intention of drawing up plans for a gallery in Florida, the woman was missing the point altogether. It didn't seem possible that she could have lost her affinity for owning a gem like Hirsch in so little time. The gobs of money Sterling had dumped in her lap must have helped, and yet, he wasn't buying her act. To him, that's all this was—an act. He knew very well she had the funds to make this happen and then some. Perhaps he needed to peel away the layers to uncover the core reason why she needed the gallery in her life.

"Your legacy," he finally said and locked eyes with her.

She returned her glasses to her bosom. "My legacy?"

"Exactly." The architect left the drawings where they were and led her back onto the porch, his arm tucked under her elbow. Once she was seated, he stood over her for a moment and wagged his finger. "You can't fool me, Margaret. That gallery is in your blood and that's crystal clear." In three short strides he returned to his chair. "So, what are you going to do about it?"

She shifted her weight to one side and pulled out her handkerchief, which had been on the seat when she'd sat down. "You have me so flustered I'm sitting on my own hanky," she said.

"Not to worry. That's why I'm here. To work all of this out."

End over end, she folded the hanky and placed it on the low table in front of her. "You're very perceptive, I must say. The only other person who told me the same thing was Ronald, my personal assistant. He said, 'If you sell that gallery, Margaret, you'll regret it until your dying day.' And what do you know? I do regret it, only I plan to outlive that regret."

Wellington leaned forward in his chair, both elbows on his knees. "I'm guessing you didn't think it was possible to get Hirsch back in reality. But I've checked with the city of Albany's zoning board, and what I'm proposing is within their guidelines for that part of town. You"—he straightened up to look at her across the short span of the porch—"could have it all. Because quite frankly, I would hate to see the Hirsch family name fade from history."

DuPont seemed to hold her chin a little higher. "Certainly, there's that. But the question remains...what does Bobby think of your plan? Is he willing to let me squat on his café, so to speak?"

Wellington smiled. "Leave Sterling to me."

Chapter Eighteen

"Take a deep breath," Norman urged her.

Incrementally, her shoulders raised up as her chest puffed out. Limply from the wrists, she shook out her hands. "They're clammy," she muttered.

Norman placed her palms on the lapel of his suit jacket and let his hands cover hers. He stared down into her eyes. "This is the night you've been waiting for, Faye. All those months of planning have brought you to this point. It's going to be a hit, just you watch. Once the guests arrive, you can welcome them with a few words and then let everyone enjoy the show."

"Right," she said and flashed him a brief smile.

"You look magnificent, by the way."

The short black dress she wore had a pleated skirt, bunched waist, and silver studs around the neckline and at the shoulders. The scooped hemline, which ended above the knee, added a flare of elegance that matched the significance of the occasion.

"What if we have poor turnout?"

"Faye, listen to me. The entire city could walk through that door in less than three hours to view these works. Think about it. You put flyers on every brownstone on this block, right? You sent press releases to all the newspapers. I know for a fact you emailed me and Jacklyn...and probably half the world. So don't worry. People will show."

"You're right. I'm being silly."

In the dim light of the storage room, which was strewn with open crates, he grabbed her into his arms. "Look at you. You're shaking." He kissed the top of her head. "No shaking on opening night, okay? It's not allowed."

She pulled back, gave a weak smile, and quickly kissed his lips. "How can I ever thank you? Lily's art lessons contributed so much money toward the rent. You got Adler to give me my apartment back. You—"

"—I'd do anything for you, Faye. So let's just skip the listing of my heroic deeds and get you ready for tonight. Is your father coming?"

"No, I'm afraid not. And of all people, he's sending Lucinda in his place."

Norman rested his elbow on a tall crate they stood near. "Would you like me to nest the smaller crates inside the bigger ones? It would give you more room to move around. And I think it's nice she's making the trek out here to support you."

She looked him up and down. "If you were wearing jeans and a tee shirt I might take you up on it, but in that expensive get-up, you shouldn't be lugging crates around. And I suppose you're right. She could've said no."

"Of course I'm right." With his fingertips, he held out his tie. "This is cheap. It's not even silk. Lily bought it for me with her own money. I only wear it to make her smile."

"You're a good uncle. And Lily's such a sweetheart." Faye fingered her small beaded purse which sat on the shelf next to a pile of brackets. "I never told you this but Lily wants me to marry you so I can be her aunt for real. That's how she put it anyway."

Norman coughed and chuckled, simultaneously. "Oh, gee," he said. "Six year olds have a tendency to say what's on their minds. Just like her mother, it's safe to say my niece needs a filter button for her pint-sized body."

"I thought it was cute. She wants us to be together."

The question was...what did Faye want? Norman would do cartwheels to have the woman he'd admired for years seek something more with him, but he wasn't sure how he felt about having his niece grease the wheels with her adorable face and her straightforward chitchat. On the other hand, he could use all the help he could get. Faye loved him, he knew that much, but was it the kind of love that could turn romantic? Many couples had started out as friends, hadn't they? With all of his efforts to calm Faye's jittery nerves prior to the opening, he didn't have time to think about it now.

***

"Thank you all for coming. I am Faye Brooks, the director of Hirsch." She stood in the center of the gallery and held a microphone to her lips. "This spectacular crowd before me proves how vital it is to show phenomenal works of art in our area. And I'm thrilled to announce we have a special guest with us this evening—Mrs. Margaret Hirsch DuPont, the gallery's owner."

She paused while everyone clapped. "I will be brief in my remarks because tonight is about this—" and she waved one hand out to the side to incorporate the frames on the walls and the letters in the display cases. "These precious works of Vincent Van Gogh have traveled across the ocean to grace us with their beauty and to inform us with their ageless perfection. Van Gogh's use of color and the strokes of his brush present us with stunning pieces that tell his story. We have drawings and sketches, letters about his works, and even three of his smaller oil paintings for you to study.

"None of this, however, would have been possible without the kindness of our patrons, whom I'd like to thank now: Mr. Norman Maynard, Mr. Alan White, Mr. Isaac Thomas, Miss Zoe Bowen and her friends, and Mr. Ray Potter and his friends. These individuals have graciously and tirelessly raised money to allow this show to occur. I can't thank them enough."

"And as many of you know, the gallery is slipping from our grasp due to financial constraints; a business unrelated to the arts is scheduled to take over this space before long. It is our hope, however, that we can somehow raise enough money to ensure the gallery's long future right here. A donation bin has been set up in the lobby and any contribution is appreciated, no matter how small.

"So without further ado, I encourage you to view the amazing art and see what Hirsch has to offer this community. When you've looked to your heart's content, please help yourself to refreshments in the lobby. Thank you and I'm so glad you're all here."

"Well done, Faye," Mrs. DuPont said as she linked arms with her. "You are a well-spoken young lady whose passion for her work is quite evident. But I'm sure you already know that."

They walked together through the assortment of people. Some leaned over the glass cases containing the priceless letters and others stood in front of the framed drawings with their heads tilted back. The buzz of conversation seemed to echo and bounce off the ceiling.

Faye glanced at her former boss. "It's kind of you to say. I must admit, though, I didn't expect to see you here tonight."

"What...and miss this?" Mrs. DuPont threw her head back and patted Faye's wrist. "Nonsense. There's no place I'd rather be than here with you celebrating Hirsch's success. You've made me realize that great things are yet to come for this place."

Had Faye heard her correctly? Was it possible that the prestige of showing Van Gogh's works had opened the heiress's eyes to Hirsch's true potential? Faye could only hope, unless she was completely misreading the woman whose shoulder touched her own. "If you're referring to the café that will soon take its place," Faye remarked, "then I beg to differ."

Mrs. DuPont wore a black dress with a wide patent-leather belt at the waist. The stiff collar and diagonal gold buttons down the front gave her an air of sophistication. She touched one of the buttons. "I've always loved this dress. For some reason, it's lucky."

Faye stopped walking. "How do you mean?"

"Well, the last time I wore it, a man offered me a large sum of money to buy this place. Only now, I think the dress is having the reverse effect on me. I feel the urge to jump on the bandwagon and see what I can do to help out."

Faye swallowed hard. "That's wonderful news. With you on the gallery's side, we're bound to fare better."

"I'm glad you think that, dear, but what I'm proposing is not my idea at all. I've merely been brought on to invest in Hirsch's future by someone who holds you in great esteem." Mrs. DuPont twisted her neck and seemed to scrutinize the crowd. "Has your father shown up this evening? I thought perhaps he would make the trip out."

Faye spotted Norman across the room and smiled at him. She wanted to wave him over, but there was no discreet way of doing it. "My father had planned to come," she began and returned her focus to the very thin brow lines above Mrs. DuPont's eyes, "only he's just gotten back from a business trip to Florida. You'll have to meet his fiancée, though. She's here tonight."

"Well, yes, of course. I'd like nothing better." Mrs. DuPont took a deep breath in, as though to bolster her resolve in meeting Wellington's better half.

"Before I introduce you two, why don't you tell me more about this person who holds me in high esteem."

The heiress waved her hand in the air. "Oh no, I'm not about to show you all my cards just yet. In due time, Faye, and not a moment sooner. Just know that things are looking brighter. You'll need to do your part, of course, but if everything falls into place, we may have more reasons to celebrate."

Ronald walked toward them. "Hello, Ms. Brooks. What a pleasure it is to see you again."

She shook his hand. "You as well."

One of the track lights cast a glare off Ronald's bald head. "Forgive me for interrupting," he said, "but I believe Mrs. DuPont will keep you tied up all night if I don't pull her away to look at some of these amazing pieces."

"How tedious you can be sometimes, Ronald, but I suppose you're right." She nodded at Faye, took Ronald's arm, and walked toward the cases of letters.

"I was hoping you could fit tonight into your busy schedule," Faye said to Alan as she walked over to him and briefly touched his arm.

He stared at a framed drawing of The Potato Eaters, a smallish, dark sketch with a single light source over a tiny table, a depiction of a peasant family consuming their meager meal of potatoes. "I love this one," he said, and turned to Faye with a faint smile on his lips. "It shows what tough times look like and how people persevere."

Faye pointed toward the cases several feet behind them. "Later on, check out his letters. A couple of them reference the final painting. In particular, he wrote to his sister Willemina in Paris, informing her it was his best work. And in an earlier correspondence, he added a preliminary sketch to show his brother Theo. The English translations are right beside the original letters, so it's easy to get the gist." She eyed the sketch and focused on the peasant's faces. "Surviving by their own toil and faith...."

Alan hooked a finger under his chin and stared at a print of the final painting, hung beside the sketch. "Do you think Van Gogh used the smaller canvas size to make it more intimate for the viewer? Essentially, we're peering in at this family having supper, darkness all around the edges."

"I believe so. Imagine it on a larger scale—it wouldn't hold the same potency." Then Faye laughed. "I have missed talking with you about art. However, that first time we met you didn't have too much to say."

"Can you blame me? I was this close"—he showed a small measurement with his thumb and index finger—"to getting tossed out on my ear."

Alan wore tan trousers with a white and blue striped dress shirt. Scattered all over his tie were mini scales of justice on a dark blue background. His crewcut left no signs of the longish hair of his past.

"That would never have happened." She pushed a lock of hair behind her ear. "And I admire your tie, by the way."

He looked down at it. "One of the partners gave it to me—the scales of justice. As amazing as this sounds, I feel attorney-like when I wear it."

"I take it your job is fulfilling?"

Alan shifted his weight. "No complaints whatsoever. Believe it or not, I might want to become a lawyer someday...join their ranks...defend the good guys." He held up his hand. "I know it'll take a while, what with me being an older student and everything, but the firm is willing to pay for some college courses and see how I do. It'd be a good way to sharpen my skills."

"I'll say. You should go for it." Faye spied Norman weaving through the crowd. "Will you excuse me, Alan?"

He nodded and shuffled toward the next drawing while Faye met Norman in three strides.

"You holding up okay?" he asked her.

"Better than okay, actually." She reached up to fiddle with his tie. "My conversation with Mrs. DuPont earlier was enlightening. Apparently, someone has encouraged her to stand by the gallery. It looks like she's considering it."

Norman cocked his head. "No kidding? Who persuaded her?"

"I'm thinking Isaac or Zoe—probably Zoe—but I really don't know."

"Ah, there you are," Lucinda said as she came up behind them. "What a completely dreadful evening! For the last half hour, I've had my ear chewed off by that DuPont woman. Good Lord, she talks a blue streak. Obviously, the poor dear has no clue that her escapades in Boca Raton are less enchanting than California's worst drought." Lucinda slid the back of her wrist across her forehead. "I'm finding out that New Yorkers and Floridians live sheltered lives."

Norman tipped his head to Lucinda. "I'd be honored to escort you for the remainder of the evening. My presence may keep the riffraff at bay. What do you say?"

Dear, sweet Norman, Faye thought. By dragging Lucinda around the gallery on his arm he was willingly taking a bullet for her. Yet again, she would owe him one. Would she ever be out of his debt? Truthfully, he made it look effortless the way he saved her skin over and over. Instead of an accountant...his profession should be miracle worker.

As the two of them waltzed toward the lobby, probably to imbibe a glass of wine and nibble on the fancy cheese and crackers, Norman looked back at Faye and raised one eyebrow. Even though her shoulders jiggled, she kept from laughing out loud. In a somewhat exaggerated way, she mouthed thank you to him. Next, she went to find Ray.

Earlier, she'd seen him with a bunch of men wearing motorcycle jackets, probably his close friends, the ones who'd lent their support in bringing Van Gogh's legacy to America. She wanted to thank them in person.

"Ray," she shouted when she spotted him reading one of the letters. There were two showcases displaying Van Gogh's correspondence at either end of the gallery. He stood off to the left.

"Hey there, Sunshine," he said, and gave her a bear hug.

Their relationship up to this point, which resembled a father-daughter one—Ray and Wellington were close in age—had mostly taken place inside the cab, with Ray in the driver's seat and Faye in the back. Therefore, she hardly knew how hulking he would appear, standing in the gallery space with his black leather jacket gripped in one hand, a clean white button down shirt straining against his muscled chest, all of his tattoos covered. Of course, she had glanced at him during her opening remarks as he stood in the back surrounded by his buddies, but now it was just him beside the case of letters. Something Bobby had said dawned on Faye right then. On the plane to San Diego he'd mentioned his encounter with Ray and how menacing the man's muscles were. And sure enough, his broad shoulders would match the width of a painting, had he been standing in front of one. It pleased her to think that good old Ray, a sweetheart through and through, had struck fear into Bobby Sterling.

Ray squeezed her once more; the tightness of his grip made a whoosh escape her lips. "It means so much to me that you're here," she said. "I thought maybe you could introduce me to your friends so I could thank them in person."

"At the moment, the whole lot of them are getting refreshments. I sent them out to the lobby on the off chance their heads would stop spinning from all this great art." He lowered his mouth toward her ear and whispered, "I may have led them to believe there'd be beer at a function like this." He straightened up and winked at her. "Eh well, the brotherhood's got to learn what to expect when a pretty little lady invites them to a tasteful event. It's not a motorcycle rally, right?"

Faye looked at him with great tenderness. "Even though it's the beginning of March, you're still my Christmas angel."

He put his arm around Faye's shoulders. "Like I said before, if I had a daughter your age, I'd want someone to look out for her." They paced forward and eventually paused in front of a large, bright sketch for Sunflowers. "You know I had a long chat with a fella named Norman shortly after we arrived. Is he the same Norman I've heard you mention—the other guy who takes you home from work?"

She smiled. "The very same."

"Well, the man asks a lot of good questions about motorcycle upkeep, but he doesn't strike me as the sort of fella to ever get one. Suit-types and bikes are rarer these days. Anyway, he couldn't stop talking about you, which got me to wondering if you're as sweet on him as he seems to be on you. I'm only asking because I really liked the guy."

Faye looked up at Ray. "He offered to do your taxes for you, didn't he?"

"Might've."

"Figures."

"Hey, the way I look at it, you're both young and attractive. He seems sensible. You seem sensible." Ray rubbed his stubbly jaw. "And most importantly, he's a better man than Bobby Sterling. I half expected to see that rat here tonight, and lucky for him I won't have to teach him a lesson right here, right now." With a dull smack, he pounded his fist into his palm.

Faye returned her eyes to the sketch and followed the inky strokes in each sunflower. "Bobby and I aren't on speaking terms at the moment. He used me, Ray."

"Aw, Faye, I'm not surprised. A man like him can't help it. He's the slime under my boot and I knew that from the start when I drove you home in tears all those months ago. Don't trust him. That's my advice to you."

"Outside of gallery business and a means of retaining this space, I don't plan to have anything to do with the man. If he dropped off the face of the earth, I'd pull out my fanciest stationary and send a thank you note to the earth."

"Good for you. That's the spirit."

Faye dragged her eyes away from the sketch and focused on a little scar on Ray's cheek. "Tell me you didn't get that falling off your bike."

He made a goofy face. "The bigger the man, the harder they fall, I'm afraid."

She crossed her arms over her chest. "Wrong answer. You need to be more careful. I won't have you tearing up your face on a patch of road."

"Understood. Next time I'll take the turn on both wheels, if that would make you happy."

She tilted her head and gave a satisfied smile. "It would."

Chapter Nineteen

The fact that Sterling was still alive—or at least vertical, coherent, and moving forward—made Wellington wonder if he'd lost his touch in working somebody over on the trail. Sterling looked about thirty-three but Wellington knew he was forty. Shorter guys always had a youthful appearance. Nevertheless, Sterling quickened his pace to match Wellington's, an observation that the older man found disconcerting. Clearly, the café owner was trying to prove a point.

The terrain rose steeply at some points and then dropped off, which forced them to adjust their footing or tumble forward. They jogged in relative silence through the trees along a dirt path. Wellington knew every inch of these California woods, which left his jogging buddy at a disadvantage.

If the businessman could be willfully turned into a pool of sweat, then Wellington knew he had to go about his plan carefully. Room for error did not exist.

It was his duty as a father to see this through, to convince Sterling to see the light. A little physical exertion was just the thing to get the blood pumping, the endorphins wriggling, and that weasel of a man to accept a solid proposal.

"You don't look tuckered," Wellington said as he dug his heels into the downward slope. "I guess jogging comes naturally to you."

"Oh, I don't know about that." Sterling slowed up and eventually came to a stop. Panting heavily, he hunched forward and put his hands on his knees. "I, uh, haven't been on a jog in a while. But I do believe jet lag is kicking in."

Ah good, Wellington thought, it was all an act. The little bugger was substantially exhausted. "I'd suggest power-walking for a mile or two to give you a breather, but it looks like you may benefit from an even slower pace. Come on, we'll keep to the right and let the joggers pass us. Plain old walking is a form of exercise, if I'm not mistaken, not that it outweighs the cardio of hiking up one's knees on the trail."

Sterling shot him a glance. "I can't be sure, but it seems like we've made the loop more than once. All the trees look the same after a while, though."

Every so often Wellington bent down, grabbed a stick off the trail, and tossed it deeper into the woods. "Every tree is unique, just like a fingerprint. You have to learn to spot the characteristics that make each one different."

Joggers pounded past them, dirt kicking up from their heels.

"This trail gets a lot of use," Sterling said as he unstrapped a small water bottle from the Velcro belt at his waist and squirted the liquid into his mouth. Then he closed his eyes and squirted his face.

"We Californians do our damnedest to enjoy the fresh air and the chirping birds. It's part of the beauty of living in this type of climate. If you can't be an outdoorsman in California then you need to hang up your running shoes or sell your boat or what have you."

Sterling stopped and leaned his back against a big tree at the path's edge. "Tell me something, Brooks. Did you call this meeting about Phase II of the café project with the ulterior motive of having an exercise partner?" He bent his knee and propped his heel against the bark.

Wellington chuckled. "Indeed, I'm getting two for one, it seems. After we head back to the office and get cleaned up, we'll spend the majority of the afternoon at the job site. I promise."

Sterling tilted his water bottle against his lips. "Good to know. I was beginning to get the feeling something might be on your mind. Either that or I've offended you in some way."

Wellington put both hands on his hips. "How perceptive of you, Bobby. And in fact there is something I'd like to run by you. But first, tell me what you may have done to offend me."

Sterling pushed away from the tree, and they began walking again. "Your daughter may have mentioned this to you, but I can't be sure. She and I met that weekend you sent her to the city with Lucinda. Anyway, with her showing up at my café of all places, I thought she might still carry a torch for me." He laughed briefly. "I no longer believe that to be the case, however."

Out with it already, Wellington felt like saying, but he wasn't about to spoil the outcome by rushing things. Let Sterling hem and haw. Let him think up excuses about why he'd tricked Faye into signing an agreement that would ban her from interfering with the gallery's fate after the Van Gogh show closed. Maybe while he was at it he could explain his reasons for picking that building, of all the available structures in Albany.

"Wouldn't you know I went out on a limb and invited her to dinner at my apartment," he continued. "Things went really well at the beginning, but by the end of the night, it was safe to say Cupid's arrow was not pointed in our direction. Apparently, I'd said and done all the wrongs things. There was no going back after that."

Wellington had the bastard where he wanted him. It was about time that pipsqueak of a man fessed up to what he had done. To allow Sterling to clear the air would make room for concessions, the type that would benefit the gallery. "So you displeased my daughter? Is that what I'm to make of your attempt at winning her heart?"

The trail narrowed slightly, so Sterling stepped off the path to give a man and woman who jogged by more room. "Well, yes and no," he said and glanced at Wellington. I'd hoped to hear from her by now, but it doesn't look like she's inclined to give me a second chance."

"Second chances," Wellington replied, "can be difficult to come by."

Sterling kicked a stone with his foot; it shot forward and skipped along the dirt. "My goal was to make her take stock of the situation, but you probably know better than anyone she's impossible to reach. I would've had better luck grinding coffee beans with my teeth than making her be realistic, even for a moment. Honestly, I think she'll be shocked when the gallery closes its doors. Her heart's too wrapped up in this whole thing."

"Oh I don't doubt that. Faye's as stubborn as a mule when it comes to Hirsch." Wellington scooped up a stick, snapped it over his knee, and hurled the two pieces between the gaps in the trees. "She probably wouldn't be my daughter if she was willing to give up without a fight."

Sterling turned his hands up. "So I have you to thank for her steely resolve?"

Shafts of early morning sunshine slanted through the trees; bright blotches struck the path. "I suppose you do. But I'm a reasonable man, Bobby. Back when you accompanied Faye to my engagement party I took you aside. Do you remember that?" Bobby nodded, so Wellington went on. "I let you in on a little secret that afternoon. Well, the time has finally come to reveal the nature of what I was trying to do."

"I can't wait to hear this," Bobby said as he rubbed a tiny towel over his head and then looped it through the belt beside his water bottle.

With a grunt more forceful than the clearing of his throat required, Wellington began, "Uh ahem...I've found a way to appease all parties. Margaret DuPont is on board, and now we only need you."

Sterling grabbed the bottom edge of his tee shirt and fanned it in and out, probably to cool himself down. "I'm intrigued.... Our conversation from that afternoon involved an addition to my building, correct? At the time, the sketches you showed me were rough. I doubted you'd pursue it any further."

Wellington's mouth dropped open. "There you go again—underestimating a Brooks—but really, I had no choice."

Sterling knelt down to retie the laces on his sneakers. When he stood back up he said, "Please, go on."

"I've taken the liberty of showing the blueprints to Margaret. Fortunately, my trip to Boca Raton was well worth it. Instead of letting her family's name evaporate into the wind, she's willing to cover the costs for the addition, which will house the gallery. The concept, I think you'll find, is fresh and new. The way I've structured the upstairs gives it a loft experience on one side, a mezzanine, if you will. Patrons of the café can look up and glimpse a portion of the artwork just as gallery goers can look down and decide which coffee to buy after their tour."

Wellington clasped his hands behind his back and added, "There won't be a direct means of entering the café from the gallery and vice versa. A set of stairs will run from the lobby to the second floor. The overlooking balcony of sorts will be the gallery's connection to the café. In my opinion, it's a fresh take on the old café-art hangout whose time has come. We could be making real waves in the art and beverage industries."

Sterling looked over his shoulder down the path. "So DuPont would retain ownership of the new gallery, then?"

"She would."

"And Faye would stay on as director?"

"That's right."

"And all of this hinges on my saying okay?"

"It does."

"I don't suppose you have the blueprints stashed behind one of these trees and as we get closer to the spot you'll disappear for a second and then come out with them unrolled for me to approve?"

He put his finger in the air. "Had I thought of it, that would've been a viable option, but no. The drawings are back at my office. I'm fully prepared to wait on your decision until you review them."

"I've got to hand it to you, Brooks. I've never seen a father go to such great lengths for his child. That alone is impressive, but"—they came to an incline so steep they had to ascend it sideways—"does Faye know?"

Toward the top, the architect handed himself over the hill and waited for Sterling. "For obvious reasons, I've left Faye in the dark. It would be silly to build up her hopes if this all came to nothing."

"And if it does come to nothing"—he took one more step to reach Wellington at the top—"I'll be the one to blame?"

"You said it, not me." Wellington checked his watch. "We'd better run the rest of the way if we plan to get any work done today."

Sterling secured his water bottle at his waist and jogged forward until he matched Wellington's pace. "You know I had a visitor at my headquarters not too long ago."

Although he had a feeling where this was going, Wellington remained silent.

"Maynard was his name. Norman Maynard. I got the impression he'd do just about anything for Faye, which accounted for him coming on rather strong. The majority of it was bravado, but still...."

They jogged through the winding path, a slight breeze at their backs.

"I've met Norman on several occasions," Wellington commented. "He's not your average accountant; I can tell you that."

Suddenly, Sterling was not quite in line with Wellington, so he grunted and sprinted forward. Neck and neck, he said, "The man gave me an ultimatum. I either did what he asked or he promised I'd regret it."

"I've never known Norman to spew out empty threats. Are you sure you didn't misunderstand him?"

Sterling's voice shook from exertion: "The guy pounded his fist on my desk and told me to wise up. He said no café was worth ruining Faye's life, and then he picked up the edge of my desk and let drop down with a thud."

In an attempt to hide his smile, Wellington sped up again, which left the shorter man to cycle his legs and kick up more dirt. "I wouldn't worry about Norman if I were you."

"Oh yeah, why's that?"

"Because I get the feeling you're going to like the plans I've drawn up and agree to come on board."

"Ha, gee, I can't say I share your enthusiasm, but I'm willing to keep an open mind. It hasn't escaped my notice how many people are itching to slap my face, punch me in the jaw, trip me going up a flight of stairs, and so on, if I don't."

"You make us sound like a band of thugs."

"Just persistent. And headstrong. Thug-like, maybe."

Wellington pumped his arms. "I can deal with that."

The closer they got to an outlet through the trees, the final stretch of their run, the more he regretted easing up on the businessman. The respite he'd permitted Sterling—a chance to wipe his sweat and sip some water—had given the forty-year-old a second wind, and every time their dissimilar leg length caused a gap to widen, Bobby the Bulldog chased him down and closed it.

***

At the art emporium, Faye rearranged the narrow gallery space one more time. To earn extra money, she'd committed to working there three weekends a month. In addition to a modest salary, the owner paid for her train fare and meals, and provided accommodations. A staircase led to a tiny room above the emporium, an attic-type space with a single bed, nightstand, dresser and lamp, which suited her just fine for a couple of nights' stay. So far, her decision to give up her weekends to moonlight in the city was working out better than expected.

She slid a pedestal across the floor and nodded her head when she liked how it looked. Then she stretched her arms out wide to lift a canvas off the wall. There was greater breadth at the back of the gallery, so she would try it there.

As she worked, she replayed her conversation with Mrs. DuPont from the night of the opening; with good reason, she cautioned herself not to count on whatever the heiress had planned. It was better to keep earning money toward the gallery's survival than to rely on something that hadn't been fully explained to her yet.

The hours dragged on without a single visitor. In contrast to Hirsch, the humble location and mediocre artwork in the emporium's gallery kept it deprived of guests. If Faye hoped to see interested patrons walk through that door, she needed to curate a better selection of art. And so, she could hardly wait for Anouk to arrive.

If Anouk De Ven, the assistant to the curator at the Van Gogh Museum, agreed to an extension of the show, then pieces from Hirsch could travel here before heading back to Amsterdam. Of course, not all of the work would fit in the small space, but half of it would. That could create a decent show for the emporium.

Faye had to admit things were looking up. She'd gotten lucky that Anouk was in America on business—in New York City, in fact, to deal with the Metropolitan Museum of Art. The Dutch woman had suggested meeting Faye at the emporium before the close of business, and it was almost that time.

"Norman, it's Faye," she said into her phone. "I'm still waiting on Anouk, but I just realized something. I may have left my curling iron plugged in but turned off. Would you mind running over to my apartment to check?"

Norman grumbled before he said, "Faye, you've got to be more careful. Adler would have both our heads if he found out about this. I'll go over there, but if I see flames shooting out from under your door, I'm calling the fire department."

A petite, blonde woman who wore a belted coat walked into the gallery. She held a small leather portfolio in her hands and smiled at Faye.

"Norman, I have to go. She's here."

"You must be Faye," she said and walked forward with her hand out.

Faye grabbed it. "It's wonderful to meet you. May I take your coat?"

Anouk's pretty blue eyes sparkled. "Oh, no thank you. I'll wait until the chill wears off."

"Certainly. Is this your first time in New York City?"

Anouk set the light brown portfolio on the high counter of the attendant's desk. "I've been several times before, but this trip has been the most exciting. On behalf of my boss, I am in negotiations with one of the Met's assistant curators to swap some key pieces for a year's duration. It thrills me to think this may be happening."

"Completely understandable," Faye said. "The pieces you loaned Hirsch excite me every time I look at them. Please, let me show you around."

Faye did one loop around the gallery with Anouk at her side. She pointed out the inadequacies of the space but mentioned its potential. Anouk seemed to appreciate the configuration of the items Faye had spent all morning rearranging.

"So, am I to understand that once you get your hands on a gallery it transforms itself through your hard work and zeal? I don't believe I've met such a passionate curator in a long time."

Faye smiled. "You're being kind. Deep down I don't have it in me to give up on a needy gallery, especially one that's in a forgotten corner of this building. It's time someone brought it out of the shadows."

Anouk marched forward and stopped in front a small, figurative sculpture. "Not a bad little piece," she said. "It might work well in a show with more of its kind."

"My thoughts exactly," Faye replied, "but for now I'm working with what I have. Angie, the owner, is committed to letting me acquire more balanced selections in the future."

Anouk spun around with her finger on her chin. "I'm curious. Am I your first visitor today?"

Faye gave a weak smile. "Is it that obvious? On occasion, people from the emporium pop their heads in after buying a print, but there's nothing on the walls to engage them, which means they head out immediately."

"Over the phone you mentioned a desire to bring a handful of the Van Gogh materials here. What's your plan? How will you gain people's interest if they have no prior good experiences with this shoebox gallery, if I may call it that?"

Faye placed one hand on her hip. "Ideally, the Van Gogh work will jumpstart this place—get people talking about it and visiting regularly. Ten to fifteen pieces would be adequate. I'd advertise extensively beforehand to build up interest. Posters all over the city would only cost me an afternoon of putting them up. Angie's got a screen printer in her storage room. I could print a batch myself in a few hours."

Anouk untied the belt at her waist and left her coat open. "And you think people would come out for Van Gogh to this little place?"

"I do. City people need art in their lives. It's a matter of connecting them with that spark of inspiration." She took in the space with a quick turn of her head. "It'll be a jewel of a place before long—one of those little creative dives you can't stay away from because you don't know what intriguing thing will come there next."

"And if I were willing to take a chance on this place and allow a portion of the works to travel here, then what?"

"Then I'd work out a plan for security. Isaac, my gallery guard in Albany, may be helpful in that area. Also, I'm pretty sure Angie has some money squirreled away that we could tap for transportation expenses...."

"Sounds like a good start...and I did run your request by the board last week. They're comfortable with me moving forward with the arrangements as I see fit. So what would you say to 'Let's make this happen'."

Faye didn't even have to think about it. She blurted out, "I'd throw my arms around you."

Anouk leaned forward. "Well, have at it because you've convinced me."

She squeezed the Dutch woman's shoulders. "I can't wait to get started on the fliers."

"Seeing as I don't head back to Amsterdam until the day after tomorrow, I'm offering you another set of hands to pull the squeegee."

"You're going to let me put you to work?" Faye raised an eyebrow as she locked the gallery's exterior door and slid the deadbolt across. "Gee, maybe I should play the lottery today, too."

They made their way through the main emporium, past the numerous stacks of prints, around the sales counter, through a fabric curtain, and toward the storage room.

Each of them tossed an apron over her neck. Anouk, who wore a red knit dress with a black gem necklace, folded her coat and set it on a chair. Faye grabbed a jar of photo emulsion off the shelf and handed it to her. Anouk smeared a layer of the thick liquid over both sides of the screen and used the squeegee to spread it evenly.

Faye sat down at the computer and wiggled her fingers across the keyboard. Before long, the text for the flier came together. She printed out a test page to show Anouk.

"That'll work," Anouk said as she closed off the water at the utility sink and rubbed a towel over her wet hands.

"I'll print out a good copy on transparency paper."

By that time, the emulsion had dried on the screen. Faye laid the transparency down, as straight as she could, and carried the screen into a darkened room, the back closet, to expose it to light. The image would transfer onto the screen after a fifteen-minute exposure.

While she waited, Faye made a sag of her apron and toted the inks off the shelf and over to the table. Anouk unrolled a length of wide, sticky tape, and cut it into strips. They would use it to mask off different parts of the image. It was best to pull the least-used color first, and work up to the predominant tone, which was always the final pull of any screen print.

"Even though it's more work," Anouk said, "I'm glad we're hand-printing the announcements. People will appreciate the artistic flare on these big posters."

"I'd offer you some wine while we do this," Faye said when she came back with the screen in her hands, "but I'm afraid they'll turn out less than perfect if we do that."

Faye watched Anouk pull up the edge of the transparency slowly. "In Amsterdam, wine makes people more productive."

Faye held back a chuckle. "In America, it makes them sign agreements they wouldn't otherwise sign. But maybe I'll tell you about that after we get rolling."

"Please do. I'm intrigued."

Chapter Twenty

"I found this in the window of my café," Bobby said as he headed toward Faye, the screen-printed announcement in his hand.

Faye stood behind the attendant's desk at Angie's small gallery. She held the brown leather portfolio that Anouk had left behind yesterday in her hand. "Well, I didn't put it there. Anouk took half of the posters to distribute."

He looked at Faye. "Who's Anouk? Should I assume she's your new boss and this is your new place of employment? Are you calling New York City home now?"

"I work here on the weekends, if you must know. And I'll take the poster back if that's why you've come."

Sterling hadn't seen Faye in weeks. Her skin looked dewy, as if the city air affected her like country air would another woman. She appeared remarkable to him, especially when her upper lip curled in anger. He'd missed her feisty nature. "You can't stay mad at me forever," he said and stared into her eyes.

She shifted hers and seemed to observe the faded edges of the leather portfolio, which she'd placed on the flat surface. "Can't I?"

"I could ask what I've done to deserve this cold reception, but I think I know. And yet, it surprises me that I'm not off the hook after the negotiations I made with Norman. We have a clean slate, Faye. The agreement you signed has been torn up, all copies destroyed. What else do you want?"

She looked at him with a cold stare. "Never to see you again, for starters."

He blinked several times. "You don't mean that."

She stood up a little straighter. "Oh, I think I do."

This was going to be harder than he'd thought. Apparently, Faye had no intention of budging. If she wouldn't meet him halfway, he might need to think up another way to her heart, perhaps one that involved chocolate and flowers. And yet, he hated to be so stereotypical in his apologies—chocolate and flowers—so he went with his second idea.

"Have dinner with me tonight."

Faye cocked her head. "Oh, no you don't. I'm not falling for that again."

Bobby leaned his elbow on the high counter which formed the front part of the desk. "There's no trick involved here. I legitimately want to share a meal with you. No strings attached. And I like your tee shirt, by the way."

Faye hung her head to look at her own shirt. "After we printed up the gallery announcements, we ran a few on fabric. Walking advertisements are just as valuable as stationary ones, even more so."

He read the shirt aloud. It mimicked the text on the poster. "Join us at The Angela Weiss Gallery for an exhibition of 15 works by Vincent Van Gogh." Dates and times were printed below it and many of the words alternated fonts, which gave the message a funky vibe, perfect for art lovers. "So how did you pull this off."

"I got lucky. The woman from the Van Gogh Museum in Amsterdam happens to be in the city on business and I bent her ear about letting some of the images travel here after the Albany show closes."

"Is there anything you can't do?" he asked, his voice a bit high.

She cracked a smile. "I do what I can...and sometimes it works out."

He ran his hand along the counter. "More than sometimes, I

would imagine. Look at you; it seems like you've already gotten this hole in the wall some attention."

"This hole in the wall, as you so kindly put it, has a lot to offer. Once I dusted off the cobwebs, it was clear to me that this place has just as much potential as Hirsch."

Bobby walked over to the nearest painting on the wall. Over his shoulder, he said, "You still haven't told me how you came to be here...in this gallery...in my city."

Faye came to stand beside him. "Lucinda knows the owner. Somehow she got Angie to offer me a job. I've only agreed to three weekends a month. Hirsch is still my top priority."

"Of course. But doesn't this prove you have room in your heart for more than one gallery?"

She folded her arms across her chest. "So what if I do?"

Bobby moved to the next painting. "Are you going to fight me every step of the way, Faye? Can't we just have a normal conversation?"

"Define normal."

Bobby tossed his hands in the air. "At least tell me you've spoken to your father recently."

"As a matter of fact, he left me a message last night. I haven't had a chance to return his call. Why?"

"He flew me out to California last week. After running me ragged on the trail, he proposed a way to save the gallery. I'll have to admit, it's a feasible plan that solves our problem. And with DuPont supplying the greenbacks, it won't cost me a dime."

Faye's eyes narrowed. "Wait a minute.... Am I the last to know about this? At the opening, Mrs. DuPont alluded to having something in the works, but she didn't explain any details. What has my father cooked up? Tell me right now."

He held up his hands. "Okay, okay. Your father has drawn up plans for an addition to the existing gallery, a second floor actually. The gallery will be above the café but on the entrance side, so people viewing the artwork can see down into the café area. It's quite brilliant, a money-maker, if I'm not mistaken."

Bobby watched the expression on Faye's face change from anger to bewilderment.

"And Margaret DuPont is willing to fork over the cash to make this happen?"

"Your father convinced her it would be a disservice to her family's name to let the legacy die, and she took the bait."

"I can't believe this is happening." In a whisper, she added, "Hirsch is saved."

Bobby stuck his hand out and Faye seemed to stare at it for a long time. "If you don't shake it," he said, "I'll take that to mean you want a hug instead."

She grabbed his hand, pumped it up and down, and smiled. "Thanks for telling me the news. I'm sure that's why my father was calling."

"I only let him know yesterday. He'd given me a few days to think it over. Looks like he phoned you right away with the outcome."

It looked to Bobby like Faye could use a drink. The poor thing had been carrying around the gallery's burden for so long that she appeared lost without its weight on her shoulders. She should lock up this place, he thought, and head over to a bar with him. The two of them could get tipsy on champagne in the middle of the afternoon, the best way to celebrate a meeting of minds—a triumph for the gallery and the café, equally.

"We should celebrate," he finally said.

She didn't reply right away. Instead, she walked behind the counter and grabbed her purse. "Fine, but I'm buying."

Bobby smiled. "I like a woman who takes charge."

Just as they were about to leave, the door opened. "I forgot my portfolio yesterday," Anouk said and popped inside.

"It's behind the counter. Let me get it for you." Faye took a few steps, but then stopped to point toward Bobby. "Anouk De Ven please meet Bobby Sterling."

The two shook hands.

"So the poster in the window of my café was your doing?"

Anouk shrugged her shoulders. "Could be. I darted into more establishments than I care to remember last night. Next time I'll change into flats first." She glanced down at her high heels.

"If I had to take a guess, I'd say you're Faye's partner in crime now."

With a slight shake of her head, Anouk answered, "We printed one hundred posters in under three hours. Neither one of us escaped without ink in our hair and under our nails. Basically, it was a bonding experience like none other. I doubt there's anything that can come between us."

Faye handed her the portfolio. "That's right. I couldn't have managed without Anouk's help."

"You should join us, then," Bobby said. "We have reason to celebrate and we're just heading out to a bar. We can fill you in on the particulars once we all have a drink in our hands."

Anouk cinched the belt on her coat. "Sounds fun. Lead the way."

"You two go ahead," Faye said. "I have something to take care of first. I'll meet you there shortly."

***

Faye left a third message with her father's secretary. Apparently, he'd been in meetings all morning, but that didn't lessen Faye's need to hear the details about the structural addition to the building from him. A part of her struggled to believe the nightmare was over—Hirsch would have its second chance.

"Excuse me," a woman said as she poked her head through the door. "I'm looking for The Angela Weiss Gallery." She peered down at the poster in her hands. "The address says—" and she read it off the bottom of the sheet.

"You've found us," Faye said as she clasped her hands together on top of the counter. "How can I be of assistance?"

The plump woman's red hair framed her face. She undid the scarf at her neck and peeled off each glove. "I'm on a spy mission, I'm afraid," she said, and heaped her winter garments on the counter. "Wouldn't you know, I'm from The Guggenheim. This morning I was strolling down East 89th Street on my way into work, and a poster, which must've blown from somewhere, landed on the sidewalk. If it hadn't been for the nice screen print, I might've stepped over it. But it caught my attention, especially the part about Van Gogh. Not to hurt anyone's feelings," she went on as she removed her coat, "but I've never heard of this place."

"We've kept it under wraps until now," Faye said, a gleam in her eyes. "But that's all about to change."

The woman faced away from Faye for a moment, her coat draped over one arm. "A quaint little show this is." She turned back to Faye. "Not quite up to Van Gogh's standards, is it? Doesn't seem possible you can go from rubbish like this to authentic works by the master. Is that the catch? The Van Gogh's you plan to display are reproductions? Because honestly, who would lend genuine Van Gogh's to an underwhelming place like this?"

"I understand your skepticism," Faye said as she took the woman's coat and hung it over the back of her chair. "Really, I do. But I've just begun to work here on the weekends. Before I showed up, the owner didn't have an attendant or a curator, so she focused on the emporium and left the gallery to manage itself, which basically allowed for its slow decline."

"You don't say. Galleries need looking after. They certainly don't run themselves. How reckless of anyone to think they could." She set her purse on the counter beside her scarf and gloves. "I assist with the permanent collections at The Guggenheim. Vanessa Hargrave."

"Faye Brooks. So please, tell me more about your secret mission in coming here."

Vanessa's hazel eyes sat on top of her rounded cheeks. "My aim is to find out how in the name of good art you got someone to lend you Van Gogh's. From what I can see this place hasn't welcomed a piece of decent art in quite some time, and I mean no offense by that." She turned her head. "If it were any narrower, I could stretch out both arms and touch the walls with my hands.

I can't justify a Dutch master's canvases residing in a venue such as this."

Faye motioned for Vanessa to join her as she did the circuit around the small space. "Everything you've said is true...to a point. This gallery hasn't had a chance to shine, but that doesn't mean it can't take center stage if given the chance. Right now I'm showing a large selection of Van Gogh's letters and drawings, and a couple of minor paintings, back in Albany where I'm the director of Hirsch Gallery. I convinced the assistant to the curator at the Van Gogh Museum in Amsterdam to allow a portion of those works to travel here once that show is done."

Vanessa bobbed her head. "Golly, where's your magic wand hidden? You don't look old enough to have been in this business very long. How'd you make a connection with someone in Amsterdam?"

Faye stopped in front of the pedestal with the figurative sculpture on it. "I knew if I wanted to make a name for myself in the museum business, it would mean attacking my goals from the very beginning. Five years ago I was lucky enough to get a directorship at a brand new gallery. The owner allowed me to follow my passion, and the next thing I knew, my creativity was soaring. I'd visited Amsterdam a couple of years before that and spent the majority of my time viewing Van Gogh's drawing and letters and paintings in awe." Faye sighed. "Hirsch has taught me so much."

Vanessa moved toward the front counter to put on her scarf and gloves. "Quite an impressive young lady you are. If every curator of a small gallery had your gumption, galleries and artists would prosper, wouldn't they?"

Faye lifted Vanessa's coat off the chair and handed it to her. "You don't know the half of it. An entire team of friends and relatives have just saved Hirsch from extinction. Granted, it's a larger gallery than this one, but...it took several months and an incredible amount of hard work to resolve the issue."

With only one arm shoved into her coat sleeve, Vanessa glared at Faye. "You've gotten my attention. You're a highly competent curator...what went wrong?"

"A café, that's what."

Faye invited her to sit behind the counter where there were two folding chairs. The woman took off her coat again and placed it in her lap.

"Hirsch's owner was offered a lot of money for the building," Faye began, "and in the blink of an eye, the gallery's five-year run screeched to a halt. The trouble was, with the owner's backing assured, I'd spent months negotiating for the Van Gogh exhibit. Phone calls, correspondence, proposals and counter-proposals, paperwork at every turn. If the gallery closed, that would put an end to the show of a lifetime—and to my career. So, I met with Bobby Sterling, the man who'd bought the building, and somehow I convinced him to let me rent the gallery for the duration of the show. However, he set an exorbitant monthly fee, $7,000 per month for a place which should have cost $2,500. Three months' rent had me scrambling to make the payments."

Vanessa fingered a strand of beads at her neck. "What did you do?"

"I swallowed my pride and let other people help. Zoe, my gallery attendant, raised money with a garage-band concert, and a cabby I'd just met did the same by collecting donations from his biker friends. Another new acquaintance who'd taken a few wrong turns in life, wrote up a grant that eventually won half the requested amount. I sold my car and contributed the money. Isaac, our security guard, banned me from buying him muffins to save cash. My good friend Norman doled out way too much money for me to give his niece art lessons. It really turned into a team effort. And fortunately, Mrs. DuPont, Hirsch's owner, agreed to give me, Zoe, and Isaac a severance package which allowed us to continue our work for the duration of the show. She provided funds for the shipment of the artwork from Amsterdam, too."

Vanessa's chubby legs were crossed at the ankles. "So contributions allowed the show to run, but who or what exactly saved the gallery?"

"My father." Faye dipped her head into her hands, rubbed her face, and then sat up. "He's an architect in California. He got an idea to build upward—a second floor, with the gallery above the cafe."

"Brilliant."

"The really amazing part is that Mrs. DuPont has committed to funding the addition. And the building's new owner, Bobby Sterling, agreed to let the gallery exist above his one-hundredth café."

Vanessa wiggled in her chair. "Who knew gallery-life could be so intriguing. At The Guggenheim we don't deal with Bobby Sterlings. I have had some interesting characters bequest a famous piece of their great-great aunt's, though. Art can bring out an individual's generous side."

Faye smiled. She hadn't realized how relieved she would feel to tell the tale to someone from the beginning. To think the ordeal was finally over brought new waves of excitement over her. Sometimes she wanted to jump up and shout, "We did it!"

A broad smile lit up Vanessa's face. "I think it goes without saying that I'll return for the Van Gogh show. I wouldn't want to miss this little gallery's transformation into a butterfly. Because that's what you've done—given this place wings."

They shook hands at the door. "Thank you for stopping by, Vanessa."

"You have a friend at The Guggenheim, Faye. Don't hesitate to make use of me."

She waved goodbye, and just as the door closed, a tabby cat snuck through the gap and raced to a hiding place. Faye crouched down to locate the animal. "Here kitty, kitty.... There's no need to hide from Auntie Faye; come out little kitty."

Out of the corner of her eye, she spotted the tail curled around the leg of her chair. In a quick snatch, she scooped up the cat, fully planning to toss him back outside. But as she stroked his back and scratched behind his ears, he stared up at her with big green eyes. "I know what you're doing...trying to act all cute to get me to like you...to turn my insides to mush. Well, you don't have a collar or a tag, which could mean you're a street cat who needs a home. Do you belong to anyone, huh little guy?"

The tan and black striped cat meowed and purred in her arms.

"I bet you'd like some milk, wouldn't you? Maybe Angie has some in the back. Let's go see."

Chapter Twenty-one

"I'm just asking you to watch him for three days, tops," Faye told Norman as she handed him Vincent from the doorway.

He held the cat under its front paws so the rest of its body was stretched out. "Why can't you leave it in your apartment? Cats love to be alone. They thrive on their own company."

"Not this one," Faye said as she brushed past him and headed for the kitchen. "And he has a name, Norman. Please call him by it."

He rested the cat against his shoulder and patted him awkwardly. "Cats and I are not simpatico, Faye. I believe we've discussed this before. How exactly am I going to get any sleep with a cat lurking about?"

Faye took down a plate from the cabinet and then opened the refrigerator door. She tucked a jar of mayonnaise under her arm, stacked two packages of cold-cut meats on her plate, and in two strides, plopped everything down on the table. "Hand me the bread, will you?"

"While you make yourself a sandwich," Norman said as he grabbed a loaf off the counter and set it beside her plate, "I'm holding a dirty, smelly cat against my good tie."

Faye looked up from smearing the mayonnaise on her bread. "Don't be ridiculous. Cats give themselves baths all the time. He's probably cleaner than Benjamin."

"Oh, wait a minute. I'd babysit my nephew any day over a cat.

Cats can't make you a card at school that says 'I love you, Uncle Norman,' now can they?"

"Of course not. They're too busy writing their memoirs."

Norman held the cat away from his body again. "Stop joking around, Faye. Where do I put this thing so it doesn't crawl all around and burrow into anything?"

"Oh just give him to me." Faye sat the cat in her lap and finished piling turkey on her sandwich. Vincent pawed at the loaf of bread.

Norman pointed with his mouth open. "Do you see that? He's touching perfectly good bread. Now I'll have to throw that away."

"Don't be wasteful, Norman. It's wrapped in plastic. It's still edible. Vincent didn't poop on it." She lowered her head toward Vincent's ears. "No, you did not, Vince. What a good boy."

Still standing beside the table, Norman crossed his arms over his chest. "I warned you about this...but you didn't listen. Was it all in vain that I told you about the woman who used to rent your apartment?" He lowered his voice, "It all starts with one cat."

Faye bit into her sandwich. "Do me this one favor, will you, Norman? Anouk's going to be staying in my apartment while I'm gone, and I don't want her to have worry about Vince."

Norman sat down across from her. "So she'll give the lecture while you're in California?"

"Yes. If my father wouldn't be disappointed in me, I'd say I couldn't attend Lucinda's bridal shower on account of Anouk agreeing to extend her stay in America. The lecture she plans to give on the Van Gogh pieces should raise enough money to cover the expenses of moving the show to the city when the time comes—that along with the donations, especially from the night of the opening."

Faye passed her sandwich to Norman for him to take a bite, but he waved it off. "I find it hard to believe that she rearranged her flight to help you out with this," he said.

"It was her idea. After all, she knows everything there is to know about those drawings. I'm thrilled we can offer this kind of event to the community."

Norman got up and brought a bag of potato chips to the table. "And there's nothing going on between Anouk and Sterling, then?"

Faye smirked. "By the time I got to the bar that day, the two of them seemed pretty chummy. She touched his arm a dozen times, and he leaned over to whisper things in her ear. They looked like a couple to me."

Norman popped a chip into his mouth. "So you think Anouk is delaying her departure to spend time with him? A lecture would be a good excuse to linger."

Faye kissed the top of Vince's head. "The lecture will be great for the gallery. If Anouk can get some fancy dinners out of Sterling in the meantime, I don't see the problem."

Norman pushed the bag of chips into the middle of the table, but Faye didn't take any. "Is she taking the train up?" he asked.

"No actually, I think Bobby's going to drive her. He knows the area and she's never been to Albany."

"Uh huh, and I don't wear a tie to work every day. Oh come on, Faye, he's putting the moves on her big time. This should be a cause for concern, especially if he does something to annoy her. She'll forget about giving any lecture if it comes to that."

With Vince in the crook of her arm, Faye brought her plate to the sink. "If there's one thing I've learned in the past three months, in the process of saving Hirsch, it's that some bridges have to be crossed when we get to them...and not before. So, my dear Norman, I'm going to leave you two alone, and run across the hall to pack my suitcase."

She kissed Norman on the cheek, handed him the cat, and then blew a series of kisses to Vince as she walked backward out the door.

***

"Oh, I can't wear this," Lucinda said as she held up a black-lace nightie someone had given her. "Or can I?"

The roomful of high-society women erupted in laughter. Faye marveled at their stylized way of laughing, their lips barely upturned, minimal wrinkles appearing around their mouths—a tasteful way of showing mirth while retaining their youthful appearances.

The next gift, a set of four crystal goblets, matched an etched decanter whose silver wrapping paper was decked out in ribbons. The theme appeared to be expensive things to pour or drink liquor out of, or garish, inappropriate lingerie. Faye crossed her fingers that Lucinda opened her gift last...or better yet...not at all; but she doubted she could walk by the gift table and nonchalantly shove a medium-sized box under her blouse.

"What do we have here?" Lucinda said as she reached for the smallest box in the pile. She shook it. "It's a bit on the heavy side...but I can't make out what it could be."

Here we go, Faye thought. Lucinda would open her gift and be disappointed. Perhaps it was better to get it over with—to let the scowls from the other guests meet her eyes, to let Lucinda make her pointed remarks.

First, she opened the card. "Oh dear, it's from Faye." Delicately, she waved her fingertips in the air as she tried to spot Faye. "Thank you, Faye. I'm sure I'll love it." Slowly, she slid the box out of the paper and took off the lid. "Oh my goodness. Look everyone. It's a picture frame."

It wasn't just a picture frame. Faye had printed an image from their weekend in New York City to go inside, the one of herself and Lucinda at the spa, seated in white leather chairs, their feet soaking in little tubs. The esthetician had snapped the shot with Faye's phone.

"And look," Lucinda said as she dabbed a tissue at her eyes, "it's engraved. Lucinda and Faye in the Big Apple." She turned the frame around for everyone to see. "My most cherished gift," she said with a hitch in her voice, "that's what this will be."

Faye smiled, a direct reaction to everyone turning in their seats to stare at her. She wondered if Lucinda truly liked the gift or if she felt compelled to put on a show for her snobby friends. Either way, Faye's contribution toward her stepmother's happiness had been made and now she could breathe a sigh of relief.

Angie, who sat beside her, leaned toward her. "Laying it on a little thick, aren't you? An engraving to boot!"

Faye whispered, "Bridal showers call for thoughtful gifts, Angie. A silver frame was the least I could do."

"Indeed," Angie said, "but between a person like Lucinda and a soon-to-be stepdaughter like you, I thought there might be some animosity. Tell me I'm wrong."

"She loved my gift. Let's leave it at that."

Lucinda set a large box in her lap. "This one's from my good friend Angie." She tore off the paper and used scissors to cut through the tape along the box flaps. Her arms dove into the box and pulled out a patterned clay pot. "An ancient artifact worth millions, am I right?"

Everyone laughed, but this time they looked down their noses at Angie instead of Faye. "It's worth twice as much as you think it is," Angie replied, "but that's all I'm at liberty to say."

Lucinda howled. "Leave it to an art emporium owner to box up one of her treasures." She placed the object on the table next to the other gifts. "Officers of the law won't come looking for it, will they?"

Angie guffawed. "In the coming weeks? ...I doubt it."

Faye excused herself to use the ladies' room. She wanted to sneak in a quick call to Norman to see how Vince was adjusting without her. "Norman, it's me. Just checking in. Call me back in the next five minutes if you can. Kiss Vince for me."

By the time she climbed the long staircase to her room and plopped down on the same bed she'd stayed in for her father's engagement party, her phone buzzed. "Hey, how's everything going?" she asked.

"He crawled into bed with me last night," Norman said, a stiff tone to his voice. "I set him on the floor three times before I had no choice."

Her mouth dropped open. "What did you do?"

Norman's tone evened out. "I put a pillow in the bathtub and closed the door."

"Norman! You left Vince alone all night in the bathroom? How could you?"

"In the tub," he said plainly, "with a pillow."

Faye sat up on the bed. "You're going to traumatize him. If you care about me at all, please let him sleep with you tonight. Trust me, the two of you just need to bond. Give it a chance, Norman. For me...please."

"You don't know what you're asking.... He's a different cat with me. Like a small tiger if you want my true opinion. But I promise to try...if I have to. How are things going there?"

The pleats in Faye's short skirt were rumpled from her position on the bed. She smoothed them out with her hand. "Well, you know, fine, I guess. Lucinda just opened my gift and appeared to like it."

"See that, she appreciated your extra touch with the engraving. Have you seen your father yet?"

"He's hiding in his den, I think, until everyone leaves."

"You need to sit down with him, Faye, and thank him for all the trouble he went to for the gallery."

Slowly at first and then somewhat faster, Faye paced in front of the bed. "I plan to...as soon as the party's over. Put Vince on, will you?"

Norman made a humph sound and then there were several minutes of silence. "Here he is, Faye. Say hello, Vince."

The cat meowed. "Hi little guy," she said. "Now listen, I've spoken with Uncle Norman and he's promised to let you sleep with him tonight, okay? Don't you worry; everything will be fine. Uncle Norman just has to fall in love with you, that's all. And he will. Kisses."

Back downstairs, one of the ladies had stuck all of the bows on a paper plate and was attempting to tie it onto Lucinda's head as a tacky hat when Faye took her seat. "What did I miss?" she asked

Angie who nibbled on a cream-filled pastry.

"All hell broke loose a moment ago. Lucinda retched into my pot, wouldn't you know. A shade of green came over her face and a look of panic in her eyes, and a second later she reached for the pot."

Faye stared at Angie's profile. "She looks fine now. Something she ate must not have agreed with her. Those seafood finger sandwiches tasted too fishy to me."

Thick and stiff, Angie's blonde hair stuck out around her face. As she shook her head, her hair remained firm. "Boy, you don't pick up on any clues, do you kid? Your step-mommy is going to give you a little brother or sister. I hate to be the one to break it to you, but how pitiful of you to turn a blind eye to it."

Faye fixed her gaze on Lucinda who tilted her head this way and that in the hat made out of bows. "I-I can't believe it. How can you be sure? You must be mistaken."

Angie patted Faye's thigh. "All the signs are there. Your days of being an only child are over. Prepare yourself for a baby shower. That'll be next."

The woman owned an art emporium, and as far as Faye knew, she had no children of her own. Obviously, her weekend employer had jumped to conclusions. Lucinda couldn't possibly be carrying a child. No notion could be more absurd. Faye, after all, was thirty-two, long past the age to gain a sibling, and Lucinda, at forty-something, seemed a bit overripe to be a first-time mother. For whatever reason, Angie was goading her. What other explanation could there be?

"Excuse me, will you?" Faye said as she took her plate off the empty seat next to her, and carried it into the hallway. The plate was her excuse to leave. She would bring it into the kitchen to do her part to clean up. If she happened to run into her father along the way, she would ask him point blank about Lucinda's health.

Dark except for sunlight shining through a pair of French doors at the far back corner of the kitchen, the massive granite island gleamed dimly; it looked like the best place to deposit her dish. She set it down and spun around, only to realize that the thought of going back to the party made her head ache. To hide out in the kitchen for five minutes wouldn't do any harm. Besides, it might give her a chance to think.

She pulled out a high stool and rested her elbows on the cool granite. If life would stop throwing her curve balls, she would surely appreciate it. She wondered if Lucinda's fainting spell in that boutique in the city had had anything to do with gestation.

"There's my baby girl," Wellington said as he entered the kitchen. "Aren't you supposed to be oohing and ahhing over the gifts in the other room with all the ladies?"

Without a smile, she replied, "I managed a brief escape."

Near the deluxe stove, her father took a pastry off a three-tiered tray. Then he put one finger over his lips. "You're my only child, Faye. So shh...please don't rat me out to Lucinda. She's gotten the idea that my wedding tux won't fit if I indulge in sweets."

"I'm not about to tattle on you. Here—" She motioned to the stool next to hers.

"I suppose I have a few minutes to sit with my favorite girl who's not about to tell anyone what she saw." He held out the pastry before bringing it to his mouth.

Patches of sunlight skipped across one end of the granite surface. Faye and her father sat on the darker half of the island.

"I promised Norman I'd thank you for the blueprints and for talking Mrs. DuPont into financing the addition. It doesn't seem possible that Hirsch is in the clear, but thanks to you, it is."

Wellington put one hand on his knee and twisted to look at her. "It means a lot to me that you appreciate my help, but I got lucky that Margaret was pliable enough to budge on the matter. And Sterling could have squashed the whole thing if he'd said no. We got lucky on all counts. How is Norman, by the way?"

Faye put her hair behind one ear. "He's learning to share his apartment with a temporary roommate." Her father gave her a quizzical look, so she explained. "I may have brought home a stray cat from the city, and Norman's watching him while I'm here."

"That sounds about right," he said.

Her face contorted. "What's that supposed to mean?"

Wellington twisted the exercise band on his wrist. "You try to save things, Faye. That's who you are. It's not a bad thing. But now that you've saved the gallery, this cat seems to be your next project."

Both of Faye's forearms rested on the granite; she tapped the fingertips of one hand on the hard surface. "That's ridiculous. A cat and a gallery don't compare."

"Maybe not in your eyes, darling, but there are similarities. But oh, forget I said anything. Catch me up with Angie's place. Have you turned that into a gem yet? And please don't tell me it's in danger of closing, too. I'm not sure my heart can take it."

Faye couldn't help but smile. "No, it's not going to close. But I did get the attention of a woman from The Guggenheim. She handles one of their permanent collections. Last weekend she stopped by to check out the space and to introduce herself."

"Well good. Obviously juggling both galleries isn't too much for you. But remember, you're going to be a parent to that cat now. You'll have less time for other stuff. What did you name him anyway?"

"Vince. After Van Gogh."

"I like it," he said. "It's a good name for a cat...or a son, I suppose."

She remained silent for a while. Was there a way to ask her father if she was also going to be a sister to his new child and not just a parent to a tabby cat? Maybe in his own way he was hinting around at it, but she couldn't be sure.

"Um Dad, I don't know how to ask you this, but is Lucinda...is she...with child?"

"She told you? Oh, what a relief! I was going out of my mind trying to think up a way to break the news to you. So you're not angry? Oh Faye, isn't it wonderful? I'm getting a second chance to be a dad."

The stunned feeling that welled up in her gut threatened to show on her face, so she stared toward the window, her face turned away from his. "I'm a little surprised," she finally said. "Lucinda's older and I had no idea you wanted more kids."

"It just happened, Faye. But I have to tell you, I'm glad it did. Now I can try my hand at parenting again, and maybe get it right this time."

She turned back to him. "What do you mean by 'get it right this time'?"

Wellington's mouth went slack, but then he spoke. "After your mother died, Faye, I did my best for you, but somehow, it never seemed to be enough. In looking back, it was neither of our faults. This time I want it to be different. Your little brother or sister will have two parents and you. We'll be a family, Faye, all four of us."

On some level, her father's excitement about having a child with Lucinda perplexed her, and yet she understood his desire to begin a new life, one without the gap in the role of 'mother' that they had both known too well.

"Tell me you're happy about this, Faye. I need to know my best girl is looking forward to becoming a big sister."

That glimmer of sadness that was always present in her father's eyes diminished when he talked about the baby—and suddenly Faye realized how this monumental change in circumstances could mean happier times for him.

"What's not to love?" she said, and threw her arms around his neck.

"That's my girl. I knew you'd come around."

Wellington's phone buzzed, so he leaned forward to pull it from his back pocket. "Brooks, here. ...Yes, I remember who you are. Uh huh...I see. When did this happen? And there were no warning signs? Is that right...you've been with her that long? ...Very sad. I'm sorry to hear all of this. Please give my condolences to the staff and to her family.... All right...I appreciate your calling. Will do. Goodbye."

Faye turned sideways on the stool, rested one elbow on the counter and her other hand on her knee, and waited for him to explain.

"A bit of sad news, Faye." He patted her hand. "Margaret has died suddenly. A heart attack they believe. That was Ronald calling to inform us."

"Poor Mrs. DuPont. How terrible.... Is Ronald holding up all right?"

"He's worked for the woman for twenty-five years. It'll take a period of adjustment, I'm sure."

"I can't believe it." In the next moment, she wondered what all of this would mean for Hirsch. The addition. The financial backing. "Now may not be the right time to ask," she said softly, "but how will this affect the gallery?"

Wellington took Faye's hand in both of his. "The paperwork was being drawn up. I was scheduled to fly down next week for Margaret's signature. I'm afraid all may be lost now. None of us saw this coming. We couldn't have known."

"So Mrs. DuPont verbally agreed to fund the addition, but not on paper?"

"I'm afraid so."

Chapter Twenty-two

"Ah, Ms. Brooks," Spencer Adler said, a suspicious smile lifting his droopy mouth. He'd stopped Faye on the staircase leading to the second floor—him coming down, her going up. "I've met your guests," he said with a shake of his head, "a woman with a strange name, and a shorter fellow. So tell me, when will they be leaving?" He stretched his neck forward to peer down at Faye, who was on a lower step.

"Oh gee, Anouk has already left," she said, "and I've just arrived home from California myself." Faye glanced at her suitcase, balanced against her knee on the next step up.

"Ah yes, have you? Well, it's good to hear they're gone. You know how I feel about long-term guests. If a week goes by and they're sleeping and eating in an apartment of mine, well then, they ought to pay rent. I shouldn't have to remind you of these things, but that's why I'm here."

"It's just me now, Mr. Adler. Anouk has gone back to Amsterdam."

"And the fellow? Why haven't you mentioned him? Don't tell me he's hiding out in 2A as we speak?"

Could he be referring to Bobby, she wondered? Had Sterling frequented her apartment while she was gone to spend time with Anouk? It was quite possible.

"He's gone," she said finally.

Adler squinted. "Well good. Let's keep it that way. You can

expect me to stop by tomorrow and have a look around."

"Okay, sure. Whatever you like. Have a good day, Mr. Adler."

Faye continued up the stairs and turned toward her apartment. She set the suitcase down in front of her door and then traipsed over to 2B to retrieve Vince. She'd missed him terribly. With any luck, the tabby hadn't sensed Norman's dislike of him.

She had barely knocked once when Norman cracked the door, and then opened it wider. Vince appeared to be asleep in his arms. "Please tell me everything went well with you two," Faye said as she tried to transfer Vince into her arms.

Norman stepped back to retain hold of the cat. "Little Vincey is sleeping," he whispered. "You're going to wake him."

"Little Vincey?" Faye repeated with a lopsided grin. "Am I to assume from this display of affection that you've grown fond of my cat?"

"He's not just a cat, Faye. The other night I told him I was going to make us some popcorn and he rushed into the kitchen ahead of me and meowed right in front of the cabinet where I keep the kernels. Smart doesn't even begin to describe this little guy."

Faye followed him into the living room. She noticed how gently he eased himself onto the couch cushion, not to jostle Vince. She slid a magazine out of the way and sat down on the opposite loveseat. "I ran into Adler on my way up here. The man thinks I'm planning to stow Anouk away at my place. He's afraid of getting gypped out of rent for a two-person occupancy."

Norman smiled. "Could you talk quieter? Vince really needs his sleep. He spent all morning playing with a pompom that fell off Lily's winter hat the other day."

She lowered her voice. "Anyhow, he mentioned some guy being at my place with Anouk."

"Right, right. Sterling walked Anouk back after their dinner date. I happened to see them on the stairs when I headed out to grab some kitty litter." He looked down at Vince curled up in his lap and then at Faye. "The next morning I saw him leave around eight."

"The next morning!" Faye shout-whispered. "The two of them spent the night in my apartment? In my bed? Oh God, there isn't enough bleach in the world to fix this."

Norman put his hand up. "Hold on, Faye. I wouldn't be surprised if they spent all evening talking. I know Sterling is a jerk, but Anouk—it seems to me—wouldn't treat your home disrespectfully."

"You're probably right. Maybe I won't have to take a scrub brush to every inch of the place...at least not until I talk to Anouk and find out the whole story."

Norman reached for a bottle of water on the end table. "You haven't told me yet. How was the shower? Lucinda loved your gift...I know that much. What else went on?"

"It's a toss-up where I should begin. Let's see, maybe it's best to start with the baby."

His eyes popped out of his skull, just about. "You're pregnant?"

"Not me. Lucinda."

"Lucinda? Isn't she, um, too old for that sort of thing?"

"Apparently not. Of course, my father's over the moon about it."

"Good for him. Wellington deserves a bit of happiness." Norman took another sip of water. "You thanked him for the blueprints, right?"

"About that...." Faye removed her wedged heels and curled her feet up on the sofa. She slanted her calves to one side and massaged her feet with one hand. "There's been a bit of a snag. You see, my father was planning to get Mrs. DuPont's signature on the documents which outline her financial contribution to the building's addition sometime next week. However, something major has happened."

"By major you mean...?"

"I mean the poor woman has died."

"Dear God, Faye!" he whispered. "How? Why?"

She shook her head. "Heart attack. And I don't know why. The only thing I know is that we're back at square one."

"Geez, Faye, I'm sorry."

***

A chubby woman with a short red bob hairstyle strolled around Hirsch. She carried a navy blue coat over her bent arm, stopped briefly in front of each framed drawing, and then lingered at the cases with the letters inside. "This is quite the collection of Van Gogh's correspondences," she said over her shoulder to the young woman who sat at the attendant's desk.

"You're not the first person to tell me that," Zoe replied. "Most of our visitors are pretty amazed at the great art we show here."

The redhead wandered toward the desk. "A reputation for excellence is not a bad thing for a gallery to have. And how do you like working here?"

Zoe fingered the piercing at the tip of her ear. "Faye's terrific. She's my boss. And while I'm in art school, this job suits me perfectly."

The woman laid her coat on the edge of the high counter. "And is your boss around? May I speak with her?"

"Not today. Isaac and I run the place on Sundays."

Vanessa's round face expanded as she smiled. "I see. Might there be a way to get in touch with her? She and I met in the city and I'd like to say hello."

Zoe rummaged in a knapsack under the desk. From one of the small side pockets, she yanked out her phone. "Actually, Faye only lives a block away, just down the street. I could call her if you like."

"Marvelous, thank you. Please tell her Vanessa Hargrave is here to see her. We have business to discuss."

"So what do you think of the place?" Faye asked Vanessa fifteen minutes later as they shook hands.

"It's a far cry from the emporium's gallery. Hirsch is impressive in every way that the other space is not. But I'd argue you'll fix that in the coming months—work your magic, so to speak." Vanessa walked slowly toward a corner of the gallery and motioned for Faye to join her. "I'm sure you're curious why I've come. Before I hopped on a train to seek you out, I stopped at the emporium. I was told it was your weekend off."

Faye nodded. "I only agreed to three weekends a month. Thankfully, Angie accepted my terms, which gives me a free weekend to wash clothes and do grocery shopping."

"Ah, the basic necessities," Vanessa said as she stopped near the far wall. "Since I saw you last I've done a bit of soul searching. Your commitment to providing the community with outstanding artwork has impressed me. In our line of work, a curator who waits for spectacular things of beauty to come her way is left emptyhanded. Exerting oneself to capture rare finds is essential. Some artwork has to be lassoed and dragged in...and it looks to me like you're willing to do just that. The Guggenheim could use a person like you."

Was Vanessa offering her a job? It sure seemed that way, only she didn't want to jump to conclusions. "What do you have in mind?"

"Isn't it obvious? I want to hire you as my assistant. To watch you blossom with the new responsibilities of museum-quality art and all the dealings that go with it. That is something too good to pass up. What I'm prepared to offer you in terms of salary and benefits is competitive."

Faye maintained an even expression. How could she commit to a job that would pull her away from Hirsch at the very moment it needed bailing out again? And yet, if the gallery had no more life to breathe into the second-floor addition, then a job at The Guggenheim would certainly fast-track her career. It left her in a difficult position.

"To say I'm flattered would be an understatement," Faye said as she clasped her hands in front of herself. "But I'm hesitant to leave Hirsch in the state it's in."

Vanessa lifted an eyebrow. "Didn't you tell me last time we met that Hirsch's owner agreed to fund an addition? That alone will secure its future. You've brought this place as far as you can, Faye. Now your talents require the strokes of a broader brush."

Faye bowed her head. "Unforeseen circumstances have arisen, I'm afraid. The project to relocate the gallery upstairs has failed. You see, Mrs. DuPont just died, and the formal paperwork had not been completed. There's no way to continue without a new source of funding."

Briefly, Vanessa put her hand over her mouth. "Shocking news, I'll grant you that. But all the more reason to accept my offer. Hirsch has run its course. You gave it your best shot. Life intervened, however."

In a way, Vanessa was right. It had been months of work to get all the pieces in place to save the gallery, only for the heart of its owner to give way. Maybe the best thing she could do was move on and start fresh; but shaking off the dust from Hirsch wouldn't be easy, if she could do it at all.

"You make a good point," Faye began, "but my vested interest in this place may outweigh what's best for my career in general."

Vanessa parted her lips slightly. "Hmmm.... This isn't something you should decide right away. Give yourself time to think. Call me at the end of the week with your decision."

***

Faye offered Ronald a seat. For him to show up at her apartment with two coffees in his hands was quite unexpected. She supposed there might be gallery business to finalize, not that she could think of any offhand. What other possible reason could he have to materialize on her doorstep?

"You must be surprised to see me," he said as he sat down on the sofa.

"Let me say how sorry I am about Mrs. DuPont. My father mentioned how long you've worked for her."

"I appreciate your sentiment, Faye. And just for the record, I didn't agree with Margaret's decision to sell Hirsch to that Sterling fellow. In my capacity as her personal assistant, I'd advised against it. However, Margaret was as strong-willed as they come. Once she got an idea in her head, it was tough to sway her. God knows I tried on several occasions."

Faye sat in a small antique chair with wooden legs and arms. She had discovered it at a flea market in the city two weekends ago. Angie had reupholstered the seat and back for her, and Norman had driven his car down to pick it up. She looked over at Ronald. "What will you do now?"

He rubbed one hand over his bald head. "You ask the important questions, don't you, Faye? Well, everything's a bit up in the air right now, but I suppose I'll have to look for other work. You wouldn't happen to know anyone who needs a personal assistant, now would you?"

Faye smiled. "...Only if you know someone who can fund an addition for Hirsch."

He set his coffee on the low table in front of the sofa. "Let's say I do. Now what?"

Honestly, she couldn't tell if Ronald was being serious or fooling around. The expression on his face hadn't changed; his eyes remained focused on her. "Okay, I'll bite. If you know someone worth millions, my next question would be what makes you think that person will want to invest it in Hirsch?"

"I'm fully prepared to answer that. But first, you'll have to indulge me for a moment." He leaned forward. "Doesn't your father live in California?"

"San Diego, yes."

"It has always been a personal dream of mine to reside in California. Ideally, we could help each other." Ronald unbuttoned his suit jacket and took it off.

"I'm not following. Did one of Mrs. DuPont's relatives put you up to this?"

"My being here is completely voluntary. You see, I took it

upon myself to safeguard Hirsch's future. A few weeks ago, Margaret suffered a bad case of indigestion. Nothing too serious, but it got me thinking. The next day I scheduled for her attorney to drop by so she could update her will."

Faye tilted her head. "You've grabbed my attention."

"I thought I might." He wiggled the knot of his tie and then continued. "Your father did his part by convincing Margaret to pay for the addition. I went a step further and persuaded her to bequeath a large sum of money to Hirsch, in the event of unfortunate circumstances."

She moved to the edge of her seat. Was she hearing him correctly? Had Ronald actually saved the gallery? Were there enough words in the human language to thank him if he had?

"I see you're stunned," he said. "But believe me, the only formality that remains is the reading of the will. And that will occur next week. Faye, there's no need to worry about Hirsch any more. The gallery is taken care of. Margaret's legacy will live on."

For a little while, she let her mouth hang open. "Oh my goodness, I don't know what to say. Yesterday, I nearly admitted defeat. It seemed impossible to save Hirsch a second time. And now, you've given me the most wonderful news. How can I ever repay you?"

Ronald reached for his coffee. "Put in a good word for me with your father. The man runs a successful architectural firm. I may be of use to him."

"I haven't a clue what his employment needs are, but I'm willing to find out. Considering his fiancée's expecting a baby, I wouldn't be surprised if Lucinda hired you to run errands once the child is born."

"Wellington's on the verge of fatherhood again? How nice to hear."

Faye made a face. "Hearing the news about that probably shocked me more than what you just told me."

Ronald put his hands on his knees. "That's understandable. You're a grown woman with a life of her own. I can't say I blame you."

"In a way, it made me realize I need to start thinking about settling down. But tell me, are you headed back to Boca Raton?"

"Have to for now. Once everything is tidied up there, I'll send my resumé to a temp agency and see what they come up with. I'm not as young as I once was...so starting again with a new boss may be difficult. It takes time and patience to learn another person's quirks. I hope I have it in me to go through all that again."

Faye pushed a few strands of hair behind her ear. "We've known each other for five years, Ronald, and you still look as vibrant to me as the day we met. And I'm not just saying that because you rescued the gallery."

"Sweet-talk comes in many forms, Faye, but you ought to know I'll take it any way I can get it." He winked at her. "Just remember, kiddo, you made Margaret proud even if she didn't say it often enough. Every step in the right direction Hirsch has taken is an accolade for you."

She looked down at her lap. "I feel a bit guilty, though. Just the other day I was offered a lucrative position at The Guggenheim. Knowing that Hirsch is out of the woods financially gives me greater peace of mind, but whether that's enough to help me relinquish my role as director...I don't know."

"And your father's thoughts on the matter?"

"You're the only person I've told."

"Opportunities like this don't come around too often, do they?" He stretched his legs under the coffee table. "I don't envy you the tough decision, but someday you might regret not branching out. If Hirsch is meant to be a stepping stone for you, then take that leap."

A flash of tan fur popped out from under the sofa and sprang onto Faye's lap. "Have you finally warmed up to our visitor, Vince?" She stroked his head. "Thankfully, I have a few more days to come up with a decision."

Chapter Twenty-three

Dimly lit, Bobby's café on Lexington had its usual evening crowd of sophisticated professionals. Some sat at the bar while others pulled up chairs to squeeze eight people around a table for four.

Anouk sat across from Faye and dipped a biscotti into her coffee. "After I left your apartment, Bobby suggested I spend a few more days with him. The lecture went so well that I didn't mind rearranging my schedule one more time. I'm sure my boss doesn't see it that way, but he'll get over it...eventually."

Faye sipped her latte and then licked the foam off her lips. "Things have become serious between you two?"

"You could say that. He's hinted around about me relocating to New York. The obvious drawbacks would be finding employment here and leaving my family and friends back home."

"Did Bobby mention he and I dated?"

Anouk shook her head yes. "I heard all about a roasted lamb dinner he cooked for you. My ears perked up when he got to the part about you throwing a glass of wine in his face."

Faye gave a sly smile. "Do you happen to know if it permanently stained his shirt?"

"I believe so. Does that make you happy?"

"Exceedingly."

Anouk's blonde hair, pulled back in a ponytail, appeared duller in the weak light. "Bobby mentioned the sad demise of the gallery's owner. What will happen now?"

The curved handle of Faye's coffee mug grazed the tops of her knuckles as she brushed some crumbs off the table. "As it turns out, Mrs. DuPont made provisions for the gallery in her will. Because of that, Hirsch can move into the second-story addition as soon as it's built."

As she leaned forward, a gleam came into Anouk's eyes, a reflection from the candle in the center of the table. "Bobby didn't mention anything about a will."

"Oh, I haven't told him yet. I thought it might be best to let him stew a while longer."

"You're terrible, Faye. Let me tell him at least."

Faye stared down into her mug. "If I say yes, you have to do me one favor."

Anouk wiped the corners of her mouth with a napkin. "Which is?"

"Don't tell him I've accepted a job at The Guggenheim."

"Oh my goodness, Faye, what incredible news! When did this happen?"

"Very recently. I was approached by a woman who manages one of their permanent collections. I'll be working as her assistant. Which leads me to my next point. There'll be an opening for a director at Hirsch. The first person who came to mind to fill it was you."

"Me? The director of Hirsch? Oh Faye, I don't know. Bobby lives here in New York City. Hirsch is three hours north. How could that possibly work?"

Faye pushed her mug aside and set her hands in its place, the table still warm from the coffee's heat. "Bobby's rich. Every weekend he can commute to see you. It's the perfect scenario, if you'll just think about it."

"There are benefits to it, I suppose." The look of confusion on her face faded. "The primary one being it's a lot closer than Amsterdam." They both laughed. "Ideally, I'd like to discuss it with Bobby, but obviously you want him in the dark. But why?"

"Playing it safe, I guess. Mrs. DuPont's death has shaken things up. I don't want Bobby using that bump in the road to back out of the addition. Legally, I don't think he can, but I want to be sure. And if you agree to become the director of Hirsch, I'll be relieved to leave the gallery in good hands. Who knows, maybe Bobby will move to Albany and the two of you can run the newfangled café and gallery together."

Anouk shook a packet of sugar into the little shot of espresso the female server had set down in front of her. "Could we live in your apartment, then?"

"My apartment? I hadn't thought that far ahead. Adler would probably jack up the rent. I'd be breaking my lease."

"Oh yes, we met that man one evening. He's a bit creepy if you ask me."

"Oh you could ask anybody...he's definitely creepy."

They laughed until Anouk put her hand up. "Espresso almost shot out of my nose. Don't make me laugh when I'm drinking."

"My apologies. Next time I'll only talk about creepy men when you set your cup down on the table."

Anouk nodded. "Thank you. I would appreciate that."

Faye crossed her forearms on the table. "You know, I almost declined Vanessa's offer. The Guggenheim is a big step. What if I'm not ready?"

"I haven't known you for long, Faye, but the look of passion in your eyes when you discuss art...well, it means you're ready."

"Norman doesn't seem happy for me. When I told him the other day he got very quiet."

Anouk straightened the little packets of sugar in the ceramic holder. "His best friend won't be across the hall anymore. Of course he's upset."

"Norman's been a big part of my life these past five years. I don't know how I'll get along without him."

"Isn't he an accountant? I'm sure they could use another number's guy in Manhattan."

"Oh, Norman can't move down there with me."

"Why not? You two like one another. He's a terrific guy. Have you even asked him to come along?"

"Lily and Benjamin adore their Uncle Norman. He'd never agree to put distance between himself and them."

"So they can hop on a train to visit. Little kids love that sort of thing, adventure and all of that."

"I'm telling you Norman won't leave his life here, and I don't think he should. Maybe this is something I have to do on my own."

"At least give him the option of joining you. He deserves an invitation."

Faye pushed her chair in. Two people at the table behind them were settling in. "I heard Bobby's bringing you to my father's wedding."

"Okay, I'll take a hint. No more talking about Norman. And yes, I've agreed to go. California will be a new experience for me."

"You'll love the place. San Diego is wonderful, except for the expensive price tag to live there."

"Bobby tells me your father's home is exquisite. I can't wait to see it."

"An architect who thinks big usually ends up with a mammoth house. And that is definitely the case with my father. The man doesn't know the meaning of the word understated."

"I look forward to meeting him. And his fiancée...what's she like?"

"Lucinda? Uh, well, if you'd asked me five months ago, I might have been hard pressed to find a kind word to say about her. But now, I believe she's the type of person who grows on you over time. Which isn't to say I like her a whole lot, but I'm beginning to realize she makes my father happy. And the latest bombshell...they're having a baby."

Anouk giggled. "No way? You're going to be a big sister? It'll be quite the age gap between you two, but my brother's only fourteen months younger than I am and he's absolutely no fun at all. You'll have the upper hand for quite a while, too—being taller and stronger."

"Either you're making me feel better or worse, I haven't decided which."

"Perhaps the Dutch look at things differently," Anouk said as she twisted around to greet a woman who squeezed between her chair and another one, and then passed by. "For the most part, we take everything in stride."

Faye wrapped her hands around her mug but most of the warmth had gone. "Not a bad philosophy, but cutting back on the number of surprises in my life would suit me just fine."

Three hours later she got a text from Norman. I'm downstairs. Come let me in. That was odd. Why would he drive down to see her? She'd be home tomorrow evening. The oval window behind her bed looked down on the emporium's entrance, two-stories below. She saw him pace in front of the door and occasionally glance down the street, perhaps at his car along the curb.

"Norman, hey, what's up?" she said, opening the main entrance for him. She stared at the duffle bag in his hand.

"Can you put me up for one night?" he asked.

She kissed his cheek. "That depends. Have you come to talk me out of my decision to move here permanently?"

"Just the opposite."

Vince emerged from the shadows and Norman scooped him up. "Hiya buddy," he said. "Is Faye remembering to feed you those little treats shaped like fish? Huh, is she?"

"Even when I hide the box, he sniffs them out. Soon I'll have to tape the lid shut and lock it in a drawer."

Norman lifted Vince under his front paws until they were face to face. "You like them that much! What a little piggy you are. If I had known, I would've brought another box with me."

Faye wondered where Norman planned on sleeping tonight. That weekend he'd driven down to get the antique chair for her apartment, she'd shown him the living quarters. Had he forgotten about the single bed? And what was so urgent that he had to see her tonight?

Vince scampered off as soon as Norman put him down. "You're probably wondering why I'm here."

"It crossed my mind."

Except for a few recessed lights in the corridor, the emporium was dark. She retreated through the storage room and ascended the back staircase. Once in the room, she offered him a seat on the bed.

He sat on the edge and crossed one ankle over his knee. "I support your decision to move here. I want you to know that. ... It's not exactly easy for me to admit how much I'm going to miss you."

She eased down next to him. "So you came all this way to tell me that?"

"My reasons for coming are twofold. Firstly, I wanted to tell you that. Secondly, I wanted to do this." Between his large hands he held her face, and then kissed her lips softly.

When the connection of their lips broke, their foreheads remained touching.

"Norman...."

"Faye, I want more. That's really why I'm here. To find out if you want the same thing."

Her lips were inches from his. "I care about you, Norman. You got me through months and months of turmoil with the gallery. When Adler kicked me out of my place, you took me in. And what about those tangled lights at Christmas? I've never seen anyone unknot a mess like that so quickly. Everything you do amazes me. And just in case you thought I didn't notice, you overpaid me dearly for Lily's art lessons, every single time." A tear ran down her face. "Don't you see? I don't deserve you."

Norman slanted her head onto his shoulder. "Faye Brooks, you listen to me. I did all those things out of love for you. I wasn't looking to be paid back. If necessary, I'd do it all again. Keeping you safe is important to me. We're a team."

She put her hand on his thigh. "You're my best friend, Norman. I think I've been scared of what we have. Maybe deep down

I'm afraid our friendship will suffer if we start dating."

"I'd rather try than never know what could've been." He kissed the top of her head. "Besides, we have a better shot than most. We can actually stand each other's company."

Her smile curved into his shoulder. "So where do we go from here?"

"Well, first of all, I didn't think this through." He peered down at the bed. "I forgot you had a single."

"If we both sleep on our sides, it might work."

"The first time you toss and turn, I'll end up on the floor. Do you think there's a cot somewhere we could dig out?"

"Let's find out." She went to her overnight bag on top of the dresser, plunged her hand to the bottom, crawled her fingers around, and finally hit into a solid object that wasn't clothing. "This should help," she said and dragged out a flashlight. "Angie doesn't want me keeping the emporium lights on after closing. But if there's any bedding to be found, we'll uncover it."

They started in the storage room. Norman held the flashlight while Faye rummaged through the first of two closets. The shelves were packed with miscellaneous items: a portable heat press for smoothing out wrinkles on smaller prints, rubber rollers, wooden drawing models, empty bins stacked high, splotchy drop cloths folded haphazardly, rolls of masking tape, a boxful of thumb tacks, postcards wrapped in plastic with the label New York City Skyline on them....

A broom leaned against the wall and aprons dangled from a hook near it.

"Nothing useable in here," she said and backed out of the closet.

In the second closet they found a rolled up length of green-and-orange-striped fabric on a stool, which turned out to be a hammock with eyelets on each side, heavy strings looped through them. Norman laid it out on the floor to get a better look. "It's not a cot, but this'll do."

Faye put one hand on her hip. "How good is a hammock if we

don't have two trees to secure it to? Is your plan to sleep outside and let the elements of the city attack you in your sleep?"

Norman tugged on the fabric. "Durable enough. No holes or tears." He lugged it toward the stairs. "With any luck, we'll find something to latch it to in your room."

"Like what?" she asked, following behind him.

The edge of the hammock skimmed each stair tread. "I'll know when I see it."

The two of them stood in the doorway and gazed at the small space. The bed, nightstand, dresser, and lamp were all they had to work with, in addition to a fancy knob by the oval window, some sort of ancient crank to open it.

Norman hooked his thumb under his chin and tapped his index finger along his jaw. "Hmmm...yup...okay...I think I see a way to suspend this off the floor. Maybe a little of this"—he wrapped the string around the window crank—"and a little of this"—then he unrolled the fabric toward the dresser—"and some of this"—and finally he secured the other end to a narrow piece of wood where the dresser's mirror attached to the section of drawers.

He stood back. The hammock swooped from the window to the dresser. "The only problem is I doubt it will take my weight if the drawers aren't full. The dresser might pitch forward when I lie down." So he yanked open several drawers, all of them empty. "We need to fill these to add weight and stability."

"Two changes of clothes," Faye said, "that's all I usually bring for the weekend. Rarely do I have time to take them out of my bag." She tilted her head to think. "We could carry up a bunch of stuff from the closets downstairs."

"My thoughts exactly."

It took them under an hour to laden the dresser with the heaviest items from the emporium. A pair of plaster Buddha statues squatted next to Faye's bag; they added at least ten pounds to that side of the dresser. A thick ceramic pot fit perfectly in the bottom drawer, some hardcover art books alongside it. Cast iron candle holders, small enough for the narrower top drawer, bore images of Frank Lloyd Wright's Fallingwater.

The items from the two closets hadn't been of much use except for the heat press, which Norman hefted to the landing and then halted. "This thing weighs a ton. I may not catch my breath until next week."

"Bellyaching won't position it in the middle of this dresser, now will it?" Faye said with a smile.

Norman grunted and stepped onto the threshold. The press rested below his belt buckle, his arms clearly straining. "Explain to me why we're doing this again?"

"So you have somewhere to sleep. Set it down right here."

He released the press onto the dresser with a small thud. "That felt like I just carried my car up here."

She peered out the window. "Nope. It's still at the curb."

"The moment of truth," he said and gently eased himself onto the hammock. "If I crash to the floor, please don't laugh. It might damage my pride."

Faye shook her head and rolled her eyes. "Laughing will be the natural reaction to whatever happens next. If you can balance yourself on that thing, I can hold back a guffaw or two. If you can't, all promises go out the window."

He held his arms out to the sides and reclined further; his head touched the tiny pillow. "So far so good. A deep breath might change that, but for now I don't plan to take in a lot of oxygen."

"Probably not a good plan, but let's see how long you'll last." She stepped closer. "Will it hold me, too?"

"Honestly, a feather might tip the scales. I'm reluctant to move a muscle."

"Maybe I should sleep on that and you take the bed. I'm lighter. It makes more sense."

"I'm trying to be a gentleman, Faye. Don't go spoiling it by tempting me."

Once or twice she woke up in the middle of the night and saw Norman in the same position as when she'd turned out the lamp. To think he'd come all this way to profess his love for her elicited her smile in the semi-darkness. Moonlight shone through the oval window behind the bed. Bits of light licked the pair of Buddha statues on the dresser.

Chapter Twenty-four

"It's no trouble at all," Jacklyn assured Faye as she accepted Vince into her arms at the front door. "Lily will be thrilled to have him as a playmate...once she returns from her grandparents', that is."

Faye followed Norman's sister into the living room, a stylish space with wooden beams that climbed the peak of a vaulted ceiling. The blue-gray furniture created a square in front of the fireplace, an oval light fixture looming over one end of the sofa. Along the far wall, built-in display shelves held picture frames and glass figurines.

Next to her foot was a doll on the carpet, so Faye stepped over it on her way to sit down. "We'll be gone less than a week. My father asked us to stay for a few days after the wedding, and I couldn't say no."

Jacklyn perched on a wing-back chair across from Faye and released the cat onto the floor. "Norman tells me he made his feelings for you clear. It's about time he took my advice."

Faye dropped her purse onto the seat cushion. "So does that mean the spice-rack story is true? A while back Lily mentioned you bought it for Norman to lure ladies into his web."

With a quick motion of her head, Jacklyn tossed her dark hair over her shoulders. "That's right. And clearly, it worked. Just another instance of me being right and my brother being wrong."

Faye laughed. "But you're not keeping score, right?"

"It's all in here—" and she tapped a finger to the side of her head. "Silly Norman doesn't realize I know what's best. He seems to think he should be in charge of his own love life. If he could do a good job at it, I wouldn't much mind, but he has a tendency to mess up when it comes to matters of the heart. Guiding him by the hand is the only way, I'm afraid."

"Well, I'm pleased he agreed to go with me to the wedding. It'll be less daunting with him there."

Jacklyn eased back in her chair and crossed her legs. "Norman hasn't been to California since we were children and our parents took us on vacation."

"He told me about the trip to the San Diego Zoo. You were scared of the elephants."

"Is that what he said? Well, it was the other way around. I believe Norman wet his pants when he saw the bear exhibit."

"Your story sounds more believable," Faye said as she watched Vince paw at the doll on the floor and then roll around next to it.

"Women need to stick together," she replied. "But tell me, what's going on with the gallery? Norman let it slip that you're packing for a move."

Faye spoke slowly and fingered the lowest button on her sweater. "I've been offered an assistant position to a permanent collections manager at The Guggenheim. It's a huge boost for my career."

"I'll say. Congratulations, Faye. And this will mean Albany's a part of your past, then?"

"Oh, I'll visit. Norman will be here. Every weekend I'll take the train up."

Jacklyn's eyes fluttered. "No you won't. You'll be too busy with work. And that promise of every weekend will turn into every other weekend, and then once a month. It's nobody's fault. It's just how these things work."

"Not if I hold myself to it. The job doesn't have to take over my whole life."

"But it will and you know it. Faye, honestly, have you asked

Norman about relocating?"

"His job is here. You, Lily and Ben are here. I couldn't ask Norman to leave all of that for me."

"You couldn't or you won't?" Jacklyn leaned forward and rested her elbows on her knees. "If I'm not mistaken, Norman wants to start a life with you. Give him the chance to do that. Ask him to go with you."

Maybe Jacklyn had a point. If she shut Norman out now, there'd be less of a chance for their relationship to succeed. The two of them could rent a teeny tiny place in Manhattan, supremely overpay for it, and see where day-to-day life took them.

***

Faye inspected the tightly-packed clouds. They'd been in the air for an hour already. Anouk rose from the seat next to hers and switched places with Norman.

"Had enough girl talk for now?" Norman asked Faye.

"Anouk wants to chat with Bobby for a while."

"Good. The man tells too many stories. The only one I found interesting was Wellington outrunning him on a wooded trail last month when he flew down for business. Your father drives a hard bargain. I'm surprised any man can survive his athletic camaraderie."

"I've warned him to stop doing that, only he doesn't listen."

"Your father's a civilized man, Faye. But when it comes to you, I think he presses himself and others to the limit."

She gawked at the stubble on Norman's jaw. "Does that make me lucky or unfortunate?"

"It makes you the daughter of Wellington Brooks."

The airline blanket covered her legs; she gathered the edge and pulled it toward her shoulders. "A nap sounds pretty good right about now."

He tapped her shoulder until she opened her eyes. "I get the distinct impression you're avoiding talking to me," he said, his voice low.

"That's not true."

"Oh no? So that look of disappointment in your eyes when Anouk returned to her own seat had nothing to do with how close we'll be for the next few hours? Something's on your mind, Faye, and if you'd tell me what it is, maybe I can help."

Oh, she doubted he could help. Her own indecision about asking him to move to the city with her had created a mental conflict, one that mushroomed in her head. On the one hand, she would like nothing better than to share a flat with this considerate, intelligent man, but she feared it was selfish to ask. Norman might say yes not to hurt her feelings when he really wanted to stay put at his reliable job, surrounded by relatives, in a neighborhood he adored. She couldn't risk cornering him with a decision that would affect his livelihood, relatives, and environs.

"I don't know if the wedding present is right," she finally said. Above their heads in the carry-on compartment was the bag with the gift, swaddled in bubble wrap to prevent any damage.

Norman's face relaxed. "The candle holders? That's what you're worried about? Faye, your dad's going to love them. He may even freak out when he sees they have Frank Lloyd Wright's masterpiece emblazoned on the fronts. Really, don't give it another thought."

"Maybe you're right. I'm being silly."

He kissed her forehead. "Glad I could clear things up for you. That's why I'm good to have around."

"Beep, beep," Anouk said as she stood in the aisle next to Norman's seat. "Could we trade places again? I thought of more questions to ask Faye about the inner workings of Hirsch."

Norman raised his eyebrows at Faye and then vacated his seat.

"So...did you ask him?" Anouk said as she twisted in the seat to look directly at Faye.

"Ah well, no, not exactly."

"Why not? That's why I left you two alone. You promised me you'd ask him."

"I know, I know, but I lost my nerve."

"Are you afraid he'll say no?"

"It's more like I'm afraid he'll say yes."

Anouk scrunched up her face. "Sometimes you make no sense at all, Faye."

"If he ends up hating life in New York City, it'll be my fault." She fiddled with the tray on the back of the seat in front of her.

Anouk set her hand on the arm rest between them. "We're friends now. It's my duty to tell you to put that out of your mind and let him decide."

With Jacklyn, Anouk made the second person who'd told her to ask Norman to uproot his life and follow her to the Big Apple. Either both of these women were wrong or she was overthinking the situation. Norman deserved the opportunity to make his own decision; they were probably right about that. When he reappeared in the seat next to her, she would bring up the subject. Before they landed at San Diego International Airport, she would have her answer, one way or the other.

"You win, Anouk. I'm determined to ask him before this flight lands. So, why don't you pick my brain about Hirsch in the meantime?"

"Will Zoe and Isaac stay on once I become director? I can't tell you how useful it would be to have them around until I learn the ropes."

"Zoe graduates in May. If she can't find another job right away, I'd imagine she'd want to stay. Isaac's retired but I doubt he'll ever stop working. The man likes to have a place to go every morning. He says it keeps him out of trouble."

"Fantastic. That's one less worry for me. And while the construction's occurring for the second story, I'll tie up all the loose ends in Amsterdam. I should be in good shape to take the reins very soon."

"And what about Bobby? Has he agreed to move to Albany?"

Anouk wore a short corduroy skirt with dark tights. She crossed her legs, ran her hand over the skirt, and said, "Get this. He wants to look into adding a third story to the building so we can live on the top floor. He plans to ask your father about it while we're in California."

"A third story? Gosh, the building may never stop expanding at this rate."

"It suits me just fine, actually. I'll have an American boyfriend and a place to live."

"Anouk, I'm really glad all of this is working out. I wouldn't feel comfortable leaving the gallery in anyone else's hands but yours. Good ole Hirsch will remain at its very best, and it's all because of you."

"I'd like to take credit, but being near Bobby had a lot to do with why I accepted your offer to run the place. That man has me spellbound. And if anyone had ever told me that one day I'd move to America and run a gallery, I would've laughed in their face. But it seems like it's going to happen."

Faye looked across the aisle, the edge of Norman's sleeve just visible. "I know what you mean. When Norman expressed his love for me, I felt like my life had finally started."

"That's my cue," Anouk said. "Ask him, Faye." She stood up, smiled, and then turned her back.

"Seems like I'm getting my exercise on this flight," Norman said as he sat down next to Faye. "So what'd you two talk about?"

"The gallery mostly. Although Anouk got in a few amorous remarks about Bobby. I just hope she knows what she's getting into...."

"I got the same from him. He couldn't say enough charming things about her."

"There is something else we discussed that you may find interesting."

He leaned his head against the seat. "Oh yeah? What would that be?"

Faye studied the clouds for a moment. "Believe me, I know it's a lot to ask—and you can say no—but please consider coming with me to the city. We could find a small place and see how it goes. On a trial basis, of course."

Norman looked up and down the aisle and then at Faye. "Do you mind if I tell the whole plane? I mean, this is terrific news. We should share it with the rest of the passengers."

Faye rolled her eyes. "You're impossible. But seriously, what about your job?"

"I have it on good authority that accountants set up shop in the Big Apple twice as much as anywhere else. It's a haven for people like me."

"So you don't mind? Have you considered Jacklyn and the kids?"

Norman took her hand. "It's a toss-up whether I'll miss babysitting or not. Those two can be a handful, especially when they're at each other's throats over a toy. But we can visit and so can they. Fortunately for me, you're not switching jobs with Anouk, in which case I'd have to move overseas."

Her mouth dropped open. "You'd follow me to Amsterdam if that's where I was going?"

"To the ends of the earth, Faye. I know that sounds corny, but I'm signing on for the long haul. You mean everything to me. It's about time you realized that."

***

A golf ball sailed through the air and swooped down near the farthest yardage marker. "Whoa," Wellington roared, "did you see that?"

Norman and Bobby, with clubs in their hands, exchanged glances. It had been Wellington's idea to spend the morning before his wedding day driving balls onto the grass at the back of his property. He'd transformed that part of the acreage into a driving range, complete with a golf cart that had gotten them out there.

"Impressive, Brooks," Bobby replied.

"I don't know what to say," Norman offered. "A shot that good leaves me speechless."

Wellington's club, still frozen in the arc of his swing, finally came down when he released the pose. "I don't put wings on the balls. They just fly out there on their own."

With his feet planted in a golf stance, Bobby took a practice swing, and then whaled on the ball. It teetered through the air in an uneven arc and eventually sunk to the ground several markers closer than Wellington's. "What a pitiful display of my skills," he commented. "Perhaps I should've let Norman go next."

"I know a thing or two about golf," Norman admitted. "Everybody stand back. Let me amaze you with my power and accuracy." The ball zoomed toward the sky and continued to sail.... It touched down one marker closer than Wellington's.

"Ah ha, my boy," Wellington said and slapped Norman on the back. "You had me panicking for a minute there, but it seems my record's safe."

The vastness of the range allowed them to spread out and take simultaneous shots. Three white dots crisscrossed in the air—Bobby's rode the lowest. "I used to be a better golfer," he said. "Looks like I've gotten rusty."

"Don't blame yourself," Norman remarked as he set up another shot. "Everybody bemoans their game when teeing off with Wellington. It's a fact of life...he makes any athletic competition look easy."

"This is an athletic competition?" Bobby asked, his voice higher than normal. "I would've tried harder if I'd known someone was keeping score."

Wellington laughed. "Friendly competition is good for the soul. I'm a firm believer in that." He bent down to retrieve another ball from the bucket. "Besides, I'm still waiting for one of you to tell me about Faye. If Lucinda got it right, her friend Angie suspects my daughter has accepted a position at some highbrow museum. Do either of you know anything about that?"

Bobby raised his wrist to his mouth and used his teeth to bite the edge of his golf glove, apparently to make for a snug fit. "All I know is that Anouk is replacing her at Hirsch."

"And you, Norman? What information can you give me?"

Norman pulled a hybrid club out of his bag. "Faye's the best person to tell you the details. I wouldn't want to speak out of turn."

"It's just us buddies out here," Bobby said as he straightened up after a shot. "Tell the man what he wants to know."

Now the accountant held a club in each hand, as if he couldn't focus on which one he needed. "Faye plans to tell you herself. Exciting news like this should come from her."

"Well you're not denying she was offered a position, so that tells me my girl is moving on. It's about time she branched out and let New York City have a taste of her expertise. I'm guessing that's where the museum is located." He paused to watch Bobby pull back his club and strike the ball. "If it hadn't meant so much to her to save Hirsch, I would've taken its original closing as a sign that her talents were being wasted there, but it turns out I hadn't looked at the bigger picture."

Bobby, with his head tilted back, focused on the ball until it landed. "Which is?"

"She needed to save Hirsch, of course. Only then could she let go of it...and save herself."

"You've lost me," Bobby said as he adjusted his hat.

"I think what Wellington means is that Faye can expand her career now that she knows Hirsch is in good hands."

Wellington sunk another golf tee into the ground. "Faye's future has always been bright. But as her father, I can tell you she takes the hard road every time. It's in her nature."

Bobby stacked his palms over the tip of the club's handle and stood there silently as Wellington sliced off a shot to one side.

"Damn fool shot," the architect howled. "Why don't I watch my aim, for crying out loud! If word of this gets out, I'll be thrown off the firm's team before I know what hit me."

"Stop grumbling, Brooks. Ninety-nine percent of the time you ace it. I'd settle for half of your golf savvy and die a happy man."

Norman hefted his bag onto his shoulder and closed the three-foot gap between himself and Bobby. "Wellington gets rattled when his game's off," he said quietly. "Might be best to change the subject."

Bobby reversed his cap so the bill was at the back. "Listen, Brooks, I want to run something by you and now's as good a time as any." He tamped his club head on the ground. "The gallery's gaining a second story, which leads me to wonder if a third story might give it a grander appearance."

Wellington yanked the towel out of his belt loop and wiped his face. "A third story? I've only gotten approval for two from the zoning board. What would its use be?"

"Living quarters for me and Anouk. One bedroom, two baths ...nothing too fancy. Maybe an exposed brick wall for character and some high-end finishes when the time comes."

Wellington tossed the towel onto the top of his bag. "This means I'll have to go back to the drawing board and sort this out. Not an impossible feat, by any means, but let me draw something up and we'll take a look at it together."

"Fantastic," Bobby said as he tossed a golf ball in the air and caught it with one hand. "I'll let Anouk know we have your blessing."

Wellington wouldn't go that far, but he was pleased that Sterling hadn't ended up with his daughter. Maybe now Faye would have the good sense to see Norman as a potential mate. Any father could do worse in the son-in-law department than a hardworking accountant like Maynard. Perhaps he could sweet talk Lucinda into having a chat with Faye about it. Weddings, after all, were a time when people thought more about love. Now that his daughter had gotten her career on the right track, it might be nice for her to give her love life a fair shot.

Chapter Twenty-five

Bewildered as to how he'd actually gotten her to do it, Norman began to relax as Faye rubbed his shoulders. Sure, he'd mentioned how sore they were from golfing, but he hadn't expected her to automatically climb onto the bed behind him and start working her fingertips at the base of his neck.

"I could get used to this," he said.

Faye raised up on her knees to work her knuckles across his shoulders. "You can pay me back after my first day on the job at The Guggenheim. Throw in a foot massage and we'll call it even."

To give her access to a knot along his collarbone, he slanted his head. "Have you told Angie about the job offer?"

She stopped rubbing for a second. "I hinted around at it. You know, just to give her a heads up."

"How likely is it that she shared the information with Lucinda?"

Faye hung her head over his left shoulder, their cheeks touching. "My father said something today while you boys were golfing, didn't he?"

"Might've."

"Such as?"

"He knows you've been offered a job, only he doesn't know where."

"Okay. Did you bring him up to speed?"

"Was I supposed to? Because honestly, Faye, I think you

should be the one to tell your father the good news. Your career is at a turning point. The details are yours to share."

She sat back on her heels and moved her hand along his back. "I'm not opposed to telling him. Although I wonder if he'll be upset. After all of his efforts to save Hirsch, it may look like I'm bailing out."

"I doubt he'll see it that way. From what I could tell, he's glad you're giving yourself more options."

"Does he know you're coming with me?"

Norman put his hands up. "I haven't said a word; he needs to hear it from you. It might make him feel like he's actually a part of your life if you include him in what's going on."

She leaned back against the headboard. "Is Bobby a good golfer?"

"Let me put it this way—" and he scooted back to sit next to her. "The man can run a café, but he doesn't know the first thing about whacking a ball with a club."

"That probably thrilled my father. He likes to be top dog."

Norman dangled his hands over his bent knees. "All in good fun, I guess. But Bobby did ask your father something interesting. He wants him to look into putting a third story above Hirsch. I'd have to say Wellington took the request like a champion; he said he'd draw up some plans."

"Anouk told me the same thing on the plane. She and Bobby would live up there."

The duvet was pulled back halfway. Norman wiggled his toes under it. "I forgot to tell you...while we were chipping up the turf, Lily phoned me. She's having the best time with Vince. As a matter of fact, she told me a cat is way better than a brother."

"Poor Benjamin. She's ready to trade him for a tabby."

"Sounds about right."

Faye peered up at the ceiling. "I have to hand it to my father. Every detail in this house amazes me." Shadowy in the dim light, the circular dome above the bed faintly showed interlocking vines with fruit.

"You amaze me." Gently, he pushed back a wave of Faye's hair and kissed her on the neck.

"Is that right? Would it be too much to ask for a list of my amazing qualities? Let's say the top ten."

He smiled as his lips grazed the delicate skin near her earlobe. "Hmmm...I'm a little busy right now. Can't we extol your virtues later?"

She didn't answer and he knew why. Faye had waited as long as he had for their pairing. He knew by her short panting breaths how she longed to be in his arms. So when she placed her palm on his cheek and kissed his lips fiercely, he tickled her ribcage. "You're quite a woman, Faye. And I plan to make this quite a night."

***

"What is it you wanted to see me about?" Wellington asked Ronald as he offered him a seat in the den.

Ronald removed his fedora and placed it over his kneecap after he sat down. "You're a busy man, Mr. Brooks, and in a few hours you'll be a married one. It's safe to say I'm hesitant about bothering you on the morning of your nuptials, but I was thrilled to receive your invitation to the wedding. Furthermore, your offer to let me stay here for the duration of the festivities was remarkably generous."

From the stool behind his drafting board, Wellington angled his legs out and crossed his arms over his chest. "It was Faye's idea to invite you. I didn't have a problem with it, especially since you played a major role in the gallery's survival. For that, I'm exceedingly grateful. Margaret bequeathed that money because of you, and now Hirsch has its second chance. So...please...tell me what's on your mind."

Ronald's bald head gleamed under the recessed lighting. "With Margaret's untimely demise, you see, I find myself without a vision for my own future. At my age, it isn't easy to pick up the pieces and find a new employer. My set of skills is invaluable, but only to the right people. Working for just anyone does not appeal to me."

"I see. So you think I may know someone—one of my clients, perhaps—who could use a personal assistant?" Before Ronald could answer, he added, "I'll put the word out, no harm in that."

Ronald switched his hat to the other knee. "Just look at me, Mr. Brooks. I'm still wearing black from head to toe. Margaret's dress code is embedded in my brain. If there's any chance of finding an employer who can reprogram the dried old man I've become...I'd be more than willing to move across the country and start work immediately. Problem is...I need a human software update—badly."

Realistically, Wellington could probably find him a new job with one of his business acquaintances. He could ask around and that would be the end of it. But something Lucinda had said kept replaying in his mind. Once the baby comes I'll need some help around here.

"Ronald," Wellington said, and then paused. "Your flexibility about relocating has got me thinking. How would you like to work here...at the house? Lucinda's going to need someone to run errands—grocery shopping, picking up the dry cleaning, that sort of thing. Would you be interested?"

"Is our current discussion my informal interview?"

Wellington rested his elbow on the drafting board. "I don't see why not."

"And my title will remain Personal Assistant and not Nanny?"

"Certainly."

His eyes looked hopeful. "Should we hash out salary and benefits?"

Wellington twisted around and pointed in the direction of the window. "About three-hundred yards that way is an open area among the trees, an ideal site for a guest house. It'll be rather secluded and have its own pond." He pulled a set of rolled blueprints out of a cubbyhole beside his board and laid them flat. "Come take a look. I've got men scheduled to dig the foundation in another month. After the footings are poured and the decking gets underway, we'll be in good shape. I expect the framing to start before summer."

Ronald traced his finger over the rooms. "Master bedroom, great room, kitchen…. What's not to like?"

"Good, because that's where you'll be staying. I assume you'll find it comfortable."

"Thank you, sir. I believe I will." Ronald walked over to the window.

The drawings rolled in on themselves the moment Wellington removed the paperweights from each side. He set the two lumps of clay, shaped into wobbly hearts, at the top of his board. "Faye made these in the third grade," he said in a low tone, "and I've never found sturdier objects for holding blueprints open." He pivoted on the stool and found Margaret's former assistant mesmerized by the view. "If Lucinda finds me in here when I should be getting ready I doubt she'll be pleased."

Ronald broke his gaze out the window and turned around. "Oh, yes, of course. I've kept you too long. But before you go, let me congratulate you on Faye's big break. You're her father. Some of the credit belongs to you."

Wellington scratched his chin. "Oh right, the job offer."

Ronald plucked his felt hat off the armrest of the sofa. "Let's face it, The Guggenheim is a bang-up assignment. So tell me…how does it feel to have your offspring in the thick of the art world, making her way like one of the greats?"

The Guggenheim, he thought. Ah, Faye's big secret. It rather surprised him that Ronald was privy to where Faye would work next—obviously the man thought he already knew—but his daughter would reveal her latest accomplishment to him in her own time. "Faye's a step above in her field. I suspect she'll do the museum proud."

"My thoughts exactly, Mr. Brooks."

***

The wedding speeches were long and drawn out. Rows and rows of white chairs dotted the grass in front of an altar with trellised sides, pale yellow flowers climbing up them. Earlier in the morning, an army of men had bombarded the backyard to set the thing up; Faye had watched from the bedroom window. Now she sat between Norman and Anouk, the afternoon sun beating down on her head.

"Lucinda looks beautiful," Anouk said into Faye's ear.

Faye nodded and glanced at the bride. Her ivory gown reached the tips of her designer heels; the Swarovski crystals that cascaded down the front shimmered in the natural light. It reminded her of that weekend in the city when Lucinda had rejected most of the dresses she'd tried on, except for the one she wore now—thin layers of overlapping silk in a soft rose color.

Norman put his hand on her thigh and leaned in. "You look prettier than the bride," he said.

Pinned up, her honey-colored hair appeared graceful, two tendrils falling past her ears on either side. "You'd better not let the bride hear you say that."

He gave her a lopsided grin. "If Lucinda corners me, I'll be forced to deny everything."

Ronald sat beside him and poked his arm. "Do me a favor...please stop talking. Mr. and Mrs. Brooks are my new employers. They're up there getting married. So shush!"

Norman made a gesture of buttoning his lips. Then he turned to Faye and rolled his eyes.

It took another thirty minutes to complete the ceremony. Angie tossed rose petals as the couple stepped down from the altar and marched along a white linen runner in the grass. Faye supposed she'd outdone herself by handing off that duty to Angie. Otherwise, it would've been her up there strewing the delicate petals on the newlyweds' heads. Thankfully, she'd seen a way out and had taken it.

"Shouldn't you be the one doing that?" Bobby whispered to Faye. He sat next to Anouk and leaned over her lap to ask the question.

"Angie pleaded with me to let her do the honors. What can I say...I gave in."

Bobby knitted his brows. "Huh, yeah, I doubt that. You paid her. Am I right?"

Faye looked down at the bright white tips of her fingernails. "Fifty dollars."

"Thought so." He eased back in his chair.

A good distance from the altar the couple stopped and began accepting congratulations from the guests pouring out of their seats to hug them. Wellington must've shaken one hundred hands while Faye observed from her seat. "My father loves this sort of thing," she said.

"He's in the spotlight, all right," Norman agreed. "Shouldn't we head over there to wish them happy returns?"

Most of the guests had left their seats by now. "Let the others disband and then we'll go over."

Norman picked up Faye's hand and kissed it. "You're happy for your father, aren't you?"

She avoided looking into his eyes. "Of course I am. I really am."

He stood up and yanked on her hand. "Come on. No time like the present." As they got closer to the happy couple, he whispered, "Just remember I'm right beside you."

Faye embraced her father first and then Lucinda. "My congratulations to you both. The ceremony was lovely. You look stunning, Lucinda."

"Oh, Faye," Lucinda said as she dabbed under her eyes with a tissue. "I promised myself I wouldn't cry, but we're so grateful to have you here with us."

"It's our pleasure to be here," Norman said for the both of them. "And if Wellington doesn't mind, I'd like to escort the bride toward the champagne." Norman held out his arm to Lucinda and they advanced toward a horseshoe-shaped bar at the far end of the lawn.

"Maynard's a great fellow," Wellington said once they'd moved off. "I suppose it's none of my business, but are you ever going to give him a chance to be the man in your life?"

Faye tilted her head, the tendrils of hair on either side of her face slanting. "Actually, I've been offered a position at The Guggenheim and Norman's agreed to come with me."

"The Guggenheim," he repeated. "They're lucky to have you." He nudged Faye's elbow and they started to walk slowly toward the altar. "How did all this come about?"

"Vanessa Hargrave stopped by Angie's. She's a fixture at The Guggenheim. Anyway, we got to talking. I told her about Hirsch and the Van Gogh show. Then, one Sunday she showed up in Albany. The next thing I knew she offered me a job as her assistant."

"That's quite a story," he said and sat down on the edge of the altar, to the right of the stairs.

Faye sat sideways on the top step and stared at her father's profile. "Fortunately, Hirsch will be in good hands with Anouk. There's nothing to worry about on that front."

Wellington looked straight ahead. "You know, Faye, I couldn't be prouder of you. I think it's time you tried your hand at a museum. The Guggenheim could lead to The Met, right?"

She toyed with the flimsy ribbon at her waist. "Let's not get ahead of ourselves. I'm content to see where this goes. After that, who knows."

"And Norman? He's scampering off to the city with no job?"

"His company has a Manhattan office. There's no room for him to transfer there at the moment, but as soon as a spot opens up, he'll grab it."

"Seems like you two have it all worked out."

She put her hand over her father's. "As excited as I am about all this...I'm equally terrified I'll disappoint Vanessa or Norman ... or you."

Wellington rested his foot on the bottom stair tread and unbuttoned the jacket of his tuxedo. "The only way you could disappoint me is if you stopped telling me things like that. I'm your father, Faye. My love for you doesn't revolve around your success. And Norman's not going to let you down either. The man has loved you for a while, if I had to make a judgment call. So don't give any of it a second thought. The city is where your life needs to be at the moment. That much is pretty clear."

Faye turned her head and caught sight of Norman leading Lucinda around the yard with a champagne glass in her hand. "Norman's one of a kind, isn't he?"

"You won't hear any opposition from me." He sunk his elbows onto his knees and appeared to study the grass around his shiny black shoes. "By the way, we've got ourselves another pair of hands around here. A seasoned personal assistant, in fact."

"Ronald?"

"I've hired him to help out. He needs a job and has no qualms about moving across the country. I plan to set him up in the guest house."

"You don't have a guest house."

"One's in the works. Should be ready for occupancy in the fall."

"Why doesn't that surprise me? The next time I come for a visit you'll have this whole place built up."

"You can't take the architect out of the man, I'm afraid."

Faye focused on two reflections in the grass, oblong specks of light from her father's cuff links. "Isn't it enough for you to draw up plans for other people?" she asked, still following the bright spots which danced when he moved his arms. "Case in point, I heard Bobby's interested in adding another story above Hirsch."

Wellington finished adjusting his wire-rimmed glasses and brought his arms down. "A third story would balance out the facade. Why not make things look nice? There's no harm in providing a flat for the owner. But is he really serious about Anouk? The poor girl's home is across the ocean."

"They're willing to give it a try. Anouk's intelligent and sweet. I think she's eager to move to America. And Bobby seems genuinely taken with her."

"Could be I just don't understand young love these days."

Faye laughed. "You've just gotten married."

"So I have. With a baby on the way, no less. I seem to be two for two. But we're not a young couple with stars in our eyes. Perhaps that's the difference."

"I'd like it if you came out to see Norman and me in the summer. Maybe by then we'll be settled and ready to entertain."

Wellington put his hands on his knees and stood up. "I'd like nothing better. But for now...let's go mingle. I want my best girl to meet more of my guests."

She rose and wiggled her hips until all the layers of her dress lay flat. "Have a heart and only introduce me to the interesting ones, please."

He wrinkled his brow. "Am I to understand my Faye is being choosy? Not all of my friends and clients appreciate art, you know. We are bound to stumble upon one or more chaps and their lovely wives who consider cultural pursuits irrelevant. I have a fair idea of who thinks this way, so in that regard you're safe. But put on your best smile, Faye, and hang onto my arm. I promise I'll let you abandon me if the seas get too choppy."

Chapter Twenty-six

"Come hold this end," Faye said to Norman as she tried to hang a curtain over the door to the balcony.

He reached up to balance the rod. "Why don't you take a break from decorating and join me for a glass of wine? We could drink it out there. That's why we chose this place, right? Because it has some outdoor space."

They'd spent several weeks after their return from California finding a place to live in the city. Most of the apartments they'd seen lacked green space. Of course, Faye's checklist of wants failed to match up with their budget, and it hardly took into account the cost of living in Manhattan. The places they toured were tiny but expensive, drab and noisy. One day the real estate agent took them to a third-story walk-up with a balcony that overlooked rush-hour traffic. Horns tooted in every direction and Faye had wondered if a bit of fresh air was more trouble than it was worth. But in the end, she and Norman had fallen in love with the place, primarily because it was clean and affordable. "This could be home," she'd said and Norman had agreed.

Faye stood back and looked at the curtain. Then she joined Norman on the balcony. "Will Jacklyn and the kids come up next weekend?" she asked.

"Please tell me you haven't already invited them. We need more peace and quiet before we have visitors. Just call her back and say another time would be better."

"I'm not going to do that, Norman. They'll feel unwelcome."

"Oh brother, you're really going to fight me on this? You know how pushy Jacklyn is to begin with.... Just give her an inch and you know the rest. Think of it as building up suspense. We're doing her a favor by making her wait to see our new place."

"I doubt she'll see it that way."

The width of the balcony was only a foot longer than the folding chairs they sat in, which allowed the railing to act as a higher-than-normal foot rest. Both of them propped their feet on it as they clinked glasses. "Here's to our new place," Norman said.

A stone's throw away were more apartment buildings. Faye gazed at the terrace directly across from theirs. "I can't believe our luck, actually. What did it take? Three weeks? Now we've got a place...and you're set up in the Manhattan office."

"Maybe you and I have good timing. Either that or the universe is on our side."

She smiled. "I'd like to think it's both."

Norman settled his wine glass on the slant of his thigh. "Have you heard from Isaac or Zoe?"

"Zoe phoned me the other day. Get this—she thinks Anouk's a fun boss."

"And did she qualify that by saying 'not as fun as you'?"

"No, she did not." Faye made a face and then threw her head back laughing.

He patted her arm. "I'm glad you're taking it so well."

"Everyone's getting along, which makes me overjoyed. I was thinking we should invite the gallery gang, your sister, Alan, and Ray to a little get together soon."

"Will they all fit in the apartment? If not, I may need to buy some hooks and cables. We could suspend the guests we like least from this railing."

She smacked his arm. "Oh stop it, Norman. There'll be plenty of room."

He crossed his ankles on the railing. "If you say so."

"And if it's all right with you, I'd like to invite Vanessa and her husband over for coffee tomorrow evening."

"Ah, so I finally get to meet your boss? Leave it to me, Faye. I'll give her an earful about your work ethic, your love of art, how you saved Hirsch with grace and style, and how cute you look right after you fall asleep. By the time I'm done chatting her up, she'll think you're Picasso's daughter."

"Leave out the part about me asleep, okay? I don't imagine she much cares about the adorable way I slumber."

"Oh, are we calling it slumber now?" He tickled her ribcage.

She held up her wine. "You're going to make me spill this." Then she swatted away his hand with her free one.

He retracted his feet from the railing and straightened up. "Let's say you finish that wine so I can take you inside. We bought that mattress at a bargain price and I think it would be wise to test it out some more. You know, to make sure it's still firm."

She emptied her glass. "Oh, I agree wholeheartedly."

***

"Let me take your coat," Faye said to Vanessa as she entered the apartment. Her boss's husband hadn't worn one, just his suit jacket.

The men shook hands and eventually went out onto the balcony. Faye had imagined Ted differently, perhaps shorter and pudgier, but in reality his height exceeded his wife's by a foot or more, and his weight was average. The tweed suit jacket provided a distinguished air, along with his glasses and white hair.

Faye toured Vanessa around the place. "It's a small kitchen, but it meets our needs," she said. "Someday we'll switch out these countertops for granite."

Vanessa rubbed her hand over the surface. "Is that a hint to let me know you'll need a raise fairly quickly?"

Faye laughed. "If that were the case, I would've shown you the outdated bathroom first."

"So tell me," Vanessa began as she followed Faye toward a room at the back, "how do you like the job so far?"

"Going from a gallery to a museum...there's a learning curve, but I like mastering the details. The job itself is exciting, and the circular building, well, I'll never get tired of that."

Vanessa looked around. "Goodness, you barely have room for a bed in here. Even without any effort on your part, I'm weakening about that raise. The two of you need more space. I'd feel awfully guilty if I uprooted you to live in a shoebox."

"Trust me, we'll manage. I've already told Norman his ties can't go in the closet."

"Is that why you have the largest tie rack I've ever seen behind your bathroom door?"

"It may look out of place, but I reasoned with Norman that it'll be a timesaver in the morning. He can jump out of the shower and get dressed."

"And he bought that?"

Faye grimaced. "Yes and no." She grabbed her phone off the dresser. "I want to show you something." She scrolled to the correct spot, and then tilted the screen for Vanessa to see. "It's a closeup of a pair of candle holders. You can just make out the depression for the candle. I purchased them from Angie for my father's wedding present. The image of Fallingwater on the front really made him smile. Anyway, I was thinking, since Frank Lloyd Wright designed The Guggenheim, maybe we could add reproductions of these to the merchandise in the gift shop."

Vanessa's round cheeks puffed up when she smiled. "That shows real initiative, Faye. It's clear to me you wish to improve the museum goers' experience. Honestly, it's moments like this that remind me of what excellent foresight I had in plucking you from Albany."

Vince pranced into the room and Faye hoisted him to her chest. "Hey Vince, I want you to meet Vanessa. She's my boss."

"Hello, little fellow," Vanessa said as she stroked his head. "What a pleasure to meet you."

"Faye," Norman called to her from the sliding door. "Ted and I are eating most of the cheese and crackers out here. So if you two want any, I suggest you hurry."

Faye eyed Vanessa. "You heard him. We need to lay claim to our share of the food." She set Vince down on the bed. "Let's make our way out there."

The two of them squeezed onto the balcony. Norman and Ted stood on either end to let the ladies occupy the chairs. "Ted," Vanessa said to her husband, "don't you know a handyman who could remodel this place for my assistant and her boyfriend? For heaven's sake, that tile in the bathroom is older than I am."

Ted pushed his glasses down his nose. "My wife enjoys putting me on the spot. You see, I'm the handyman she's referring to, and there's not a day that goes by that she doesn't commit me to some project or other." He rested his hand on the railing. "Not that I mind. I'm retired now. You're looking at one of the few archival librarians who knows how to wield a hammer." He bent his arm at a ninety-degree angle and made a fist, only his tweed jacket camouflaged any muscles that might have protruded under the surface.

"Very impressive," Faye said as she reached out for Norman's hand. "I would like to throw Norman into the ring, too." She batted her eyelashes at him. "You'd like to help out with some light renovations, wouldn't you?"

"If it's going to make more room for my tie collection, I'm in."

Vanessa leaned toward her. "See, that wasn't so hard, was it?"

Faye brought a cracker with a wedge of cheese to her lips. "Surprisingly easy, I'd say."

"You two boys can stir up dust here," Vanessa said, "and in a few months' time, who knows, maybe this place will have the facelift it needs."

On the city streets below, cars honked and drivers shouted obscenities. "I think I need more wine," Ted said as he peered over the edge of the balcony. "I plan my best renovations after two glasses."

"That's not true, darling. Remember, I counted once. Three glasses are what you'll need to be worth anything to these two."

Faye went inside to retrieve another bottle, and Norman excused himself to assist her. "I won't hold you to helping with any renovations," she said as he came up behind her and grabbed her around the waist.

"I meant what I said. If swinging a sledgehammer and doing a little tile work makes more room for my ties, you won't hear a single complaint from me."

She turned in his arms and kissed his chin. "I doubt that's going to happen, but somehow I think you know that."

The tip of his finger ran underneath her blouse. "Even so, I couldn't be happier."

"And why's that?"

"You have to ask?"

"I like to hear you say it."

He kissed the tip of her nose. "Because I love you, Faye Brooks."

She tucked her honey-colored hair behind her ears, flashed him a smile, and schlepped more wine onto the balcony.

"Ted wanted to send out a search party," Vanessa remarked. "I told him you'd be back soon enough. The man has no patience."

"Blame, Norman," Faye said. "He was too busy making a case for his ties to share our bedroom. Otherwise I would've been much quicker."

Norman took up his former spot against the railing. "In my defense, I think I'm weakening her resolve."

Vanessa laughed. "You've known Faye longer than I have. However, we have a new saying down at the museum. Remember Hirsch. It means if Faye sets her mind to something, it'll happen."

"So there's no hope for my ties?"

Faye didn't respond until she'd refilled everyone's glass, and then she said, "None whatsoever."

Norman bent down and kissed the top of her head. "That's okay. I'm flexible."